ETERNITY RING

Titles by Patricia Wentworth

ETERNITY RING

PATRICIA WENTWORTH

HarperPerennial
A Division of HarperCollins*Publishers*

This book was originally published in 1948 by J. B. Lippincott Company.

First HarperPerennial edition published 1991.

ISBN 0-06-097442-7

91 92 93 94 95 WB/RRD 10 9 8 7 6 5 4 3 2 1

CHAPTER 1

Maggie Bell stretched out a hand and picked up the telephone receiver. It was a thin, bony hand with jutting knuckles and it moved with a jerk. Maggie did everything in jerks. She was twenty-nine years old, but she had not grown or developed very much since she had had what was always alluded to with some family pride as her "accident." A car had knocked her down in the village street when she was twelve.

She lay all day on a couch drawn up to the window in the room over Mr. Bisset's Grocery Stores. That was what Mr. Bissets called his shop, but actually it sold a great many things that could not possibly be classed as groceries. The term might of course be stretched to cover the liquorice bootlaces, a sweet now extinct in many parts of England and concocted by Mrs. Bisset from a family recipe, but it could not apply to the mohair or leather varieties which hung from hooks on either side of the entrance. Onions, tomatoes, apples, pears, and nuts in season were of course quite in order, but a row of cotton overalls and a pile of strong boots, lads' and men's, could only be accounted for by the fact that Deeping was a village and that Mr. Bisset's "Grocery Stores" was in fact its general shop.

On a good day Maggie could look from the window above the entrance and check up on nearly everyone in Deeping. Most of them would wave a hand and give her a "Good-morning!" or a "Hullo, Maggie!" Mrs. Abbott from Abbottsleigh never missed. She'd wave her hand and smile, and Colonel Abbott would look up and nod, but if it was Miss Cicely she'd come running up the stairs with a book or a magazine and stay a little. Maggie read a great deal. You had to do something, lying there all day. That was the way she put it to herself, having grown up in circles where reading was synonymous with idleness.

Miss Cicely brought her real nice books, and not the improving kind neither. Maggie had a sharp eye for being improved, and an impenetrable armour against it. She liked the age-old success story—the barefoot boy who sells papers in the streets and becomes a millionaire, the girl who starts so plain that nobody will look at her and ends up a raving beauty or a duchess. She liked a good murder, with all the corpse's friends and enemies suspected in turn. She liked travel books with people crossing rope bridges or wading in swamps where snakes, crocodiles, lions, tigers, and enormous apes might at any moment burst upon the view.

Abbottsleigh was a treasure-house. Mrs. Abbott had been known to remark that she possessed a larger library of rubbish than any other woman in England—"so reposeful after two lots of war literature to say nothing of the papers—so dreadfully up-to-date, if you know what I mean."

Maggie didn't read all the time. She could sew when she was propped up, but she couldn't keep on at it. Her mother was the village dressmaker, so of course anything Maggie could do was a help. Buttons and buttonholes, hooks and eyes, and all the odd finishings—these were her share of the work, done in a series of jerks but quite neatly. Mrs. Bell was clever and got quite a lot of custom from the big houses round. She had got through the war on turning and making over the ransackings of old laid-away things which had certainly never expected to be haled from their seclusion. Her proudest moment, and Maggie's, was when Mrs. Abbott brought her old Lady Evelyn Abbott's wedding-dress to see what could be done with it for Miss Cicely. "Because of course you simply can't get stuff like that now, and Cicely has a fancy for it. I shouldn't have wanted to get married in my grandmother's wedding-dress myself, but there's been rather a fashion for that sort of thing, and of course it is lovely stuff."

The folds of deep creamy satin had filled the room. That was the long Court train with roses worked on it in pearls, but the dress was plain, to show off the flounce of Brussels point which draped it. Maggie had never seen anything so lovely in her life. It made her tremble to think of touching it. Pity about Miss Cicely being a little brown thing. Funny too. There was the Colonel, a handsome upstanding gentleman, and Mrs. Abbott not what you'd call a beauty but what Mrs. Bell called a fine woman that showed her clothes off, and there was Miss Cicely a little bit of a brown thing with big eyes and nothing much else. And all that beautiful cream satin for her wedding-dress. Well, it hadn't brought her luck. There she was, back at Abbottsleigh, and Mr. Grant Hathaway at Deepside, and talk of a divorce. Nobody knew what had gone wrong between them—three months married and a split like that. Even Maggie didn't know what it was all about, and Maggie knew most things, because when she wasn't sewing or reading she was listening in on the telephone.

Deeping possessed that invaluable source of private information, a party line. The dozen or so houses with telephones had this line in common. Anyone who chose could listen to a neighbour's conversation by merely lifting the receiver. This should have made everyone very careful, but familiarity breeds indifference if not contempt. It is difficult to divest oneself of the illusion of privacy when one is using one's own telephone in one's own private room. Maggie knew all the best times for listening and she managed to collect a good deal of information about a good many people, but she never found out why Cicely Hathaway had left her husband. The nearest she ever came to it was the evening when she lifted her receiver and heard Grant Hathaway say, "Cicely—"

There was no answer for such a long time that Maggie wondered if there was going to be any answer at all. Then a little cold voice said,

"What is it?"

Maggie was listening passionately, her bony hand clutching the receiver, her long, sharp nose quivering at the tip. She heard Grant Hathaway say,

"We can't go on like this. I want to see you."

"No."

"Cicely!"

"I have nothing to say to you, and you have nothing to say to me."

"That's just where you happen to be wrong. I've got plenty to say to you."

There was another of those long pauses. Then Cicely Hathaway said,

"Nothing I want to hear."

"Cis—don't be a fool!"

Cicely Hathaway said a very odd thing. She said,

"A fool and his money are soon parted. You can have it."

And hard on that a slam which shook the whole party line. It was Mr. Grant who had banged down the receiver, because when the tremor on the line had died Maggie could hear Miss Cicely catch her breath a mile away at Abbottsleigh. Then she hung up too.

That looked as if the quarrel had something to do with money. Well, Miss Cicely had plenty, left her direct by old Lady Evelyn after she had quarrelled with everyone else in the family. And Mr. Grant hadn't any at all, as everybody knew—only the big place and his farming experiments which hadn't begun to pay but he was quite sure they were going to.

Maggie thought dispassionately that Miss Cicely was cutting off her nose to spite her face. If a man married a rich wife he expected to get something out of it, didn't he? And whatever

4

the rights of it were, there he was good-looking enough to turn any girl's head, and there was Miss Cicely, just a little brown thing, and if she didn't take care, somebody else would get him.

Maggie put the receiver to her ear and heard a woman's voice say with what she thought was a funny accent,

"Mr. Hathaway—I wish to speak to Mr. Hathaway."

CHAPTER 2

It was on the following afternoon, which was a Saturday, that Frank Abbott was taken out to tea with Miss Alvina Grey. He was spending a week-end with his uncle and aunt, of whom he was more than a little fond. Colonel Abbott was so extraordinarily like his own father as to provide a sense of coming home for the holidays, whilst Mrs. Abbott, warm, inconsequent, made a particular appeal to his sense of humour. With Cicely he had been on teasing terms until she married and became almost at once someone behind steel bars. Nobody seemed to know why the marriage had broken up. Monica Abbott mourned to him about it.

"You'd think she would tell her mother if she didn't tell anyone else, but not a word, not a single word, except of course that she never wanted to see him again, and how soon could she get a divorce. And when Mr. Waterson told her she couldn't unless there was another woman or something like that—well, really, Frank, I thought she was going to faint. He said Grant could divorce *her* for desertion, but not for three years, but she couldn't divorce him unless he gave her cause, and all she said was, 'He won't,' and walked straight out. And of course it really would be better if she would go away and let things settle down, but she says why should she let herself be driven away from her home. And I see her point—but, my dear Frank, so dreadfully awkward, only we're getting hardened—at least I suppose we are. He didn't come to church at all regularly—at least not until he was courting Cicely. She plays the organ, you know. The Gainsfords gave it as a memorial to the son who was killed in 1915. It's a lovely instrument and she plays it beautifully, and whether that's why he comes, I don't know, but there he is every Sunday, and comes up to us afterwards as if nothing had happened. Only of course Cis isn't there, because she goes on playing for ages and he doesn't wait, just comes up to Reg and me and says something, and we say something, and everyone stares—really people have no manners—and then off he goes in a sort of seven-league-boot kind of way. And Cis probably playing a funeral march or something like that inside and coming home late for lunch—and nothing makes Mrs. Mayhew lose her temper worse, except not eating anything, which she considers an insult to the food—and looking as if she'd just seen seventeen ghosts." Mrs. Abbott paused momentarily for breath and added with renewed vigour, "I'd like to knock their heads together."

Detective Sergeant Frank Abbott raised a pale eyebrow.

"Why don't you?"

She laughed ruefully.

"They're never near enough. I did ask him what it was all about. We met in the Lane and there wasn't anyone there, and he said, 'Hasn't Cicely told you?' So I said, 'No, she hasn't.' And he said, 'Nothing doing, ma'am,' and he took my hand and kissed it and said, 'Mothers-in-law out of the ring!' So there was nothing more I could do, was there? He's sweet, you know, and I think Cis is a fool—I don't care what he's done. I'm a fool too, because I cried, and he lent me his handkerchief—mine's always lost when it would be the slightest bit of good. Oh dear, why did I talk about it? Too stupid of me when I'm going out to tea. Oh, my dear boy, thank you!"

Frank watched her dab her eyes with his neatly folded handkerchief. When she had leaned her nose against it and sniffed once or twice, and he had assured her that neither it nor her eyes were red, she smiled a little shakily and began to tell him about Miss Alvina.

"The late Rector's daughter. He lived to be ninety-seven. She has what used to be the sexton's house, only she calls it Rectory Cottage now—just beyond the church and most convenient, because she does the flowers. Only of course we rather wish she wouldn't, because she just crams them in, and she has a passion for marigolds. Not that I mind them myself, but not with pink sweet peas, and with Miss Vinnie you never know. She is distressingly fond of pink, which is all very well, but you can have too much of it. Just wait till you see her room."

It was just as they were starting that Cicely came up the garden with the dogs at her heels—an old liver-and-white spaniel, and a black dachshund with melting eyes and an insinuating manner who was trailing a lead. At the moment he was full of virtue because, having been put on the lead just up the Lane, he had avoided his usual scolding for chasing Mrs. Caddle's cat.

"He always does," said Cicely, releasing him. "And she doesn't like it—Mrs. Caddle, I mean, not the cat—so I've taken to putting him on till we get past the Grange. Of course the cat's perfectly all right." She screwed up a little cross face which would have been attractive if it had been allowed to smile. "Cats always have the upper hand, and this one's the fierce stripy sort—a regular tiger. She sits on the wall and mocks at Bramble, and of course he goes mad." Her eyes glinted at Frank for a moment, then sank again into gloom as she turned them on her mother. "I met Mrs. Caddle when I was going out and she looked like nothing on earth."

Monica immediately displayed the true village spirit.

"But, Cis, she's at Miss Vinnie's until five. Are you sure it was Mrs. Caddle?"

Cicely gave a short, hard laugh. Everything she did these days was jerky and abrupt.

"Of course I'm sure! It's getting dark now, but not too dark to recognize people, and anyhow it wasn't dark then. She was coming down the Lane as I was going up, and she looked as if she'd been crying her eyes out. It's that Albert, I expect. I can't think why he couldn't have got shot or something when the war was on, instead of coming here to break poor Ellen's heart." She turned back to Frank, a sudden flame in her look. "She was Gran's head housemaid—the nice comfortable middle-aged sort—and she went and lost her head about Mark Harlow's chauffeur who'd been in the Commandos, and was ass enough to marry him. And now God knows what he's been up to, but she looks like death. Aren't women fools!"

She stamped her foot and ran from them suddenly in the dusk, Bramble barking wildly and snatching at her ankles, the old spaniel following at a walk. She did not stop running until she reached her own room, where she banged and locked the door. But of course it wasn't the slightest use, because she had to open it again for Bramble, who was a spoilt toad, and if you didn't let him in, all he did was to sit outside and blow under the door until you did. Even after this brief separation it was, as far as he was concerned, an occasion for pouncing, barking, and the endearing kind of nibble which was the way he had of kissing. The worst of it was that he made her cry. She made haste to lock the door again, because nobody—nobody had seen her cry since she was five years old. Nobody except Bramble, who had now bounded on to the bed and with lightning rapidity gone to sleep like a black snail on the green eiderdown. Certainly not Grant.

Certainly—certainly not Grant. The flame of her anger against him came up in her again and dried the tears. He had shown her something unimaginably beautiful—and murdered it. No, it was much worse than that—he had shown it to her, and then she had found out that what he had shown her was a sham. She could have borne to have her beautiful thing and lose it. What kept her in torment night and day was to know that she had never really had it at all.

She walked up and down in the room. The curtains had been drawn. She had turned on the lamp by the bed. Its green shade gave all the light in the room a wavering under-water look. Cicely walking up and down in it wasn't really there at all. She was going out with the dogs, walking up the Lane, stopping at the Grange to put Bramble on the lead.

Mark Harlow came out of the back gate while she was doing it. She straightened up to see him standing a couple of yards away and looking at her.

"Going for a walk? You've left it a bit late, haven't you?"

"I like walking in the dusk."

"It will be dark before you get back."

"I like walking in the dark."

"Well, I don't like your doing it." Then, as her chin lifted, he broke into laughter. "Not my business? I suppose you're right!"

"Yes."

He came near enough to touch her lightly on the shoulder. Bramble growled and pulled at his lead—if you came out for a walk, why didn't you go for a walk?

Mark said in a softened voice,

"Proud, cold little thing—aren't you?"

She looked up at him, her eyes dark.

"Yes."

"Mayn't I come with you?"

"No, Mark."

"Why?"

"I don't want you. I don't want anyone."

He laughed, and turned back to the gate again. Cicely went on.

As soon as she had gone a little way she let Bramble off the lead and ran with him, old Tumble plodding behind. Bramble was very funny when he ran. His ears flapped, and every now and then he did a sort of spy hop which extended his view. There might be rabbits, there might be birds, there might be another cat, there might be a weasel or a stoat—there might even be a badger, arch-enemy of his race. Immemorial generations of little hounds bred for hunting the badger stirred in him to sharpen the zest with which he snuffed the air.

Cicely ran as lightly and almost as fast as he did. The colour came to her cheeks. She meant to go no farther than where the driving-road cut across the Lane between the Harlow land and Grant Hathaway's. Before everything happened the dogs were trained to stop on the edge of the road and wait for her "Hi over!" The Lane went on on the other side. It went all the way to Lenton. Bramble couldn't understand why they didn't hi over any more. He and Tumble halted obediently at the edge of the road, but instead of crossing it they had to turn. It was too dull. Tumble didn't mind of course. He was old and fat, and he no longer cared for walks. It was Bramble who never had enough, and Cicely who could run as far as he did and then sink down laughing whilst he pounced for joy and nibbled at her hair.

But now there was no more laughing, and they always turned at the road. Today they turned as usual. The sun had set and a cold dusk was falling over the fields on the right, and the fields on the left, and the two high hedgerows between which they walked. And then, coming up behind them silently and swiftly, Grant Hathaway on a bicycle. He was past them before they heard him come. He was past them and off his bicycle, leaning it against the bank and coming back to a snuffing, sobbing welcome from Bramble and no welcome at all from Cicely.

Husband and wife stood looking at each other with all there was between them—a young man, broad-shouldered, with an easy way of moving, neither fair nor dark—the regulation brown-haired Englishman with eyes between blue and grey. He looked strong, and he looked as if he might have a temper. He was also what Monica Abbott had once called quite sinfully good-looking—"Men have no business to be heart-smiters—they've got too many aces up their sleeve without that." Grant Hathaway had too many aces. Perhaps Cicely would have found it easier to forgive him if he hadn't. He was smiling as he looked at her. One of the things which drove red-hot knives into her as she walked her bedroom floor was the fact that his smile could still make her heart turn over. What sort of hateful, despisable stuff were you made of for a smile to do that to you? When everything was finished, when you knew that there hadn't even been anything at all, he had only to smile and your heart flapped round like a dying fish.

He stood there and smiled, and said,

"Well, Cis—how goes it?"

She didn't say anything at all. What was there to say? It had all been said. The Lane was narrow. There was a good deal of Grant. If he wanted to stop her, she couldn't get past him, and if he touched her—if he touched her—

She would have to speak after all, because if he touched her she couldn't answer for what she might do. Horrible to feel as if everything might slip away and leave you just pure savage— a creature gone back to the wild and the weapons of the wild, clawing, scratching, biting. She said in an icy voice,

"I've got nothing to say."

"No wonder I wanted to marry you—the woman who doesn't answer back!"

She found something to say after all—the one weapon that would never fail her.

"But that's not why you married me—is it? You had a much better reason than that."

He was still smiling.

11

"Stupid of me. I married you for your money, didn't I? I keep forgetting. So easy to forget, isn't it?"

He knew how to get through her armour. And her weapon had failed her after all, because he didn't care. He was quite, quite shameless, and he found it easy to forget. She said in a low voice of fury,

"Let me pass!"

He laughed.

"I'm not stopping you." Then, as she moved, he stopped and caught up Bramble by the scruff of his neck.

As if his touch had been on her own flesh, she dropped the other end of the lead and walked past without looking back, whilst he pulled Bramble's ears, calling him by silly familiar names, and finally putting him down with a quick "Be off with you, little black mouse!"

There was a moment of indecision. Then without turning her head Cicely called "Bramble!" and he ran after her trailing his lead.

That was all, but it was enough and to spare. She went on walking up and down her room.

CHAPTER 3

Monica and Frank took their way down the Lane. It was deep dusk now and would be very dark. They came out into the village street, turned to the right and, passing a row of cottages and the Rectory, arrived at the church. Miss Alvina's cottage lay a little beyond the Rectory and was the last in the village. It was old, the once black beams of its living-room not much more than six foot above the flagstones of the floor. Miss

Alvina, considering them gloomy, had painted them a good bright rose, performing this act of desecration with great gusto from a precarious perch upon a kitchen chair. The result fully justified her boast that the room was now much brighter. She had not actually painted the window seat, but it was heaped with pink cushions. Roses as large as cauliflowers bloomed on the sofa and three chintz-covered chairs, whilst the curtains, cut down after long service in the Rectory drawing-room, had preserved to a surprising extent the vigour of a cerise stripe upon rather a bright blue ground. There was not really room upon the walls for all the treasured pictures which had once had a more spacious home, but Miss Alvina had done her best. An overmantel in poker-work assisted the mantelpiece in its task of supporting as many photographs and knick-knacks as possible. The month being January, the fine scarlet geraniums in pink and blue glazed pots which adorned the room in summer were now replaced by bunches of orange everlastings grown very successfully in Miss Alvina's little back garden.

She herself wore a pink blouse with her grey coat and skirt, and some rather tired pink cotton roses pinned to the lapel. Her bushy grey hair bulged in every direction under the black felt hat which was, like the curtains, a survival from the past. None of the young people in Deeping had ever seen her in any other hat. Cicely could remember it looking just as it did now when she was seven or eight years old and was given pink sweets for being a good little girl in church. The hair it was supposed to cover had rebelled against it then as it rebelled against it now. Under the hat and all that hair there were neat little features, very bright blue eyes, and so small a mouth that one wondered how Miss Vinnie managed to eat with it.

Frank took all this in as he shook hands, taking care not to straighten up again too suddenly in case the pink beam should be a trifle under a six foot. With some relief he subsided into a chair, whilst Miss Alvina twittered on a theme to which he should by now have been accustomed, but which always induced a feeling of savage boredom.

"So very interesting to think that you are at Scotland Yard. We must all mind our p's and q's, mustn't we, or you will be arresting us." She gave the little clear laugh which went with the high, birdlike voice, and then changed it suddenly to a cough, because, well as she knew the Abbotts, it was the first time their nephew had come to tea and at close quarters there was something a little daunting about his slim elegance—fair hair mirror-smooth, eyes of pale unchanging blue, and, oh dear, such beautiful clothes. Miss Alvina had an eye for detail. She noticed the socks, the tie, the handkerchief, the impeccable cut of the coat, and the really beautiful shoes. Not in the least like a policeman. A vision of Joseph Turnberry, the village constable, entered her mind upon heavily clumping feet. A very worthy young man of course, and a good baritone voice for the choir. She had a high esteem for Joseph, whom she had taught in Sunday school, but for the moment he added to her slight confusion. Her colour rose and she turned with relief to Mrs. Abbott, who was excusing her husband with the smoothness of long practice.

"The Clothing Accounts, Miss Vinnie—he has left them to the last moment again. I am sure you will understand."

Miss Alvina understood perfectly. Everyone in Deeping knew that Colonel Abbott would not go out to tea-parties. "A pack of rubbish! And you'll take away each other's characters much more comfortably without me." Most people had heard him say it, but the conventions continued to be observed. He was always invited, and if it wasn't the Clothing Club accounts which prevented him from coming, it would be the autumn clearing-up in the garden, the winter pruning, or the spring planting-out. There were also dogs who had to be exercised and a number of other useful refuges from hospitality. Mrs. Abbott rang the changes on them with amiability and charm.

When Colonel Abbott had been disposed of, Cicely's "I simply won't go out in a gang" had to be softened into "She was afraid we'd be too much of a party for you." After which Miss Vinnie addressed herself to the tea-table and poured a straw-coloured liquid out of a very large Victorian teapot into her best eggshell china teacups, which had no handles and were quite terribly difficult to drink out of. If the tea was hot, you burned your fingers. If you didn't burn your fingers, it meant that the tea was at that horrid lukewarm stage when it not only looked like straw but tasted like it too. Frank, like every other male visitor, was torn between a horrid conviction that it would be impossible to get through without crushing or dropping his fragile cup and an inexcusable urge to precipitate the crash and get it over.

Miss Alvina informed him that the tea-set had come from China as a present to her great-grandmother—"Only she didn't marry the gentleman who sent it, because just about then she met my great-grandfather at a Hunt Ball. They were married in exactly a month to the day, which wasn't considered at all the thing, but my great-grandfather was so impetuous. And they were married for sixty years and had fifteen children, and never a cross word between them. You can see their tombstones if you look out of the little window at the end of the room—at least you could if it were not so dark. I do hope you don't mind sitting like this with the lights on and the curtains not drawn. It's a thing I used not to care about myself, but now I enjoy it because it means that the war is over and one can think about that horrid black-out and be so glad that you don't have to do it any more. And then, of course, being right on the outskirts of the village, I think it's rather nice for anyone coming down the path off the Common—such a lonely road, especially where it runs through Dead Man's Copse."

Frank Abbott put himself out of temptation by setting down his empty cup.

"Who was the dead man?" he asked.

Miss Alvina pressed a home-made bun upon him and dispensed more straw-coloured tea. The bun was stuck full of caraway seeds and iced over all with a layer of soft pink sugar.

"Well, it's rather a horrid story, Mr. Frank, but of course it's so long ago, they would all have been dead anyway. He was called Edward Brand, and he was some sort of connection of the Tomalyns who were the family that owned Deerhurst Park on the other side of the Common. They've quite died out now, but you can see their tombs in the church. They owned all the land right up to the path across the Common, and they let this Edward Brand go and live in what they called the Forester's House, right in the middle of the wood. No one knew where he came from, or why they let him live there. He was very tall and thin, with long coal-black hair tied back with a riband. It was in the eighteenth century and most people wore wigs with powder on them, but Edward Brand wore his own long black hair. He lived quite alone in the Forester's House, and in a little while nobody would go near the place, especially after dark. It was said that he practised witchcraft. People were very superstitious in those days—My dear Mrs. Abbott, do let me fill your cup. And you really must taste my strawberry jam. Ellen Caddle made it a new way this year and it has really turned out very well."

Mrs. Abbott said, "It's delicious. I think Ellen really is a witch. I can't get my jam to taste like this. But go on—tell Frank how Edward Brand became the Dead Man."

"If you think it's a suitable subject for the tea-table—" said Miss Alvina. She turned to Frank. "Well, the stories got worse and worse. Even on the path along the Common people said bats swooped on them and they heard owls shrieking, and some of them said it sounded more like human beings, and they got to think dreadful things went on in the Forester's House. In the end there was some story about a girl who disappeared, only it turned out afterwards she'd run away from home because

16

she didn't get on with her step-mother. Everyone thought that Edward Brand had something to do with her disappearing like that. She was quite a young girl, not more than fourteen. They thought none of their children would be safe, so they went up into the wood to burn the Forester's House. My father said that when he was a boy the old sexton who used to have this house told him his grandfather was one of the men who went up from Deeping to call Edward Brand to account. He said they found the house quite empty, with all the doors and windows wide open and no sign of anyone there. There were a great many looking-glasses in the rooms, and they broke them, and pulled the doors from the hinges, and came away. There was no path up to the house, only as much track as anyone would make going to and fro. The Common path is quite a long way off. When they got back to it where it runs between the trees they came suddenly on the body of Edward Brand hanging from a long straight branch. And they buried him at the cross roads where the path comes down off the Common just outside the churchyard wall. That's what they did with suicides in those days. The Forester's House is still up there in the wood, but nobody's lived in it since and nobody likes going near it. And the place between the trees where they found Edward Brand hanging has been called Dead Man's Copse ever since."

Frank Abbott's attention was caught not so much by the story as by the fact that whilst she was telling it her small twittering personality seemed to have receded into the background. He had the strongest impression that the story itself was being passed on to him as it had been received—no absorption had taken place. He had no doubt that it came to him as it had come to her, and to her father, from the old sexton whose grandfather had seen Edward Brand hanging in Dead Man's Copse—all in the true line of oral tradition, a thing not uncommon in village life, though not as common as it used to be. He thought Miss Silver would be interested, and put it away to tell her.

The tea-party went on as tea-parties do. Half past five struck, and a quarter to six. Monica and Miss Alvina seemed to have a great deal to talk about. Frank reflected that there always was a lot to talk about in a village, because sooner or later everything that happened got into circulation and was passed on vigorously until something else took its place. Of course sometimes the thing hadn't happened at all. A pleasing element of doubt and mystery was then added to the gossip. As a good many of the people in Deeping were only names to him, he found it difficult to feel any marked degree of interest, though some of it was to come back to him afterwards. Maggie Bell and the way she listened in on the party line—Miss Alvina's indignant, "Everyone knows she does it, and I think it's high time someone spoke to her or to Mrs. Bell," and Monica's indulgent "Poor Maggie—she has so few pleasures. If it amuses her to hear me ordering the fish from Lenton or making an appointment with my dentist, I should hate to snatch it away."

Miss Alvina had become a little heated, and it was perhaps to change the subject that Monica Abbott began to talk about Mrs. Caddle, whom he identified with the Ellen responsible for their superlative strawberry jam, and who appeared to be Miss Vinnie's daily help.

"Cicely met her in the Lane when she was coming back from giving the dogs a run this afternoon—I thought she stayed all day. And Cis said she looked terrible, as if she'd been crying her eyes out. Is there anything wrong?"

The twitter returned in full force.

"That's just what I said to her, Mrs. Abbott. You know she comes at nine—I get my own breakfast—and the minute I saw her I said, 'Dear me, Ellen, what's wrong? You look as if you'd been crying your eyes out.' My exact words, and so she did. And all she would say was she'd got a headache. So then I told her she'd better go back and lie down. She said she'd rather work, so I told her to make herself a good cup of tea. But after

18

lunch she looked so bad I sent her home. And you know, she may say what she likes about a headache—and I daresay she had one, because there's nothing like crying to bring them on, is there—but it isn't the first time she's looked as if she'd been crying all night, and quite between ourselves, I'm afraid there is something wrong at home. Albert Caddle may be a very good chauffeur—and I believe he is—but it was very foolish of her to marry him—so much younger, and really quite a stranger here. However, we mustn't gossip, must we?" She turned to Frank with unsolicited information. "Her husband is chauffeur to Mr. Harlow at the Grange, and he gets his dinner up at the house. That is to say, he was old Mr. Harlow's chauffeur after he was demobilized, and when Mr. Harlow died last year and his nephew Mr. Mark came into the property, he stayed on. Mr. Mark doesn't much care about driving himself, which seems strange, because he's quite a young man. Do you know at all why it is, Mrs. Abbott? He's a friend of Cicely's, isn't he?"

Monica Abbott felt the sharp anger which always came up in her when anyone bracketted Mark Harlow's name with Cicely's. What made it a great deal worse was that she must on no account let anyone see that she was angry. She smiled now and said in her most amiable tone,

"I don't know if he is a friend—he is a very pleasant acquaintance. He is away so much that we all see less of him than we should like. I'm afraid I have no idea why he doesn't drive, but you could ask him, couldn't you?"

The church clock was striking six. Miss Alvina became a little flustered.

"Oh, I wouldn't *dream!* It would seem so—so intrusive."

"It might," said Monica Abbott.

Miss Alvina pursued the theme.

"I did ask Ellen Caddle—I don't mean to say that she would talk about Mr. Harlow's affairs, but I did happen to ask her whether she knew if he suffered from—night-blindness, I think

19

they call it. Because he does drive himself in the day, and of course sometimes at night too. Ellen said she didn't think there was anything to stop him driving if he wanted to, but I just wondered whether it could be that. Old Mr. Tolley had it—his wife always had to drive if it was after dark, and he had very good sight in the daytime. Mr. Harlow certainly has very fine eyes—don't you think so? And so good-looking."

"He is a very pleasant acquaintance," said Mrs. Abbott with finality. Then she turned her head sharply. "What's that? It sounds like someone running."

Frank Abbott had heard those stumbling, running footsteps for a full half minute before Monica turned her head. They all heard them now—desperate, stumbling, running feet coming down off the old path from the Common and across the road. There was the sound of gasping breath, the clatter of the gate thrown back. And then before any of them could reach the outer door there were hands that beat on it, and a girl's voice screaming, "Murder! Murder! Let me in!"

CHAPTER 4

It was two or three days later that Frank Abbott, off duty for the evening and very comfortable in one of Miss Maud Silver's Victorian chairs with the bright blue covers and the curly walnut legs, looked across at her knitting placidly on the other side of the hearth and broke off his narrative to remark,

"It's right up your street, you know. What a pity you couldn't have been there."

Miss Silver's needles clicked. An infant vest revolved. She coughed slightly and said,

"My dear Frank, pray continue."

He went on looking at her in the half teasing way which did not quite conceal a deep affection and respect. From her Edwardian fringe, rigidly controlled by a hair-net, to her black woollen stockings and beaded glacé shoes she was the perfect survival of a type now almost extinct. She might have stepped out of any family album to be immediately recognized as a spinster relative of slender means but indomitable character, or at a second view as the invaluable governess whose pupils, doing her credit in after life, would never forget what they owed to her ministrations.

What no one would have guessed was that Miss Maud Silver, after twenty years of the schoolroom, had left it behind her to become a highly successful private detective. Not that she described herself in this manner. She remained a gentlewoman, and she found the phrase repugnant to a gentlewoman's feelings. Her professional card described her as:

Miss Maud Silver
15 Montague Mansions

and added in the right-hand bottom corner the legend, "Private enquiries."

Her new profession had brought her modest comfort and a great many friends. Their portraits thronged the mantel-piece and a couple of occasional tables. There were a good many young men and girls and a number of blooming babies in old-fashioned frames of silver, and fretwork, and silver filagree upon plush.

As Miss Silver looked about her room her heart was wont to swell with gratitude to Providence, not only for having surrounded her with all this comfort, but for having preserved her and her possessions through six terrible years of war. There had been a bomb at the end of the street. Her windows had been broken, and one of the blue plush curtains had sustained a rather nasty cut, but it had been so neatly mended by her invaluable Emma that even she herself could hardly see the darn. A lot of dust and rubble had got into the carpet of the same bright peacock-blue shade as the curtains, but it had returned from the cleaners as good as new. Her pictures had not been damaged at all. "Hope" still turned her bandaged eyes upon some inner dream. The "Black Brunswicker" bade an eternal farewell to his bride. Millais' lovely nun still pleaded for "Mercy" in the picture which everyone used to call the "Huguenot." "Bubbles" still watched the flight of perishable joy. Cosy, very cosy, was Miss Silver's invariable conclusion. And so providentially preserved.

She said, "Pray continue, my dear Frank," and was all attention.

"Well, as I said, it's right up your street. There was this girl battering on the door and crying murder, and falling down in a dead faint as soon as she got inside. Rather a pretty girl—on the up-and-coming side, I should think, when not on the edge of being frightened to death."

"Was she known to your aunt and Miss Grey?"

"Oh, yes. Name of Mary Stokes. Demobilized from the A.T.S. and helping on an uncle's farm on the other side of the Common. Rather pretty, as I said. Rather silly and—I'm not so sure about this, but I got a sort of idea that underneath all the screaming and fainting there was something—well, tough."

"What made you think so?"

"I don't know. She came round pretty quick—I thought there were indications that the brain was ticking over. I may have got it all wrong—girls are so odd. Of course you read them like a book. I wish you had been there. Anyhow Monica and Miss Grey got her round, and after some preliminary gasping this is what she said. Her uncle has a farm on the other side of the Common—Tomlin's Farm it's called. All the land over there and down as far as Deeping used to belong to a family called Tomalyn. They've died out years ago, but the farm keeps the name. The farmer is Stokes, same like the niece. Well, she was coming in to Deeping by the path I told you about, the one running through Dead Man's Copse."

Miss Silver coughed.

"Would it be the way she would naturally come?"

His left eyebrow rose a trifle.

"It's the nearest way."

"There is another?"

"Yes, there is. It's a little longer and comes into the village farther on—in fact very nearly at the other end. It's the driving-road. No one in their senses would take a car over the other, though I daresay it's been done—there are a lot of lunatics on the road. Anyhow that's one of the things that made me feel Miss Mary Strokes might be tough. I gather that the local inhabitants don't queue up to go through Dead Man's Copse in the dark."

Miss Silver's needles clicked.

"It was dark?"

He shrugged slightly.

"As pitch. After six of a black January evening."

She said, "Go on, Frank."

"Well, this is her story. The path dips to the Copse, which is quite a dense little wood. She says she heard something and went off the path into the bushes. When she was asked why, she said because she was frightened, and when she was asked what frightened her she said she didn't know, she just thought she heard something. You can go round and round like that for quite a time without getting any forarder. When she had led the local constable round and round the mulberry bush for as long as my patience would last I suggested that we should get on with what happened."

Miss Silver's small, shrewd eyes were on his face.

23

"Did she appear to you to be trying to gain time—to collect herself, or perhaps to think out what she was going to say?"

A faint smile just touched his lips.

"It did occur to me—especially when she had another prolonged sobbing fit. When we got her going she said she heard the noise again, and this time it was footsteps and something being dragged. They passed close beside her and on to the path, and then there was the beam of a torch and she saw a man's hand and arm and—what he had been dragging. She said it was the body of a murdered girl and that is what she has stuck to up hill and down dale."

Miss Silver was knitting rapidly. She held her needles low, in the continental fashion, and hardly ever glanced at them. She looked across them now and said,

"Dear me!"

"Dear me it is—and with knobs on."

"My dear Frank—what an expression!"

"Consider it retracted. We are keeping the corpse waiting. Mary Stokes says it was a young woman, and a stranger, with fair hair and a shocking wound on the head. She was quite sure anyone with a wound like that must be dead. She says the hair hung down and hid the face a good deal. She described the clothes—a black coat, black gloves, no hat, and—here's the thing that has us all intrigued—one earring, and a rather peculiar one at that."

Miss Silver coughed.

"She seems to have seen a good deal. You say she stated that the girl's hair was falling all about her face. It seems strange that she should have been able to see an earring."

"It's a lot stranger than that. She says the man turned the girl over and looked for the other earring, and it wasn't there. She said he looked for it like a madman, turning the beam this way and that, feeling in the hair."

Miss Silver said, "How extremely shocking!"

24

"Well, it is rather. When he couldn't find it he left the body lying there and went back into the wood, and Mary Stokes came out from behind her bush and ran for her life. Well, we got the local constable, a good hearty chap, and we went up to view the spot. Mary went faint on us, so I went back to Abbottsleigh and fetched my car. That's how I know what the track is like to drive on—I'm one of the fools who've done it. When we got Mary there, there wasn't any corpse. She went on being faint in spite of a pretty nipping air, and when it came to trying to fix the spot she didn't seem to have any ideas on the subject. Just said she'd got well along into the Copse, but not far in and she wasn't nearly clear of it, but it was too dark to say for certain, and oh, please couldn't she go home to Uncle, and a lot more of that kind of thing and more tears. I said no, she couldn't, and then a County Inspector rolled up from Lenton, and he said so too. Well, we searched the place from end to end, and neither then nor next day when we went over it by daylight was there the slightest sign of anything having been dragged through the bushes at the side of the path. On the wood side there's the sort of ditch which ought to show footprints—soft sides and a muddy bottom. And nothing you could swear to from one end to the other except Mary's own footprints where there's a sort of gap and the remains of a track going off into the wood. No sign of anything being dragged there either. It looks as if Mary had come down on to the path from the bushes like she says and then come running back again. The two best prints are certainly those of running feet—the toe very deeply marked and scarcely a trace of the heel. That was the only corroboration of her story until this afternoon. There was no corpse on the path or in the wood, and no sign of one ever having been there. There was no one missing from the neighbourhood. There was no stray earring."

Miss Silver coughed.

"The other one of the pair, which I think you described as peculiar."

"Well, it was. You know the kind of ring they call an eternity ring?"

She smiled.

"An old fashion which has come back—a circle of small stones set continuously. Extremely pretty but not very practical. The stones are sadly apt to fall out."

"You know everything—I've always said so. But have you ever seen an earring like that?"

"No, indeed. It would be very difficult to arrange, would it not? You see, an earring would have to open on a hinge, or it could not be passed through the ear."

He laughed.

"I didn't think of that. But I suppose it could be managed. Anyhow Mary Stokes swears, and sticks to it, that what she saw in the corpse's ear was an eternity ring set with diamonds."

Miss Silver continued to knit, her small, quite pleasing features composed, her air attentive. After a moment she said,

"You have something more to tell me, I think."

He nodded.

"When I tore myself away on Sunday night there were two major schools of thought in Deeping. According to one, Mary Stokes had been pulling everybody's leg. Passion for the limelight. Exhibitionism—only in the country they call it plain showing-off. Quite a tenable theory, and compatible with everything except those running footprints. The other school of thought, which is adhered to by a minority, maintains that Mary was telling the truth, with perhaps some natural enhancing of the horrid details, but that the corpse wasn't dead and just upped and walked away after Miss Stokes had run screaming down the path."

"Pray continue. You mentioned this afternoon—"

He nodded.

"I did. Round about half past four we got a report from out Hampstead way. A woman had been in and said her lodger was missing—went out on Friday and never came back. Description of missing person—young woman round about thirty or perhaps less, fair hair shoulder length, hazel eyes, medium height, very slight build. Went out dressed in a black coat and black beret, both very smart. Light stockings, black shoes. And large hoop earrings *set all round with little diamonds like those eternity rings.*"

CHAPTER 5

There was a pause, yet it hardly appeared to be one, so charged was it with Miss Silver's intelligent interest. When she observed, "A truly strange coincidence," Frank Abbott laughed and said,

"Do you believe in coincidences to that extent? I'm afraid I don't."

Miss Silver continued to knit.

"I have known some strange ones."

He laughed again.

"As strange as this?"

She made no direct answer, but said,

"Who is this missing woman? The landlady must have known a little more about her than that she wore a black coat and rather curious earrings."

"Well, she doesn't seem to know very much. I went down to see her, and this is what it amounts to. The missing woman hadn't been with her very long—not more than a month. Name Mrs. Rogers. Christian name Louise. Slight foreign accent. She told Mrs. Hopper—that's the landlady—that she was French,

27

but had married an Englishman who was dead. She was nicely spoken, didn't bring anyone home with her, and paid on the nail. She told Mrs. Hopper once that her family had been very rich, but they had lost everything in the war. Then she looked mysterious and said, 'Perhaps I shall get some of it back—who knows? That is why I am in England. If a thing is stolen, the law can get it back. That is why I am here.' She went out some time on Friday morning. Mrs. Hopper doesn't know when, because she was out shopping for the week-end. Well, it was on Saturday evening that Mary Stokes says she saw a fair-haired corpse with one eternity earring in Dead Man's Copse, and Louise Rogers has never gone back to Hampstead. I asked Mrs. Hopper whether she'd ever heard of Deeping, and she seemed to think that it was a patent food or a furniture polish." He leaned forward and stretched his hands to the cheerful glow of Miss Silver's fire. "Of course, you know, if it weren't for Mary Stokes, one would simply conclude that Mrs. Rogers was week-ending and hadn't bothered to let her landlady know."

Miss Silver coughed.

"If she had intended to stay away she would have taken a suit-case. Is anything missing?"

"Mrs. Hopper says no."

Miss Silver inclined her head.

"She would be well informed. A woman who lets lodgings keeps a very sharp eye upon that sort of thing. People have a way of removing their things by degrees and then going off without paying the rent."

"Well, she says there isn't anything missing. To use her own words, 'She went off in what she stood up in, her good black coat and beret—very smart and quite the lady, though foreign.' And the question is, did she go to Deeping and pose as Mary Stokes' corpse, and if she did, where did she go from there?"

Miss Silver stopped knitting for a moment and said quite gravely,

"I do not think you can neglect the possibility that she has met with a violent death."

"I suppose not. I'm to go to Deeping tomorrow and smell round. The locals won't bless me, but it's all fixed up with the Chief Constable. They're sending me because I was there when Mary put on her act, and because I'm supposed to know the place. As a matter of fact, any knowledge I have is extremely sketchy. My uncle has only recently come back from a long stretch overseas. Monica got stuck out there too, so the only one I've seen much of in the last ten years is my cousin Cicely. I used to go down and take her out when she was at school. Monica wrote to the headmistress about it, and I got brevet rank as brother."

"I think I saw your cousin's marriage in the papers some months ago, to a Mr. Hathaway."

"Yes. They've split, and she's at home again. Nobody knows what happened. She was right on the top of the world for about three months, and then she walked in one day and said she'd come home and she never wanted to see Grant again. You know, she's a bit of an heiress. My grandmother came into a packet from her father, who was one of our shipping peers, and she left the whole lot to Cicely."

"My dear Frank!"

He laughed.

"Uncle Reg and I mingle our tears. She couldn't do him out of Abbottsleigh, because that was Abbott property, but he's got precious little to keep it up on. She quarrelled with him because he took his turn of service aboard instead of buying himself out of it. My father, of course, hadn't been on speaking terms with her for years—she was furious about his marriage to my mother. Being the second son, she'd got it all mapped out that he was to marry money. And of course the pen went right through my name when I joined the police."

Miss Silver pressed her lips together for a moment before saying,

"Did it not occur to her that she might have made it possible for you to continue your studies for the Bar as your father had intended?"

He looked at her with sardonic amusement.

"Oh, yes, it occurred to her all right. She had me down and told me just how thriftless and foolish my father had always been, and how entirely in keeping it was that he should die before he had provided me with a profession. I can see her now, sitting up as bleak as an east wind and telling me she didn't propose to put a premium on folly and incompetence by taking over his responsibilities."

"My *dear* Frank!"

His look softened momentarily.

"Blessing in disguise, I shouldn't wonder. I should probably never have got a brief—to say nothing of not meeting you. Well, that was my last visit to Abbottsleigh till Uncle Reg came back the other day." He laughed. "I told her what I thought of her in a few well chosen words and cleared out. You know, what's so charming for me is that I'm her dead spit and image. I can even see it myself."

"Is your cousin like her too?"

"Oh, no—Cis is a little brown thing."

There was a pause. Then Miss Silver said,

"Just why have you been telling me all this, Frank?"

A gleam of humour came and went. He said casually,

"Oh, I don't know—I do tell you things, don't I?"

She looked at him with affectionate severity and produced a quotation from her favourite Lord Tennyson.

" 'And trust me not at all or all in all.' "

He laughed.

"And, 'A lie that is half the truth is ever the biggest of lies,' or words to that effect. All right, I'll come clean. Monica is dying

30

to meet you. How would you like to come down on a visit to Abbottsleigh?"

She maintained her gaze.

"Are you offering me a professional engagement?"

He laughed a little.

"Not at the moment."

"What do you mean by that, Frank?"

His lip twisted.

"I don't know what I mean. State of mind quite chaotic. The nearest I can get to it is that the thing as it stands makes nonsense, and you have a way of inducing things to make sense. All quite vague and filmy, and mixed up with the fact that Monica really is dying to meet you—" He broke off, and then said quite seriously, "I'd like you to see Mary Stokes and tell me whether she's lying. Also to what extent. And why."

CHAPTER 6

Abbottsleigh was a large, rambling house of no particular style of architecture. It had, as a matter of fact, begun as a farmstead and been added on to as rising fortunes and large families suggested. A mid-Victorian Abbott with fifteen children had, after a visit to the Highlands, built on a truly frightful wing bristling with turrets in the style of Balmoral. In Lady Evelyn Abbott's day a stiff conventionality had descended upon as many of the furnishings as could by any possibility be subjugated. Her daughter-in-law, with very little money to spend, had gone up into the attics and routed there, discovering a good deal of rather nice old oak, and some chests full of charming Regency curtains with which to replace the prevailing tapestry and plush.

Several rooms had consequently been humanized, including her bedroom and Cicely's, the dining-room, and a charming small sitting-room which got all the sun it is possible to get in the middle of an English winter.

The drawing-room she had not attempted to alter. It was a room to entertain in, not a place in which anyone would wish to sit. The curtains of heavy old-gold brocade, the small gilded chairs, and the large brocade armchairs, suggested expense rather than comfort. There were a great many mirrors in gilt frames, and a number of family portraits, amongst them one of Lady Evelyn herself painted not very long after her marriage. No one could possibly help being struck by the resemblance to the grandson now decorating Scotland Yard as a rising detective sergeant. The high-bridged nose was there, too pale and thin to suit a woman's face, the chilly blue of the eyes, looking even paler because lashes and eyebrows were of the same colourless shade as the hair. The hair itself, slicked back from the brow after the trying fashion of the eighties, enhanced an already startling likeness. If there had been no other reason for not using the drawing-room, Monica Abbott would have found it impossible to relax under her mother-in-law's sardonic gaze. What Colonel Abbott may have thought remained unspoken. It is certain that he could not have brought himself to remove his mother's picture, but like Monica he probably preferred the morning-room, where the only portrait was a water-colour drawing of Cicely as a child.

Miss Silver, having been met at Lenton and driven back to a good fire and a well spread tea-table, was now comfortably at her ease. She thought Colonel Abbott a very fine-looking man, and Mrs. Abbott most warm and kind. So nice-looking too, with that wavy dark hair and big brown eyes. Mrs. Hathaway had the eyes, but otherwise was not at all like either of her parents, except for the hair which might have been like her mother's if it had not been cut. Really, with those short curls all over her head and her small slight figure, it was very hard to think of her as a married woman. Glancing involuntarily at the third finger of Cicely Hathaway's left hand, Miss Silver was really shocked to find it bare. Modern girls were very careless about wearing wedding-rings—oh, very careless indeed—though she feared that this was not a case of carelessness but of design.

As she partook of scone and honey and listened to Monica Abbott explaining that it was Cicely who looked after the bees, her eyes dwelt shrewdly and kindly upon the girl sitting on the hearthrug who drank cup after a cup of tea but ate nothing at all. Frank Abbott had called her a little brown thing. Miss Silver thought it a very good description. Hair, eyes, and skin were all brown, the hair and eyes not as dark as her mother's, but the skin much darker. As she sat there close in to the fire, her face reflected its glow. One cheek burned scarlet where the heat had caught it. The colour lent her an elusive charm. She could have had scarlet berries in her hair and gone dancing down the wind with last year's leaves.

No such fanciful thought entered Miss Silver's mind. She saw a girl who was desperately unhappy, and desperately tired of her own unhappiness. She turned to Mrs. Abbott, and was presently conducted to her room. She considered it most pleasant and comfortable, with its solid Victorian furniture and curtains of crimson repp.

Having removed a black cloth coat with rather an elderly fur collar and a black felt hat now in its third winter but enlivened by a small bunch of purple pansies, she tidied her hair, put on her beaded indoor shoes, washed her hands, looked for and found a gay chintz knitting-bag, and returned to the morning-room. She was wearing the dress of bottle-green wool which had been new in the autumn, the slightly open neck filled in with a net front and adorned by a bog-oak brooch in the shape of a rose with a large Irish pearl at its centre. There was also a fine gold chain to support the pince-nez which she occasionally used for reading fine print if the light was bad, and another chain of more massive construction which fitted close about her neck. From this depended one of those heavy Victorian lockets with a pattern of deeply cut and interlaced initials, a pious relic of the long dead parents whose A (for Alfred) and M (for Maria) formed the design. In the days when it had reposed on Maria's bosom it had contained a lock of Alfred's hair. To this had now been added a soft grey curl of Maria's. To Miss Silver Alfred and Maria were "Poor Papa" and "Dear Mamma," and she thought the locket very handsome.

Settling herself beside the fire, she took a ball of pale blue wool from her knitting-bag and began to cast on the stitches for a companion jacket to the one which she had finished the evening before. Babies really required several of these little coats if they were to be kept clean and warm. A most sensible fashion.

When she had the right number of stitches, she was ready for conversation with her hostess, and pleased to find that they were alone, Colonel Abbott and Cicely having vanished, and Frank having rung up to say that he was driving down and might be late.

"You don't know how glad I am to meet you," said Monica. "Frank adores you."

"My *dear* Mrs. Abbott!"

"Oh, he does. And so good for him, because he isn't at all given to adoring. That cold, sneering way he has, you know. Of course a lot of it is put on, but not altogether. My mother-in-law was so very bad for him. Not that he saw a lot of her, because she had quarrelled with his father—she quarrelled with everyone. But he is really too like her—it would be rather frightening if one did not know that he is quite different underneath. And then the way she behaved when his father died—I expect he has told you about it. Quite dreadfully embittering for him, poor boy. And there we were, at the other side of the world, and no idea that things were so bad—my brother-in-law left nothing but

34

debts. And of course Frank never told us, though I don't know what we could have done if he had, with Cis at school and Reg with practically nothing but his pay. Even Abbottsleigh was left to Lady Evelyn for her life—she had her husband quite under her thumb." She turned a warm smile upon Miss Silver. "So you see how frightfully good it is for Frank to adore you. She robbed him of much worse things than money, and you've been giving them back. That's why I wanted to meet you. And of course for other reasons as well. There's this murder—or perhaps it isn't a murder at all—Frank says it doesn't make sense. And it doesn't—does it? But—somehow—it's rather frightening."

To the soft click of her needles Miss Silver said, "Yes?"

Monica Abbott's colour had risen.

"It is, you know. If it was just a murder it would be horrible, and that would be the end of it—I mean it would have happened because there was a quarrel, or someone was jealous, or got drunk and didn't know what he was doing, or for money. Those are the sort of reasons why murders happen. But this one— well, you don't only not know why it happened, but you don't know whether it happened at all. It's frightening—like seeing something and not knowing whether it's really there and not being sure whether you even saw it."

In prim but rather pleasing tones Miss Silver quoted from Lady Macbeth, " 'They made themselves—air.' "

Monica Abbott gazed at her with warmth.

"Yes—that's exactly what I mean. How clever you are!"

Miss Silver smiled.

"Tell me a little more about it all. A good deal seems to turn upon the character of this girl Mary Stokes. Of course that is always the way in any crime—a story which appears quite incredible in the mouth of one person can be accepted as perfectly natural from another. Now what sort of girl is this Miss Stokes?"

Monica Abbott said slowly, "I—don't—know—"

35

Miss Silver gave her slight cough.

"Do you not?"

"Well, I've got nothing to go on. I don't like her, but I oughtn't to say so, because I've got nothing to go on. I can only tell you what you would see for yourself in five minutes. She's about twenty-four or twenty-five, but she looks—experienced. She was in one of the women's services at the end of the war. She hasn't been very much in Deeping. Of course we've only been here ourselves for a few months. We used to pay short visits before my husband went abroad, but we didn't belong."

"Does Mary Stokes belong?"

"No, she doesn't. The younger girls copy her clothes and the way she does her hair, but she isn't liked—they think she gives herself airs."

"And does she?"

"I suppose she does. Oh, I don't know—I don't think I'm being fair. You see, she isn't a village girl at all—she's something much smarter and more sophisticated. She comes down to the farm once in a way when she's out of a job or wants a change. She isn't strong and they're good to her, but I think it's a relief when she goes off again. She's been working in an office in Lenton, but she got ill and was ordered a month's rest. I believe the firm are taking her back."

"Is she pretty?"

"Oh, *yes!*" said Monica Abbott in an exasperated tone.

Half an inch of blue knitting now stood out from the needles in a frill. Gazing mildly across it, Miss Silver said,

"In what way?"

Monica laughed.

"Oh, in the good old peroxide way that gentlemen prefer. No—that's low of me. She probably assists it a little, but I believe her hair has always been fair. And she has blue eyes and synthetic manners." She threw out her hand in an expressive gesture. "Look here, it's no good—I don't like her and I can't be fair."

36

Miss Silver's eyes dwelt upon her calmly.

"Why do you not like her?"

"I just don't."

"But I think you could give me a reason if you would."

There was a moment's pause. Then,

"I think she's a snake in the grass," said Monica Abbott.

"Dear me!"

Miss Silver pulled at her pale blue ball, releasing a yard or two of the fleecy wool. She found Mrs. Abbott very picturesque, very attractive, but was more concerned with the matter of her judgment. She did not appear to be the sort of woman who would be hard upon a girl, but you never could tell. There might be reasons. She wondered whether it was possible that Mary Stokes had had anything to do with the break-up of Cicely Hathaway's marriage.

In a perfectly artless and natural manner she induced the conversation to drift in Cicely's direction. Having first remarked upon the cosiness of the room and enquired whether the charming water-colour on the farther wall was a representation of Durham Cathedral, she turned to the portrait above the mantel-shelf.

"Your daughter of course. A most speaking likeness."

Monica sighed. Those nursery days seemed far enough away.

"Oh, yes—it's Cicely at seven. It's very like her still, only—she doesn't look happy any more."

"No—"

"She's had a quarrel with her husband—I expect Frank told you. I don't know why one has children, I'm sure—and they go on and on about putting up the birthrate! If she would only tell us what it's all about, we might do something to help her, but she won't say a single word. When you think of its being the creature you used to wash and dress, and put in the corner, and slap when it was naughty—though I don't believe in slapping children, it spoils their tempers—well, it's simply devastating. But she always was the most obstinate creature, even when she was six months old. Rather sweet, you know, but definitely aggravating."

Miss Silver knitted.

"And you have no idea at all of the reason for the quarrel?"

"She won't say a word, and he won't either."

"But sometimes one may have an idea. Is it at all possible that there was—another woman?"

"I don't know—I don't think so. But, oh dear, of course there's always another woman if you look hard enough—one just can't afford to go hunting for skeletons in cupboards. I mean, it was too soon after they were married for there to be anyone *fresh*— at least you'd think so, wouldn't you? Only three months, and they seemed so happy! But of course if you go delving into the past—" She leaned forward and spoke impulsively. "The plain fact is, I don't know. Cicely has locked herself up, and I don't know anything. But if I were to start guessing I should say it wasn't another woman. But it might be the money—Cis has rather a lot, you know."

"So Frank informed me."

Monica's eyes sparkled.

"Reg's mother left the whole lot past him to Cicely. Outrageous, isn't it? And the worst of it is, the child used to be too much with her grandmother. We were abroad, and she spent all her holidays here." She hesitated a little. "I may be wrong, but sometimes I think being here so much she may have got rather a wrong idea about the importance of money. You see, Lady Evelyn thought that everyone else was as much taken up with it as she was. She believed we were all counting on it and wishing for it, and she thought she would punish us by leaving it to Cicely—and now I'm wondering whether she just didn't punish Cis."

Miss Silver coughed.

"You mean?"

"I don't know what I mean," said Monica Abbott in rather a distracted voice. "She's bitter about the money—you can't help seeing that. You know—" she hesitated again—"she couldn't look less like her grandmother, but she's got a streak of the same old obstinacy, and—oh, Miss Silver, I'm so unhappy. She doesn't eat and she doesn't sleep, and she doesn't tell us anything. She's such a warm-hearted child really—at least she used to be until she froze up like this. She doesn't even stay here because she wants to be here—she just stays because she won't let him drive her away." She produced a handkerchief and passed it rapidly over her eyes. "You must think me quite mad, talking to you like this when I've never seen you before, but I can't talk to anyone in the village, and you don't know what a relief it is."

CHAPTER 7

"Well, this is the place," said Frank Abbott.

Miss Silver alighted from the car and looked about her at Dead Man's Copse. The thought which immediately sprang to her mind was that it was very well named. She had never seen a gloomier wood or driven over a rougher track, and it did not surprise her at all that the place should be very little frequented. Something about the lie of the land and the way the road dipped to this hollow made the place even darker than it should have been. The trees were not so very thick, and they were not large—a few straggling pines; a dense hump or two of holly; the wreck of what had been a massive oak, now smothered in strangling ivy; and for the rest the sort of tangled undergrowth which springs up through years of neglect.

She enquired who owned the land.

Frank Abbott laughed.

"I believe Uncle Reg does. There's been some doubt about it. It was all Tomalyn property as far as this path. Everything on the other side of it is common land. The male Tomalyns died out more than a hundred years ago, but there were two daughters. One married an Abbott, and the other a Harlow. The Harlow property marches with Abbottsleigh. The Tomalyns' house was burnt down, and a lot of papers with it. Nobody bothered very much about this bit of land and it was just let go. There was some superstition mixed up in it, I shouldn't wonder—some idea that it was unlucky. Uncle Reg says he can remember an old boy in the village telling him the Dead Man had left his curse on the place. Anyhow neither the Harlows nor the Abbotts had the title-deeds, and they don't seem to have bothered who it belonged to for a good many years. Then some old paper turned up, and they settled it between them. So I suppose you may say that this delightful spot is now Abbott property."

Miss Silver had listened with attention.

"And the house? There is, I understand, a house in the wood. That would go with the land."

"I haven't seen it, but it must be a complete ruin. There used to be some sort of a path going off to it—hereabouts just short of the oak, so the local constable says, but there's not much trace of it. If Mary Stokes is telling the truth, which I don't think she is, that's where she was standing when she saw someone looking for an earring in a dead girl's hair. I wonder what she really did see. If it weren't for Louise Rogers and her earrings, I should be inclined to think she made the whole thing up. But there is Louise, and she's still missing. And look here, it hasn't rained since Saturday—you can still see where Mary came down off

40

the bank and left those deep toeprints in the mud. She was running all right."

Miss Silver picked her way across the ditch and up the bank in a very active manner. She looked at the footprints, and then turned her attention to the wood.

"How far away is the house you spoke of?"

"Between a quarter and half a mile according to the plan Uncle Reg showed me. They called it the Forester's House, and I suppose there was some sort of path through the wood in those days. There isn't one now."

Miss Silver coughed.

"The wood has been searched?"

"To some extent, I gather."

"My dear Frank!"

"Well, you know, I was merely an onlooker at that stage and I had to watch my step. The Inspector from Lenton was in charge, and I may be wrong, but I certainly got the idea that if I was stupid enough to make a suggestion I should get it smacked back in my face, so I didn't make one. I don't know if he knew I was at the Yard, but I was taking rather particular pains to be Colonel Abbott's nephew on a visit. So I'm not really in a position to know just how far the search went, but if you ask me, I should say it was fairly cursory, and that if there were any traces, it won't now be possible to identify them. The local constable, Joe Turnberry, is a bit in the steamroller line."

Miss Silver said, "Very unfortunate."

He nodded.

"As far as I had any opportunity of observing the ground myself, there was no sign of anyone being dragged through the undergrowth. I don't see how a man could have dragged or carried a girl through this sort of tangle by night without leaving unmistakable traces—it doesn't make sense."

"How far into the wood did you go?"

41

"No great distance. As I say, I was being rather careful not to butt in. Now that I'm on the job, I'm getting Smith, the Lenton chap, to come over this afternoon, and we'll go through the place with a toothcomb. But I'm not sanguine."

"What about the house?"

"The Forester's House? It's the best part of half a mile away."

"Has it been searched?"

"I shouldn't think so. You see, I'm pretty sure Smith thought the whole thing was a mare's nest—I thought so myself. Just take the evidence. A girl says she sees a bleeding corpse dragged out of a wood. There isn't any corpse, there isn't any blood, there isn't any sign of anything having been dragged. What does the plain man conclude? He thinks the girl is telling the tale, and he doesn't go very far into the wood to look for a nesting mare."

Miss Silver's expression did not change. It was, and remained, of a mild firmness.

"I should be interested to see the Forester's House."

He threw her a quick look.

"What have you got in your mind? Do you expect to find Louise Rogers somewhere in the ruins?"

"I do not know, Frank. I would like to see the house."

He gave an odd short laugh.

"Well, you shall. But in the name of sanity, why should anyone who had murdered a woman, presumably in this wood, first drag her out on to the road to be seen by Mary Stokes, and then drag her back through half a mile of undergrowth? And how did he do it without leaving any traces? The thing's impossible."

Miss Silver coughed gently.

"If it was impossible, it did not happen."

He had a quizzical look for that.

"Well, what would you like to do first—see Mary Stokes, or wander in the wood?"

"I think we had better see Mary Stokes."

It was what he had hoped she would say. Under a casual manner he was, as a matter of fact, straining at the leash. If the case made nonsense at present, this much at least was certain—Mary was either lying, or telling the truth. If the former, it should be possible to break her story down. If the latter, she might be able to produce something a little more credible than Saturday's sobbed-out tale. As to whether she was lying or not, he had a good deal of confidence that Miss Silver would be able to give judgment. But when they came face to face with her in the parlour of Tomlin's Farm he wasn't so sure that they were going to get anything out of Miss Mary Stokes.

Mrs. Stokes, who admitted them greeting Frank as "Mr. Frank," and left them there with many apologies for there being no fire, was a good hearty soul with her sleeves rolled up to the elbows. She said her niece wouldn't be a moment, but they had the best part of ten minutes to wait and plenty of leisure to observe the flowered wallpaper covered with what an eighteenth-century lady once described as "great romping flowers"; the fox's mask grinning from a dark corner; the case of stuffed birds on a three-legged table shrouded in maroon cloth and trimmed about the edge with a valance of deep cotton lace; the Toby jug and charming lustre-ware in a corner cupboard; the photographic enlargements of Mr. Stokes' parents on one side of the room and Mrs. Stokes' parents on the other, both men very uncomfortable in their Sunday clothes with high stick-up collars and ties, both ladies decorous to the point of gloom. In the case of old Mrs. Stokes the portrait had been taken after she was a widow, and the camera had done ample justice to the wealth of crape in which she mourned, and to a truly portentous widow's bonnet with long funeral streamers.

Miss Silver gazed with interest at these evidences of family life. She noticed the brass handles on a walnut bureau—delightfully bright, and the bureau itself so beautifully polished. Not a speck of dust anywhere, and a good many knick-knacks to keep.

When Mary Stokes came into the room she did not seem to belong to it at all. She was young and pretty, but when you looked at her a second time you began to wonder if she was as young or as pretty as you thought at first. There was something just a little stiff, a little set—something that reminded Miss Silver of the old nursery warning to be careful how you looked when the clock struck or you might stay that way. It might have been the effect of the artificially brightened hair, the artificially heightened complexion. It might have been the way the hair was done—the last and extremest London fashion, looking a good deal out of place on a country farm. It might have been the hard royal blue of an equally unsuitable dress, or the brooch which glittered quite as brightly as if its stones were real. Probably all these things contributed to the impression made by Mary Stokes.

She came into the room with quite a little air. When she shook hands and said "How do you do?" her voice was pitched too high to be pleasant, and the syllables clipped to an excess of refinement.

Frank Abbott said, "I have been sent down from Scotland Yard to make some enquiries, Miss Stokes—Detective-Sergeant Abbott. I hope you will not object to Miss Silver's presence."

If Miss Stokes had not been so refined she might have tossed her head. As it was, she stared briefly without looking at Miss Silver and sat down on the nearest chair, after which she crossed her legs, displaying a good pair of silk stockings, arranged the blue skirt, and fixed a pair of bright blue eyes upon the personable young man who had come to question her. Good-looking fellow and a cut above a policeman—thinks quite a bit of himself. She let her glance meet his, and then very effectively dropped the darkened lashes until they lay upon her cheek. She could feel him looking at her, and had no idea that any young man could do so without pleasure.

With a faint conscious smile she said,

"Oh, of course—I'm sure I'm only too pleased."

He had taken out a notebook, and moved now so as to rest it on one of those solid pedestal tables so much in vogue about the middle of the last century. Of finely figured walnut in a high state of polish, it supported two heavily embossed photograph albums and a large family Bible, each on its own closely crocheted mat of maroon wool. He made room for the notebook, produced a pencil, and addressed Miss Stokes.

"I have just been making an examination of Dead Man's Copse. It is quite plain that you ran down the bank and across the ditch on to the path, but there is no sign of anyone else having done so."

The lashes rose. The bright blue eyes met his.

"Well, I'm sure if Joe Turnberry and Inspector Smith didn't leave any marks, there's no reason why anyone else should."

It was quite obvious that she thought she had scored. After a brief cold stare he proceeded to counteract this impression.

"I'm afraid that is no argument. Smith's and Turnberry's tracks are both quite easy to trace. You will remember that I happened to be there when they were made. What you must understand is that there are no other tracks. If, as you stated, a man came out of that wood dragging the body of a girl, how do you account for the fact that he left no footprints either on the bank or in the mud of the ditch, and that the dragged body left no track?"

She tilted her head a little.

"Oh, well, I wouldn't swear to the dragging—it was dark, you know. He may have been carrying her."

"In which case one would expect even deeper footprints."

She gave a slight shrug.

"Perhaps you haven't found the right place."

"Your own footprints are quite clear—there is no mistake about them. You were facing the path. On which side of you did this man come out of the wood?"

She pressed her lips together, frowning slightly.

45

"I don't know."

"Come, Miss Stokes, you were going down into Dead Man's Copse, when you heard a sound coming from the wood—that's what you said, isn't it? You were so frightened that you crossed the ditch and climbed up the bank into the wood to meet the noise." One of the fair eyebrows rose quizzically. "It seems rather an odd thing to do. Could you kindly explain why you did it?"

She said quite coolly,

"I was frightened—anyone would have been."

"So you ran in the direction of the sound which frightened you?"

"Well, I didn't stop to think, I just ran—you do when you're frightened. I suppose I wanted to hide."

"Yes, but why not the bushes on the other side of the path? Why go rushing into danger? You might have bumped right into the murderer—mightn't you?"

Miss Stokes showed signs of temper.

"I tell you I didn't think—I was too frightened! I don't know why I ran into the wood that side, but I did."

"Are you quite sure that you did?"

She stared angrily.

"What do you mean?"

"Well, you know, there are no footprints of yours going into the wood."

Her breath came quickly.

"I can't help that."

"Odd—isn't it? No footprints of yours going in, and none of the murderer's coming out! I'm afraid there's a discrepancy somewhere. You didn't cross that ditch to get into the wood, you know. However frightened you were, you would hardly be able to clear it at a single bound, especially in the dark."

All this while Miss Silver had been a silent but attentive spectator. She had chosen a chair which strongly resembled those in her own flat—a slightly curved upholstered back, a slightly curved upholstered seat, and small bow legs of yellow walnut tortuously carved. A very comfortable type of chair for knitting or needlework, affording support to the back without hampering the arms. At moments like these Miss Silver missed her knitting, but she did not permit herself to fidget. Her hands, in the warm black woollen gloves which had been a Christmas present from her niece Ethel, remained folded in her lap. Her regard dwelt thoughtfully on Mary Stokes. A cheap pearl necklace hung down over the bright blue dress. At the moment it was rising and falling in quite a noticeable manner. The girl's colour was deep and angry. Miss Silver believed her to be both angry and frightened. She considered that Frank was doing very well. He was smiling a little. It was a chilly smile. Monica Abbott wouldn't have liked it at all. It would have reminded her rather painfully of her mother-in-law. With just such a smile had Lady Evelyn been wont to preface some singularly wounding remark.

"Well, Miss Stokes—what about it?"

Some of the refinement slipped.

"I don't know what you're talking about."

"I've no objection to repeating it. Let me put it quite simply. You didn't walk across that ditch into the wood, and I'm prepared to swear you didn't jump it. How did you get there?"

She was looking at him now, angrily, uneasily.

"How did I get there?"

"Yes."

She tried to laugh.

"Wouldn't you like to know!"

The tone was intended to be provocative. It failed before his ice-cold stare.

He said, "Very much." And then, "Are you going to tell me? I think you'd better. This is rather a serious matter, you know. Anyone who is not implicated in a crime is naturally willing to

47

assist the police." He smiled again, this time in a more human manner.

Mary Stokes put up a hand to the pearl necklace, displaying five blood-red nails and a turquoise ring.

"Well, if you want to know, I went into the wood farther back."

"How much farther back?"

"Oh, a good bit."

"You would still have to cross the ditch."

"Well then, I wouldn't! Because there isn't any ditch before you get down into the dip—at least nothing to speak of. And it's dry—it wouldn't show footprints."

He wrote that down. Mary watched him. Then she had to meet the pale stare again.

"You thought that out very nicely. But I'm afraid it makes trouble for you in another direction. It explains why there are no footprints of yours going into the wood, but it doesn't explain why you went into the wood at that particular spot. You said in your statement, and you have just told me all over again, that you ran into the wood because you were so frightened that you didn't know what you were doing. The reason you were so frightened was because you had heard a dragging noise. Are you sticking to that?"

Her hand was pressing down upon the pearls, and upon the upward surge of her breath.

"Of course I am!"

His eyebrows rose.

"I haven't measured the distance from the top of the dip to where you ran on to the path, but I should say it was all of two hundred yards. Are you going to say that you walked all that way along the edge of the wood in the direction of the noise which had frightened you so much?"

Miss Silver saw her pull at the pearls and tangle them.

"Why shouldn't I?"

48

"It seems a little strange."

She flared up suddenly.

"What's strange about it? Anything's strange if you like to make it out that way! There wasn't anything strange at all! I heard the noise like I said, and I ran off the road where the wood begins, before there's any ditch. Well then, I stood a bit and listened, and the noise had stopped, so I went on again, but I kept in among the bushes just in case. I'm pretty good in the dark, and I thought if it was anyone who'd had a bit too much to drink, well, I could always dodge him in the wood. When I got down into the dip I heard the noise again, so I just stood still where I was."

"I see. So you're good in the dark—"

"Nothing wrong about that, is there?"

"Oh, no—very useful. You stood there and watched someone drag a body out of the wood. If you're so good in the dark you'd be able to see whether he was dragging it, wouldn't you?"

"That's what I said."

"I seem to remember you being a little inclined to hedge. Well, what about it—was he dragging her, or wasn't he?"

"That's what it sounded like. I said he might have been carrying her, and so he might."

That light stare of his persisted.

"All right—he was dragging her, or he was carrying her. Which side of you was he—between you and the village?"

She hesitated, angry and confused.

"I tell you it was dark!"

"But you're good in the dark—you've just said so. Look here, Miss Stokes, you were coming from Tomlin's Farm and you were on the way to the village. You simply must know which side of you this man came out of the bushes—behind you, or in front of you—between you and the farm, or between you and Deeping."

"It was between me and the village. You get me all confused."

His voice took an ironic inflection.

"I should be sorry to do that. But if he came out between you and the village he must have crossed the ditch just where it's wettest, at the bottom of the dip. I'm telling you that no one could have got across that ditch either dragging or carrying a body without leaving footprints—it couldn't have been done."

Her fingers were motionless, pressing down upon the pearls. She said nothing. He went on.

"You said in your statement that he put her down on the path, got out a torch, and put the light on her."

She gave a slight shiver.

"Yes, he did."

"You saw what it was he had been carrying—or dragging?"

She looked up and nodded. Miss Silver, watching, saw the angry expression change to a sick remembering one. But there was something else as well. The hand clenched on the pearls relaxed—came back to join the other in her lap.

Mary Stokes was suddenly full of words. Her breath hurried, she couldn't get them out fast enough.

"Oh, it was horrible! She had been hit over the head—a lot of light hair, and blood on it, and her eyes open. That's how I knew she was dead. Her eyes were open, and he flashed the torch in them—and they never moved. So I knew she was dead. And there was the earring, catching up the light—a real ring set all round with diamonds."

"What size was the ring? I'd like the most exact description you can give me."

"About the size of a wedding-ring—half an inch or three-quarters—I don't know, I've never measured one, but that's what it looked like. And there was only the one, because he turned her over and looked and the other one was gone, and he went on looking for it, running his fingers through her hair."

She shuddered uncontrollably. "I tell you it turned me up! I keep coming awake in the night and seeing it!"

For the moment the careful refinement was all gone. It was a scared country girl remembering something which had sent her screaming and running to beat on Miss Alvina's door. She took a sobbing breath and said,

"If he'd caught me spying on him, I'd have been the next. The first minute he went back into the wood I ran for my life."

Miss Silver gave her slight habitual cough.

"A truly terrifying experience. It is not surprising that you should find it painful to recall. But you will, I am sure, do all you can to assist Sergeant Abbott. The man who is capable of such a crime should not be at large. He may commit others. Now I wonder—you say that the stones in the earring caught the light as the beam of the torch went to and fro?"

Mary stared, on her guard against a new questioner. She said,

"Yes."

"Then you will have noticed whether the blood on the hair was wet."

"I didn't."

Frank Abbott said,

"Just try and think. It's important."

She shook her head.

"I wasn't thinking of whether anything was wet or dry—I was thinking that she'd been murdered and as likely as not it was going to be my turn next."

CHAPTER 8

They got no more from her.

As they drove back from the farm, Miss Silver observed the scenery with interest. Undulating common land to the right and fields to the left under a cloudy sky. The air less cold than it had been for some days past—oh, yes, decidedly less cold, and with a touch of damp in it. It occurred to her that the afternoon was likely to bring rain.

Frank Abbott stopped the car where the trees began on the left-hand side of the road.

"That's where she says she went into the wood. Impossible to say whether she did or not. You see there's no ditch to speak of, and it's all as dry as a bone—it gets the wind across those fields."

Miss Silver alighted from the car and stood there looking at the scene. The wood was quite unfenced and the undergrowth very moderate. Mary Stokes' account of her actions was a perfectly credible one. She could have crossed into the wood and walked down its edge very nearly as easily as she could have walked down the path. Frank walked down it now, looking about him as he went.

When he returned, to find Miss Silver as he had left her, he could only say,

"Well, she could have done it."

She said in a thoughtful voice, "Oh, yes." And then, "I should like to get the geography a little clearer. There is, for instance, a track here between the field and the edge of the wood. Where does it lead to?"

He looked at her sharply.

"It comes out in what is called the Lane, which runs up from the village past the back of Abbottsleigh and the Grange—that's Mark Harlow's place."

"The Lane runs between those two estates and this wood?"

"It runs between Abbottsleigh and the wood. Uncle Reg's land stops where we're standing now. The fields on our left are Harlow property, and the Grange is back there behind them."

"On the other side of the Lane?"

"On the other side of the Lane. Deepside, Hathaway's place, is farther along still, but the driving-road to Tomlin's Farm cuts between Deepside and the Grange."

"Does the Lane go on?"

"Yes, it goes all the way to Lenton. It's the old direct way. The new road wasn't at all popular when it was made, because it took a bit off the frontage of all those three properties. I believe my great-grandfather cursed the place down. He had to rebuild his lodge."

Miss Silver was looking thoughtful.

"Dead Man's Copse, then, is an irregular rectangle bounded by this field track, the track over which we have driven, the village street, and the Lane at the back of Abbottsleigh."

He smiled at her.

"Answer adjudged correct."

"And the Forester's House—is it nearer to this edge of the wood, or to the Lane?"

"Oh, a good bit nearer to the Lane—and definitely nearer to this end of the wood than to the village."

"Then I would propose, my dear Frank, that we find our way to it along the field track."

He stood looking at her.

"Now what have you got in your mind?"

She smiled.

"You asked me that before."

53

"And got no answer."

"Well, this time you shall have one. I have in mind its usual furniture—a considerable variety of thoughts, some of them quite unrelated, others in a very elementary state of combination. There are only two which I can at the moment offer for your consideration, and you will doubtless have already thought of them for yourself. In the first case, Mary Stokes is lying when she says that she stood on the edge of the bushes in the dip and witnessed the carrying or dragging of a dead body from the wood on to the path. You brought that out very clearly when you questioned her. But I think it is equally clear that when she spoke of the beam passing to and fro over that poor murdered girl she was describing something which she had actually witnessed. I feel quite sure that every detail of that description is correct. She did see a murderer searching for the lost earring in terror lest it should have dropped in some place where its discovery might betray him."

"You think she was speaking the truth?"

"I am convinced of it. She witnessed that scene, and the shock and horror of it sent her running for safety in a blind panic. It was only when she had reached that safety that some other consideration operated to prevent her telling all the truth. She sobbed out her story of the terrible thing she had seen, but she lied as to the locality in which she had seen it. The tragic scene took place, but not on the track through Dead Man's Copse."

He eyed her quizzically.

"I expect you're right—you always are. Though if it wasn't for Louise Rogers, I'd be inclined to think Miss Mary Stokes a more consistent liar than you do. It's Louise Rogers and her eternity earrings that make me give her the benefit of the doubt. Otherwise I should conclude that she had just invented the whole thing.

Miss Silver coughed in a hortatory manner.

54

"No, Frank—she had seen what she was describing. It was something which had frightened her almost out of her senses. The sense of fear and shock were quite unmistakable. Did you not notice how all her affectations fell away? The girl who said 'I tell you it turned me up' was telling the truth."

He nodded.

"Yes, I noticed that. I expect you're right. Well, where do we go from here?"

If he intended the question metaphorically, it was taken in a perfectly literal manner.

"I think to the Forester's House."

"Now?"

"I think so."

She began to walk along the track between the field and the wood.

After returning to the car to remove and pocket the switch-key Frank caught her up.

"I could have driven you round by the village and up the Lane."

"Thank you, but I am an excellent walker. The air is really extremely refreshing."

After a moment he said,

"And what do you expect to find at the Forester's House?"

"We shall see when we get there."

He laughed.

"You wouldn't care to give any idea of what you expect?"

She shook her head.

"It is wiser not to indulge in expectations. There are, of course, certain possibilities."

"As what?"

"Mary Stokes must have had a reason for transferring the terrible scene which she had witnessed from the place where it really happened to the place where she said it happened. This reason must have been extremely strong—so strong, in fact, that even in the midst of blind panic it operated to prevent a disclosure of the actual spot where the tragedy took place. What would you deduce from that?"

He gave vent to a slight whistle.

"You mean it was somewhere she hadn't any business to be."

"Can you explain it in any other way? I cannot."

"But—the Forester's House—"

"Consider what we know of the girl's character. She has been staying here not from choice but because she had to. She is a town girl by choice and preference. It is quite obvious that she would find life very dull at Tomlin's Farm. When that sort of young woman is dull some mischief can usually be found for her idle hands to do, and it is sadly apt to take the form of a man. I think you would do well to enquire whether there has been any gossip of this sort about Mary Stokes."

"You think she was meeting someone at the Forester's House?"

"I think she may have been. Pray consider how convenient a place of assignation it would be. She could reach it by this path, and if anyone saw her, she would be going through to the Lane and so down into Deeping. The house itself is shunned by the village people."

"Wouldn't she shun it too?"

"She is a town girl, smart and sophisticated. She would, I think, despise the old village tales, and, as you will have observed, she is neither a sensitive nor an imaginative type. Besides, a young woman who is going to meet a man isn't thinking about things that happened two hundred years ago. She is thinking about herself—and the man."

Frank Abbott nodded.

"What about the man—is he too much in love to bother about local superstitions, or what?"

Miss Silver coughed.

"Two possibilities present themselves. There must, you see, be some reason why he cannot meet her openly. If it were a case of the ordinary village courtship, they could walk out together, and there would be no need for concealment. But the facts require a very strong reason for concealment. The man may be married, or he may belong to such a different class that Mr. and Mrs. Stokes would be scandalized by his association with their niece. Then what could be more convenient for a meeting-place than a deserted house avoided by everyone?"

Frank Abbott laughed.

"Well, you've explained that Mary didn't avoid it because (a) she was tough, (b) she didn't really belong to the neighbourhood, and (c) she was in love."

Miss Silver coughed.

"I do not think that I should call it love, Frank."

"Probably not. But putting that on one side, I suppose you would say that we must look for a man who is also tough, and who doesn't really belong to Deeping?"

"I am inclined to think so."

"Well, there is the Lane in front of us, and here is what looks like a way into the wood."

The undergrowth was not very thick at this end of the Copse—a few hazels, a holly-bush or two, an occasional trail of bramble, and a great deal of ivy. It was plain that no forester had kept an eye on the timber for a very long time. Old trees done to death by the ivy had come down in many a winter storm to rot where they lay. Others stood as sheer hulks in a winding-sheet of green, their branches gone, their hollow trunks full of rotting leaves. Presently the bushes thinned away to what was almost a clearing—a most desolate place with a great humped mass of yew on either side of what had perhaps once been a gate. And beyond it, standing amongst rank high grass and nettles, the Forester's House.

Frank Abbott whistled.

"Well, I can think of places where I'd rather meet a girl," he said.

Miss Silver's reply startled him. In all sobriety she enquired,

"Can you think of a better place for a murder?"

He whistled again. Before the sound had ceased her hand was on his arm.

"See, Frank—I was right. Here are her footprints in that damp patch—running footprints."

They stood looking at the marks—three or four of them, very clear and distinct, the deeply impressed prints of the fore part of a woman's shoe. The damp patch of ground which had received and retained them was some dozen feet across, but the heel of that shoe had never touched it once. It was plain to see that the girl whose footprints they were had been in headlong flight.

Frank said under his breath,

"Yes, you're right. And the way they're pointing, she must have run straight through the wood and out of it where the footprints are in the ditch. I'll follow up the direction this afternoon with Smith. We may be able to trace her right away through the wood." He straightened up. "Well, what do you want to do now? I'm not at all sure you hadn't better let me take you home and ring up Smith. It looks as if there might be something quite nasty inside that unpleasant domicile."

Miss Silver coughed.

"My dear Frank, I have not the slightest intention of going home. Far too much time has been wasted already. If anything remains to be found, there should be no further delay in finding it."

They walked between the two great masses of yew and up what had once been a flagged path, cushioned over now with thick-growing moss and slippery to the foot. The house rose square before them, its roof still intact, windows to right and left of the door, two above and two below, and two small gables over all. Whether the legend of Edward Brand and the mob that had come witch-hunting here getting on for a couple of hundred years ago was true or not, it was a fact that there was no glass in any of the windows. They stared horridly, and gave the house the look of a dead, eyeless thing. One on the left appeared to be roughly shuttered. Frank remembered that, according to the story, an angry village had wrenched the doors from their hinges and gone away to hunt for Edward Brand and found him hanged and dead. The front door of what had been his house stood there, hingeless still. No, not stood, for it leaned at a crazy tilt, wedged between lintel and jamb. Whether by accident or design, after all these generations it still did its office—if it be the office of a door to deny entrance to the house it has been set to guard. If the story was to be believed, Edward Brand's door had never been wont to open in welcome to any living soul. It was not to be opened now. Gape it might, between sill and lintel, between jamb and jamb, but the weatherproof oak was sound, and budge it would not.

Miss Silver stood back and regarded the depressing spectacle. Inevitably, she produced a quotation from her favourite poet, the great Laureate of the Victorian era.

" 'Portions and parcels of the dreadful past,' " she observed.

To which Frank Abbott replied with cheerful irreverence,

"Some parcel—isn't it!"

They went round to the back, and found an empty rectangle half hidden by crowding bushes. Frank went in first and held them aside for Miss Silver to follow.

"Take care—there may be holes in the floor."

But the floor was stone, laid in flags like the path. The place they had come into was a kitchen—cobwebs hanging from the beams, a mass of old rubbish mouldering under the dust of years.

But there was no dust on the flagstones between the door of their entry and the empty doorway opposite. For a three foot width the stones had been swept clean. They followed the swept path to a passage so dark that Frank fished out a torch and switched it on. Narrow and bare, the passage ran to the front door, with a stair going up no more than a yard from the entrance between a stone wall on one side and rough panelling on the other. There was no dust here either, but on the stair it lay as soft and thick as a carpet. Two narrow doorways in the space between the staircase and the wedged front door, one to the right and one to the left—one open, the jamb sagging where the door had been torn away, the other with its door intact and latched. When Frank Abbott lifted the latch, taking care not to touch it with his bare hand, it swung in easily enough.

He paused on the threshold to turn his torch upon the hinges and exclaimed,

"They're new! Look here! The door's old, but the hinges are new! It had been wrenched off like the others, but somebody has taken the trouble to patch it up."

He stepped inside, set the beam dancing, and turned to let Miss Silver pass.

"It's all right—no corpses here."

It would have been dark if it hadn't been for the torch, the rather small window being completely blocked by one of the derelict doors, which leaned against it and took the place of a shutter. Where the leaning of the door would have admitted daylight or have allowed a light in the room to become visible at night, the gap had been filled with paper crumpled up and stuffed between wood and wall.

Frank Abbott said with a sardonic inflection,

"Someone's been busy making this place light-proof." He turned the torch back into the room. "He's had a fire in the hearth too. Look at that charred wood—that's not been here since seventeen hundred and something."

The beam moved. It showed a couple of sacks lying rugwise across the hearth, and, standing where it would face the fire, a heavy oak settle, old but solid. The light, travelling over it, showed where a leg had been mended and not so long ago, the new wood showing up against the old. They moved round the big jutting arm, and Miss Silver said,

"Dear me!"

The settle had been heaped with fern and straw over which something had been spread. The beam went to and fro. Quite unmistakably the something was an army blanket.

CHAPTER 9

Frank Abbott's search of the Forester's House disclosed no corpse. He came away with the certainty that Mary Stokes had fled from the place in terror, but with no further evidence as to what had caused such a headlong flight. A second certainty was that someone had been using the house—someone who had taken the trouble to rehang a door, make a room roughly habitable, and secure privacy by completely blocking the window. Without actual proof, it was impossible not to put two and two together or to resist the conclusion that Mary Stokes had a lover, and that she had been meeting him at the Forester's House. So far so good. But there is nothing criminal about a meeting of illicit lovers. However morally undesirable such a situation may be, it is not one with which a detective sergeant from Scotland Yard need concern himself. Just where the horrid apparition of a murdered girl impinged upon these certainties, or to what extent this apparition could be identified with Mrs. Hopper's missing lodger from Hampstead, he felt quite unable to say. The missing earring was as absent as the corpse of its owner, at least to the somewhat cursory search which was all he would permit himself.

"That room must be a mass of fingerprints, and until we've got them down in black and white I can't have anything disturbed. Better get home now. I'll get on to Smith and tell him to bring along the doings."

After lunch Miss Silver permitted herself to rest in the very comfortable armchair which her bedroom afforded. Frank was meeting Inspector Smith from Lenton, and her kind hostess had provided a small tea-party. "Miss Alvina Grey—the late Rector's daughter. And Mrs. Bowse—the widowed sister of our doctor, Cyril Wingfield." What Monica did not add was that the tea-party had been prompted by Frank.

"Collect your ablest village gossips and just prod them when they flag!"

Monica laughed.

"Darling Frank, they won't, they can't, they don't know how. What do you want them to gossip about?"

"Anything and anyone, but rather specially Mary Stokes and anyone she may have been carrying on with. I can't believe that Mary hasn't got herself talked about in a place like Deeping."

Monica looked thoughtful.

"Well, you know, that's the extraordinary thing. As far as I know, there hasn't been any gossip about her at all—except, of course, that everyone knows Joe Turnberry tried to make up to her and got his nose bitten off."

"Oh, well, she'd be a cut above Joseph."

"That's what poor Joe was given to understand, and not at all politely."

He looked at her, frowning.

"Look here, Monica, I think she's got a lover. I want to know who he is, and I want to know as quickly as possible. I can give you a few pointers about him. He's probably not Deeping born and bred. He's served in the Army. And he's got a cast-iron reason for keeping this affair with Mary dark. Can you help me out?"

Her eyes wandered from his. With characteristic irrelevance she exclaimed,

"But Frank—who hasn't?"

"Hasn't what?"

"What you said—served in the Army. But as to anything else, I don't know why you think I know about the Stokes girl's affairs, because I don't."

"Perhaps Mrs. Bowse and Miss Alvina will."

"They know a great many things that never happen," said Monica Abbott. "Cis had better go and practice the organ—she can't stand them." She gave a not very happy laugh. "Well, at any rate whilst they're talking about Mary Stokes they'll be giving Cis and Grant a rest."

The tea-party was a great success. Miss Silver imparted a very pretty knitting stitch to both ladies, and was promised Mrs. Caddle's recipe for strawberry jam.

"That is, of course, if I can coax it out of her," said Miss Alvina. "I have been in the kitchen when she has made it, but you know how it is, if you are not doing a thing yourself you don't take a great deal of notice. So I couldn't tell you what she does to make it quite, quite different from anybody else's and so very superior. She won't give the recipe to anyone in Deeping, and she won't make it for anyone but me. She might be persuaded if I said it was for a lady from London, but of course I can't promise—"

Mrs. Bowse, a handsome, florid forty-five, came down on Miss Vinnie's twitterings with sledgehammer common sense.

"Promise? I should say not! And as to getting a recipe out of Ellen Caddle—" she spread large weatherbeaten hands to the fire—"what a hope! She's one of the sort that would rather die than part with any of her belongings. After all, why should she? She hasn't got so many that she can afford to. That wretched Albert of hers may be slipping through her fingers, but at least she can hold on to her recipe for strawberry jam."

Miss Silver coughed, and remarked that Albert was a name which had gone very much out of fashion—"But perhaps in a village like Deeping—"

Both visitors began simultaneously to inform her that Deeping had not been responsible for Albert Caddle or his name, the robust voice of Mrs. Bowse giving her an unfair advantage. It was she who in the end completed the Caddle saga.

"Served in the Commandos, and got a job as chauffeur to old Mr. Harlow. Then when his nephew Mark came in for the property he kept him on. I believe he's very handy about the place, but he's a lot too good-looking, and Mark will always have trouble with him—I told him so the other day, and he only laughed. Of course you can't expect a young man to take that sort of thing seriously. Poor Ellen Caddle did a bad day's work for herself when she married him—more fool she. Must be at least ten years older than he is, and never was anything to look at. What does she suppose he married her for? Her savings, and what Lady Evelyn left her! It's as plain as a pikestaff—I told her so myself. 'Ellen,' I said, 'you're a fool.' And she made a face like a mule and said she'd a right to do what she liked. 'That's as may be,' I said. 'But what is he marrying you for—you ask yourself that!' "

"She's a very good cook," said Miss Vinnie.

The sledgehammer came down again.

"And he lets her go out to cook for you instead of staying at home and doing it for him! I tell you there's something wrong when a man lets his wife go out to work like that. I told her so straight out. 'He's getting good wages, and what's he spending them on?'—that's what I said. 'Or *who?* You ask yourself that, Ellen!' I said."

"I shouldn't have thought Mark Harlow could really afford to keep a chauffeur," said Miss Alvina. "Old Mr. Harlow's affairs were said to be very much embarrassed—and then of course the death duties—"

"Oh, but he had money of his own." Mrs. Bowse was emphatic.

"I never understood—"

"He couldn't keep up the place as he does if he hadn't something very substantial." She turned to Monica Abbott. "That's what your son-in-law found—wasn't it? And of course worse for him than for Mark, because he was really only quite a distant cousin, wasn't he, and that would make those wretched duties so very much heavier. Quite iniquitous of course, but we'll never get rid of them, I suppose. Now do tell me, Mrs. Abbott—is it really true that he's been selling the family diamonds?"

Monica smiled vaguely. Behind the vagueness there was a burning anger. It was a solace to reflect that Mabel Bowse could have clothed herself in no more unbecoming garment than the green-and-brown checked tweed she was wearing. It was too tight, it was too bright. It bulged where she bulged, and it clung where it shouldn't have clung. Soothed by these thoughts, she said in a dreamy voice,

"I don't know—why don't you ask him?"

Mrs. Bowse said, "Oh, well—" and turned without visible discomfiture to Miss Silver. "We're all quite devoted to Grant Hathaway and most anxious to see him make a success of his experiments. It's all very modern and scientific, and a great deal too technical for me. But of course that sort of thing just eats capital, and it's years before you can expect any return, so I'm afraid he's having a tough time. He succeeded a very old cousin, and the place had been allowed to go to rack and ruin."

Monica had the feeling that she might have been allowed to explain her own son-in-law, but being cross with Mrs. Bowse didn't get you anywhere, it just bounced off. She had passed to Mark Harlow now.

"He came into the Grange just about the same time that Grant came into Deepside, but he doesn't attempt to farm the land himself. He's not interested in that sort of thing. As he says, he spent the six years of the war working very hard and getting very dirty, and he thinks he's entitled to be clean for a change and have some leisure. Well, I don't mince my words, and I said to him, 'You know, you're an idle young man,' and he laughed and said he was. Actually, you know, he's musical—writes songs and gets quite a lot of money for them. He did the music for that revue that was so successful last year—what was it called?—all those things are so alike, I can't remember. At least I know he did some of the songs, because he told me."

Miss Silver coughed.

"How extremely interesting."

Miss Vinnie murmured, "He's really a very charming young man," but that was as far as she was able to get. The deep, strong voice of Mrs. Bowse rolled over her.

"Well, it doesn't go with farming, does it? He lets the land to Stokes, which saves him a lot of trouble, and Stokes is glad to get it because the grazing is so good. Stokes does a big dairy business. If that niece of his wasn't such a finicking fine lady she could make herself very useful there. As it is, I think they're very good to put up with her, and so I told Mrs. Stokes. 'Why don't you put that girl to a job of work?' I said. And she didn't like it a bit—got as red as if she'd scorched her face over the fire, and said Mary wasn't strong. Well, I wasn't going to put up with that, so I said, 'She's strong enough to be out till all hours, and she's strong enough to go round with the eggs and butter to any house where there's a good-looking young man.' And would you believe it, she looked as if she was going to fly out at me. I really thought she was, but she stopped herself and said she must get on with her work."

Miss Silver set down her teacup and remarked,

"So much goes on in a village, does it not? Really quite a little world. Most interesting. So Miss Stokes delivers the eggs and butter. Do you deal with her, Mrs. Abbott?"

Monica said, "Sometimes—when our hens don't lay. Mrs. Stokes is cleverer with hers than I am. But we make our own butter. Cicely makes it. She's very proud of her butter."

"Most delicious," said Miss Silver. "Country butter is always such a treat. Do your neighbours also deal with the Stokeses?"

Mrs. Bowse broke into a hearty laugh.

"Mark Harlow does, and so does Grant Hathaway. Silly, isn't it, a farmer having to buy butter? I told him everyone was laughing over it, and he only laughed too and said, 'Wait till my nursery grows up, then you'll all find out what can be done in the milk and cream and butter line!' Well, of course that's all very well for a joke, and I'm sure I wish him every success, and so will every other woman in the place. That's what I meant about the handsome young men. You don't imagine Mary Stokes goes delivering down the village street? That would be rather too much like work, and not at all in her line. Oh, no, she just comes down the Lane and does Deepside, and the Grange, and Abbottsleigh, and if she doesn't get a chance of making eyes at Grant or Mark, there's always Albert Caddle." She laughed in what Miss Silver considered a distressingly loud manner.

Miss Alvina sighed and said,

"I am afraid she must be very dull here—and after all it is natural for a girl to like young men." She twittered a little as she continued. "I really don't think it is very kind of you to talk about her like that, Mabel—and when she has had such a shock." She turned back to Miss Silver. "Mrs. Abbott will have told you about the dreadful fright poor Mary had. She and Mr. Frank Abbott were having tea with me—so very pleasant. And then such a shock, poor Mary running in like that and saying she'd seen someone murdered."

"Very startling indeed."

Mrs. Bowse said, "Rubbish! Oh, not present company, you know. But this girl's ridiculous story—pure exhibitionism the

67

whole thing! I said so to my brother. 'Cyril,' I said, 'Mary Stokes has no more seen a murdered corpse than I have. She's bored to death at the farm, and she's thought up a way of making everybody talk about her. You mark my words,' I said, 'it's nothing but showing off.' "

Miss Alvina persevered in a small determined voice.

"Of course Dead Man's Copse hasn't at all a good name. I don't know if you have heard the story."

"I should like to hear it very much," said Miss Silver.

Both ladies drew their chairs a little closer and the narration proceeded. If Frank Abbott had been there he would have been interested to notice that it varied by scarcely a word from the tale as she had told it to him.

Miss Silver listened with deep attention. When the story was done she commented on the harmful nature of a belief in witchcraft.

"It led, I fear, to many superstitions and cruelties."

Miss Alvina agreed.

"Yes, indeed! My dear father was very much interested in the subject. He collected quite a number of stories of the kind and wrote them down. There were a few copies privately printed. I have a copy if you would care to see it. Old Mr. Hathaway had one too. He was a good deal interested in the subject himself—not Grant, you know, but the cousin from whom he inherited, old Mr. Alvin Hathaway. He and my father were very much of an age—he was ninety-five when he died—and they were very great friends. He was in fact my godfather, and I am called after him—Alvina."

"A pretty and unusual name," pronounced Miss Silver.

Mrs. Bowse had been supplying Monica Abbott with a number of horrid and undesired details about the decease of the village drunkard, having reached the topic via Mrs. Stokes, whose distant relative he happened to be. She now returned fortissimo to the conversation between Miss Silver and Miss Alvina Grey.

With a burst of hearty laughter she picked up the latter lady's name and repeated it.

"Alvina—well, it is certainly uncommon. So that's where you got it—I've often wondered. I shouldn't have said thank you myself, but it's too late to do anything about it now, I suppose. Thank heaven my parents didn't wish anything fancy on to me! Mabel is a good plain name."

To everyone's astonishment Miss Alvina pecked back, not in defence of her name, but of "my dear father." A reflection on the name he had given her was a reflection on him. A gentle fury filled her breast. Her eyes were bright and her cheeks a delicate pink. She had always considered Mabel an odious name, but she would never have said so if she had not been tried beyond her strength. She came as near to saying it now as a ladylike upbringing would permit.

"A name like mine has at least one advantage—people do not become tired of it. Yours, my dear Mabel, after being sadly overdone, is now quite out of date—one never hears it, even in the village."

Mrs. Bowse did not even notice that she had been pecked. She took the last iced cake, and remarked that village children were all called after film stars nowadays.

CHAPTER 10

Cicely was playing a toccata and fugue by Bach. The great crashing waves of music swept in upon her and swept her mind quite clean. All the things which had troubled and vexed her were like small dust, which this great tide of beauty carried away. When the last notes died she came back to her surroundings—

but slowly, like someone waking from a sleep which has been so deep that it has drowned memory and pain. There is a time in such a waking when consciousness has returned but has not yet regained its power to wound. It lies smooth and bright, as the sea lies over a wreck. She was relaxed and quiet. Except for the organ light the church around her was dark. The air throbbed with that tremendous music, passed out of audible sound but present still.

She took her hands from the key-board and turned her head. She didn't know why she turned it. She thought afterwards that she must have heard him move, not consciously but with that finer sense which lies at the edge of consciousness. He was standing in the shadow where the curtain which screened the organist had been drawn aside. The odd thing was that it seemed quite natural for him to be there. She could rage about it afterwards, but at the time it seemed the most natural thing in the world—the dark church—the music still echoing in her—and Grant. And all the pain gone.

But it only lasted a moment. They looked at one another, and he said,

"Saint Cecilia—"

And that was another thing to trouble over in the watches of the night, because just how did he say it? Lightly? Mockingly? Yes—yes, of course it would be that way. But then why did it shake her heart? She turned a hot face into her pillow and gave herself the answer—"Because I'm such a damned fool about him still." At the time she just sat there looking at him, her eyes wide and the light all round her. Then he said,

"That was very fine. You've come along a lot."

"Have I?"

It didn't really matter what she said. All that mattered was not to break this moment of release. It wouldn't last, but she could have said like Faust, "*Verweile doch, du bist so schön.*" With everything in her, that was what she was saying now. But not

70

aloud. Words were too difficult. They said too much or too little. There had been too many of them already. The things she had said to Grant in love, the things she had said to him in bitter resentment, were not to be remembered now, or the moment of peace would be gone. But if she didn't say something, he would think—She came perilously near to letting everything go without caring what he might think.

It might have been some instinctive recoil from this, it might have been something simpler and more elementary, which made her say,

"Someone has been writing me anonymous letters."

It was so entirely unpremeditated that the sound of the words shocked her. She had never meant to tell anyone about the letters. She had certainly never meant to tell Grant. The words had just come out of her mouth. It was rather frightening.

The effect upon Grant Hathaway was to make him duck under the rod which held the curtain and come into the light. He looked incredulous and a little angry.

"Anonymous letters?"

She nodded.

"About us?"

"About you."

She oughtn't to have spoken about the letters. The pain was coming back. But it would have come back anyway. She must go through with it now.

He put out a hand.

"Let me see them!"

She picked up her bag from the organ stool and opened it. The letters were in an envelope stuck down. She slit it.

"I thought I'd burn them, and then I thought I wouldn't. I thought if it went on I might have to try and find out who was sending them, so I put them in this envelope and stuck it down, then I thought I'd know if anyone—well, tampered with them."

"Did they come through the post?"

"No. That's what's so horrid. They weren't even in an envelope—just screwed up and pushed in at the hall letter-box with my name on the outside." She took out a crumpled piece of paper and handed it to him. "Look—like that."

"Printed, I see." He turned it over. "And the same inside." His face hardened as he read:

"Do you want a divorce? You could get one if you knew as much as I do. He married you for your money. You know that, don't you? Why not get free?

A well-wisher."

When he came to the end he said,

"It sounds almost as if the well-wisher had been eavesdropping—doesn't it? Is there another instalment?"

Her voice was hard with pain as she said,

"There are two more. The first came on Saturday, this one two days later."

She gave him a second note. In crooked, stumbling capitals it said:

"He is quite the bachelor again. Don't you care? Ask him who came to see him on Friday night. If you had any proper pride you would get a divorce."

Cicely gave him a third note. It was much shorter than the others—no more than a single sentence. It ran:

"Some people might want to know what happened on Friday night."

When he had read it he took the envelope out of her hand, put all three notes inside it, and put it away in a pocket.

"You'd better let me keep them. Just let me know if you get any more, will you? And don't handle them more than you can help. I'd like to get any fingerprints on record."

There was a sense of relief in getting rid of the things. She shut her bag and turned to go, switching out the light and turning on a torch to see them out. As he fell into step beside her on the churchyard path he said in a laughing voice,

"Quite a new scandal for the village if they only knew—Mr. Grant Hathaway sees Mrs. Grant Hathaway home!"

She came back quickly and defiantly with,

"I'd much rather you didn't."

"Well, I'm going to, so you can put that in your pipe and smoke it. And here's something else. I don't much like your being out on your own after dark at the moment."

She managed a laugh.

"Because of Mary Stokes? You don't suppose she really saw anything, do you?"

"She seems to have had a fright."

"It's as likely as not to have been an owl, or a rabbit. You know the way those big owls swoop down at night—it really is startling, and she's not what you'd call a country girl. No— something frightened her and she started off and ran herself into hysterics. And of course when they wanted to know what it was, an owl wasn't nearly exciting enough, so she made up a story. I can't think why Frank is wasting his time over her. I should have thought Scotland Yard would have had something real to put him on to nearer home."

There was a short silence before he said,

"I didn't know your cousin was here on duty."

"I thought everyone knew that. And I just can't make out why anyone should bother about Mary Stokes."

He said, "I'm afraid I haven't thought about it at all. I heard she had had a fright, but that's as far as it went. What frightened her?"

Cicely pulled herself up with a jerk. She and Grant were not on those sort of terms, and she hadn't any intention of letting them get there. But it was frightfully easy to slip. She had felt herself slipping. She said stiffly,

"I expect it was an owl."

He made some kind of sound which might have been the beginning of a laugh. Whatever it was, it was broken off short. She thought she knew very well what it meant. She and Grant walking together in the dark and talking about Mary Stokes. As if either of them cared a halfpenny stamp what Mary had seen! She and Grant alone in the dark with nothing real to say, whilst all the things between them clamoured to be said—that was a quite unendurable prospect. She panicked in the silence and cast wildly about her for something safe with which to break it, but of all those clamouring words not one came to her tongue.

It was Grant who said in a conversational tone,

"Seeing much of Mark?"

That helped, because she could get up a little spurt of anger.

"Why shouldn't I?"

"No reason at all. He writes comic songs, you play the organ—it's bound to be a bond."

He heard her catch her breath.

"That's beastly of you, Grant."

"A bald statement of fact."

"His stuff's clever—if you like that sort of thing."

"All right, all right—don't like it too much, that's all."

"As a matter of fact I don't like it at all."

"But you like Mark. Are you by any chance trying to tell me that you love him for himself alone?"

He was baiting her, and she knew it. If she let her temper go, he would have the satisfaction of knowing that he had scored. She achieved a creditable calmness of tone.

"It wouldn't be your business if I did."

"Well, that would depend—because, you see, you can't marry anyone else unless you get divorced from me, and you can't get divorced from me unless I make it possible."

There was a horrid little pause. Then she said,

"Are you going to?"

"Oh, no."

"Then I shall just have to wait for three years."

"My dear child! What three years?"

"You can get a divorce after three years. Mr. Waterson said so."

"Exactly. He said I could get a divorce for desertion in three years' time. You see, it's you who are doing the deserting, not me, and if I choose to put up with it, there isn't one—single—solitary thing you can do about it."

She turned on him in a glow of anger.

"But you will—you will—you *must!*"

"Not a bit of it. Why should I? You don't imagine that I could possibly want to marry again—after such a very unpleasant experience?"

"It *wasn't!*"

The words flashed out before she could stop them, and she heard him laugh.

"Not altogether—not all the time? Well, that's something at any rate! Bride to groom, 'Thanks for the memory,' and all that!"

They were just at the turning. She caught her breath sharply and ran from him up the Lane. Her blood drummed in her ears, and her heart against her side. She was sick with mortification and anger. And he would know—he would know that she had run away because she couldn't bear to stay. She couldn't even run fast enough to get in before he caught her up. She fumbled at the garden gate, shaking too much to make sure of the latch.

Grant's hand came down over her shoulder. The latch clicked, the gate swung in. And then, just as she crossed the threshold, his left arm took her about the shoulders and for a moment she felt his cheek against hers.

"Thanks for the quarrel, darling," he said in a light laughing voice, and gave her a little push and was gone.

CHAPTER 11

Frank Abbott came in late, the net result of a long afternoon's work being a number of fingerprints from the interior of the Forester's House, most of them from the room where the window had been blocked and the settle drawn up to the hearth. The prints were those of two people, a man and a woman—some of them from the passage, but nearly all from the one closed room. Upstairs no prints at all—no sign that anyone had trodden the old dust.

"It's clear enough that two people have been meeting in that room. They've been coming in the same way we did, and they haven't bothered about the rest of the house. That's as plain as a pikestaff. There are no other prints of anyone at all, so it looks as if either there wasn't any murder, or as if the man did it. I wondered about a jealousy motive—the one-man-two-women triangle. What do you think about that? Suppose Louise Rogers was an old flame of the man's and butted in on his rendezvous— one of those French words which the Chief dislikes so much— he might do her in to prevent Mary knowing, or Mary might do her in out of jealousy. Only if she was there, how did she contrive not to leave any prints? I suppose the answer would be that she was wearing gloves."

He stood by the fire looking down at Miss Silver on her low chair. They had the morning-room to themselves in the half hour before dinner. She looked up across her knitting.

"If she was killed in that house, there would surely be stains, or some traces of their having been removed."

He leaned an elbow on the mantelpiece. "I know—I know. But the passage had been swept—there was a birch broom in the kitchen. Smith's taken it back with him to see if they can get any traces off it. There are no signs of the flags having been washed—Smith is prepared to swear that they haven't."

Miss Silver coughed.

"What about the sacks in front of the hearth in that room?"

"No sign of a bloodstain." He hesitated for a moment. "There's just one thing—it's probably negligible—"

"I shall be interested to hear what it is," said Miss Silver.

"You know that passage between the kitchen and the front door—on the right there is the stone wall, and on the left the panelled side of the stair. Well, fairly high up on the panelling there is just one dark stain which might be blood—fairly recent and soaked down into the wood. Smith has taken a scraping, so we shall know more about it by tomorrow, and then we shall have to find out whether the woman's prints were made by Mary Stokes."

Miss Silver's needles clicked rapidly.

"Did you find any more of her footprints?"

He bent down to put a log on the fire.

"Oh, yes—there were half a dozen more. She must have run right through the wood just about as hard as she could pelt—there's no doubt about that. And, you know, it looks to me as if she didn't bolt like that for fun. A pretty tough young woman who has been making a habit of meeting a man in a place like the Forester's House doesn't act like a scared rabbit for nothing. I say she's been making a habit of meeting someone there, because she left far too many fingerprints for a single visit. They're all over the place—on the door that was blocking the window, all round the hearth and chimneypiece as if she had been making up the fire, and on both sides of the door. Something unusual must have taken place, or she'd never have bolted like that. And anyhow, where is Louise Rogers?"

Miss Silver coughed.

"And the missing earring, Frank."

He bent a look of cold exasperation on her.

"For the matter of that, they're both missing," he said. "And so is she. And it's a week today since she walked out of Mrs. Hopper's room and never came back."

Next day being Saturday, Mary Stokes delivered eggs and butter at the three houses whose back gates opened upon the Lane. Since she neither drove a car nor possessed a bicycle she had to make these deliveries on foot, and regular exercise in the open air being one of the things recommended by Dr. Wingfield, Mrs. Stokes made no bones about keeping her up to it—not that Mary appeared at all disinclined to go. Just how she managed to take so much time over her errands, Mrs. Stokes never quite made out, but she was an easy-tempered woman and supposed that it was dull for the girl on the farm, and that she would be talking with the maids and perhaps get invited in for an elevens. Mrs. Abbott had those two nice girls under Mrs. Mayhew—sisters they were, from the other side of Lenton. And there would be Mrs. Caddle at the Grange garage, which you had to pass to get in from the Lane. Not that she'd be Mary's sort at the best of times, and a very peter-grievous poor thing these days by all accounts, but perhaps a word with Mary would cheer her up—you never could tell. And there was always Mrs. Green and her daughter up at the House, doing for Mr. Harlow like they did for his uncle. Nice steady women the both of them, but of course too old for Mary—Mrs. Green in her sixties, and Lizzie forty odd. She did wish there were more girls of her age for Mary to be friends with, but what with her having such high notions and thinking nobody good enough—well, it wasn't too easy.

Continuing up the Lane in her mind, Mrs. Stokes arrived at Deepside. Mrs. Barton, the housekeeper there, was a friend of her own and as nice a woman as ever stepped. Been there thirty years, and nursed the old gentleman to the end. And a blessing for Mr. Grant Hathaway to have such a dependable person in the house, with Miss Cicely running home the way she done. And to be hoped it would all come right—young people like that with their life before them. Mrs. Barton didn't speak about it of course, but you could tell how it troubled her. That girl Agnes Ripley, the house-parlourmaid, she wasn't Mary's sort either. Come to think of it, she wasn't much anyone's sort. Good at her work—Mrs. Barton hadn't a word to say about that. One of those moody girls, if you could call her a girl, which she must be up in her thirties, and plain at that. No notion of making anything of herself either. Not that she held with all the stuff girls put on their faces these days, but you got used to it, and there was no getting from it, it did brighten them up. That Agnes now, she'd a good figure and good hair—if you liked it as straight as a horse's tail. But that sallow skin and those dark eyes, and the way she stared at you—well, Mrs. Barton could have her. She would rather a dozen times put up with Mary, airs and tempers and all.

Frank Abbott took an early train from Lenton. "Business" was all he told Monica Abbott. To Miss Silver he was more communicative.

"I want to know if they've routed out anything more about Louise Rogers, and I want to see the Chief. So far I haven't been able to raise anything this end. If she came to Lenton by train, nobody noticed her there. It's a busy station, and of course she may have just passed in a crowd, especially if it was getting on towards dusk. But how did she get out to Deeping? It's all of four miles. Do you suppose for a moment that she walked it in the dark?"

"She would not do that."

"And how would she know the way? No, that's out. And she certainly didn't come by bus. Everyone in Deeping has heard Mary's story by now—they'd be tumbling over one another if any of them had come out from Lenton in the same bus as a mysterious stranger with diamond earrings. No, if she ever came at all she must have come by car. And where is the car? You see, whichever way you look at it, it all goes up in smoke. I've got an advertisement in the county paper and the little Lenton rag today. I can't do anything more down here till I get those results from Smith. It's practically certain that the woman's fingerprints are Mary's, but I want to put it to them at the Yard, 'Where do we go from there?' You see, it's all very awkward. The Yard isn't concerned with her morals, so how hard am I to press her about this story of hers? There isn't really a shred of evidence to connect her with Louise Rogers. I've been thinking about that a lot, and I'm going to put it up to the Chief. She ran away from that house in a fright, but we don't know what frightened her. She's the sort of girl who might enjoy working a chap up until he lost his head—it happens every day. Then she's frightened and bolts. When she has to explain herself she can't say what happened, so she pitches a tale. The only solitary link with Louise is that blighted earring, and you know there's an easy explanation for that. We don't know where Louise went last Friday. It's not impossible that Mary may have seen her and remembered the earrings. A lot of people go through Lenton, you know. Mary may have seen her there any time. If the earrings took her fancy, she'd remember them. When she wanted a story in a hurry, and an exciting one, don't you think it's the sort of thing she might fish up? Anyhow I'm going to put it up to the Chief and see what he says. What will you do with yourself?"

Miss Silver said primly, "I shall walk into the village and call on Miss Grey. There is a book she has promised to lend me."

CHAPTER 12

It was late when Frank Abbott returned—late Saturday afternoon. He came through Lenton, and saw Inspector Smith. The fingerprints collected from the Forester's House were, as they expected, those of Mary Stokes and of a man so far unknown. Inspector Smith had, as a matter of fact, gone over on his bicycle to Tomlin's Farm in order to obtain corroboration. Arriving there at two o'clock, he was informed that Mary had gone into Lenton. "Lunching with a friend," Mrs. Stokes told him, "and going to the pictures afterwards. . . . No, and I'm sure I can't say when she'll be home, Inspector. Girls don't hurry themselves to get back from a jaunt, and that's a fact. I'd be worrying myself about her coming home in the dark, for you can say what you like, it's a lonely road, but she was meeting Joe Turnberry tea-time and he said he'd see her safe. Is there anything I can do for you? . . . Something she's in the habit of handling? Well, I dunno. There's that *Picture Post*— she was looking at it last night and no one's touched it since. You're welcome, I'm sure, though I don't know what good it'll do you."

By the time Frank Abbott came into Lenton police station the proofs of Mary's fingerprints were waiting for him. There were plenty of them all over the pages of the magazine, and they were identical with the prints from the Forester's House.

"There's just one of those that looks different." Smith fished out a large, vague print. "See? It's the side of a hand—right hand print—bit of the palm, little finger, and the one next to it, all too much smudged to be any use. That came off the panelling in the passage of the Forester's House—five foot four from the ground and just above the smudge we thought might be blood, and blood it is. It looks to me as if it might be smeared from the cuff of a coat."

Frank nodded.

"Well, there's nothing else we can do tonight. The Yard are on to a man who is said to have been a pal of Louise Rogers. A little light at that end would be helpful. Meanwhile I can confront Mary Stokes with these prints and ask her what about it. It may get us somewhere, or it may not. I think we ought to go over every inch of that clearing—shift all the leaves. Some job! But if Louise was murdered there, there may be traces."

He drove back in the dark with the feeling that looking for a needle in a haystack was going to be a joke compared to what lay ahead of them.

It was when they were all in the drawing-room after dinner that Mark Harlow rang up. Cicely came back from taking the call to announce that he was coming round to spend the evening.

"He says he's got the blues. Mrs. Green and Lizzie are out. It's their day, and they've gone to Lenton to the late house at the Rex. The poor lamb has had cold supper and is fed to the teeth. I told him we could at least give him hot coffee."

Mark Harlow, duly arriving, appeared to be in the best of spirits. He drank three cups of Cicely's coffee, and then sat down at the piano and rattled off a lot of brilliant fireworks which had the effect of driving Colonel Abbott to his study, where he could devote himself to the day's cross-word puzzle in peace.

Cicely hung over the piano, talking, arguing, animated, in a house-coat the colour of rowan-berries. Presently Mark was playing one of his songs and she sang with him, making a duet of it, with nothing that could be called a voice but an odd effect of artistry.

Monica was doing embroidery, her lips rather tightly pressed together, the vexed colour high in her cheeks. Frank next to her, lazy and comfortable.

On the other side of the hearth Miss Silver, her knitting laid by, was engaged in reading the Reverend Augustus Grey's privately printed *Memoirs of Deeping and the Neighbourhood*. The volume, handsomely bound in brown calf, was light enough to hold, but it must be confessed that she was finding its contents heavy. She looked up from them occasionally and allowed her gaze to rest upon the young people by the piano.

Mark Harlow was of a slimmer build than Grant Hathaway. He lacked perhaps an inch of Grant's height, and without being dark was darker than Grant both as to hair and eyes. He had a much more mobile face, thinner eyebrows, a quick twist of the mouth when he laughed, a constant play of expression from grave to gay. There was no doubt that he had a great deal of charm, and that his playing was clever—oh, yes, very clever indeed, though according to her old-fashioned standards sadly lacking in melody. Catching her eyes upon him, he might have read her thoughts, for he laughed and broke suddenly into the "Blue Danube."

Miss Silver smiled, and Cicely clapped her hands.

"Come and dance it with me, Frank!"

He shook his head.

"Too lazy."

There was scorn in her voice.

"Bone idle!"

She picked up her long, full skirts and began to waltz by herself, as light as a feather, as light as a leaf, as graceful as a birch tree in the wind. She might be a little brown thing, but she had her charm.

Her mother watched her for a moment or two, then dropped her eyes to her embroidery. This was how Cis used to look—this was how she was meant to look. But not for Mark Harlow. What was happening to her? Where was she going? Why couldn't you keep your children safe and happy as you did in their nursery days? A sleepy head on your shoulder—God bless Mummy and Daddy and make me a good girl. The bright silks in her lap dazzled in a sudden mist. A verse which she had read somewhere came into her mind, very clear and distinct, as if she was reading it again:

> "I bore you and I nursed you, you were flesh and blood
>   and bone of me.
> I toiled for you and loved you, but you've gone from me
>   and grown from me.
> Oh, once you were my little maid, but now you've
>   travelled far.
> For it's a grown woman, a grown woman, and a stranger
>   that you are."

The tune came to an end. When it was over Monica looked relieved. Miss Silver went back to her book, emerging thankfully from a long-winded narrative about a supposed apparition in the churchyard which had in the event turned out to be no more than a strayed ewe. The Reverend Augustus was unsparingly diffuse. When at long last he had finished with the story he proceeded to moralize upon it. It was not until nearly ten o'clock that Miss Silver, turning a page, found her flagging attention revived. Mr. Grey wrote:

84

"My Excellent Neighbour Sir Humphrey Peel has permitteed me to transcribe the following interesting passage from his grandfather's Day Book. In his capacity of Justice of the Peace, Sir Roger Peel was a most respected magistrate and a most kindly and benignant friend to the poor. It may have been in either of these capacities that he was approached by a certain widow of this parish whose name is given as Thamaris Ball. This name I conceive to be a mistake for Damaris. . . ."

The Rector proceeded for some paragraphs to follow the Ball family in and out of the church register. Marriages, births, deaths, and tombstones—a very tedious performance.

Miss Silver dealt with it perseveringly, but returned with some relief to the transcription from the Day Book of Sir Roger Peel. She had just become a good deal interested in the fact that there was a mention of the Forester's House farther down on the page, and was reading a sentence which began, "This Thamaris Ball said and deposed—" when the drawing-room door was opened and the house-parlourmaid, still in her outdoor clothes, came a step or two into the room. She was flushed, and her manner nervous.

Monica Abbott looked round in surprise.

"What is it, Ruth?"

Words came hurrying and stumbling.

"It's Mr. Stokes—and could he see Mr. Frank for a minute? It's about his niece—they don't know what's happened to her. He's got Joe Turnberry with him. They caught us up in the Lane. Oh, Mrs. Abbott!"

Frank was out of his chair before she had finished her first sentence. As he shut the door behind him he heard Monica say, "Now pull yourself together!"

Josiah Stokes was waiting in the hall, square and ruddy in an old weatherbeaten coat, Joe Turnberry beyond him in his off-duty clothes, his big open face all puckered up like a frightened child. Frank took them into the dining-room and shut the door.

"What's happened, Mr. Stokes?"

"Well, Mr. Frank, we don't rightly know that anything's happened, and it's maybe I'm wasting your time and my own over nothing at all, and if it hadn't been for the stories that's been going round, and you being down here to look into them, I wouldn't have troubled you. But my wife's in a way about it."

"Do you think you could begin at the beginning, Mr. Stokes?"

Josiah ran his hand through his hair, the thickest thatch in the parish. As yellow as corn when he was young, it curled up strongly still all over his head, but the grey in it gave it a flaxen look under the hanging light. He said in a simple, vexed voice,

"I'm all put about. The fact is she went off to Lenton and she hasn't come back."

Frank glanced across at the mantelpiece. The hands of a funeral marble clock stood at twenty to eleven.

"It's not so late, you know."

"Well, it is, and it isn't. I got off on the wrong foot. Mary, she went off to meet her girl friend in Lenton and have a bit of lunch with her, and Joe here, he met them afterwards and they went to the pictures. Well, they came back by the seven-thirty bus from Lenton that gets in here at ten minutes to eight, and Joe, he sees her back to the farm."

"Then—"

"Just a minute, Mr. Frank. Joe, you tell him how long it took you."

Joe Turnberry blushed.

"A matter of twenty minutes, or maybe twenty-five."

"Well, go on then, can't you! That's what I brought you here for, isn't it? Haven't you got a tongue in your head? You carry on and tell Mr. Frank what you've been telling me!"

Joe's colour deepened.

"I took her back to the farm same as I told Mr. Stokes, and she said goodnight and went in and shut the door, and I come along home to Mrs. Gossett's where I lodge."

"That's right," said Josiah Stokes. "We heard the door, Mother and I did, and the kitchen clock made it twenty past eight—about five minutes fast it runs run mostly. My wife, she calls out, 'Mary, is that you?' but there isn't any answer. The dog gets up and walks across the door, but he doesn't bark. He'd bark fast enough for a stranger, but he wouldn't for Mary, nor yet for Joe here. My wife says, 'Well, she'll be through for a cup of tea,' but she doesn't come. After about a quarter of an hour or so my wife goes through and calls up the stair, but there isn't any answer. She leaves it a bit longer, and then she goes up to see what the girl is at. And Mary isn't there. She comes down all of a fluster, and we go through the house, but she isn't there. Then I take a lantern and go out round the house calling, but there's no one there either, so we make up our minds we're mistook. There was something shut, but it couldn't have been the front door. Must have been door or window shutting itself—happens that way sometimes in an old house. I tell my wife the girl'll be along by the next bus. Well, next bus gets in ten minutes to nine. When it comes to half past nine I walk down to the village to Mrs. Gossett's, and there's Joe Turnberry sitting in the kitchen listening to the wireless, and he tells me he brought Mary home by a quarter past eight. Well, then I think, 'She slipped out again, that's what she done, and as like as not she'll be back before I am.' So I go back and Joe comes along, but Mary isn't there. We wait about a bit, and then my wife says, 'You take and go down to Abbottsleigh and tell Mr. Frank. I don't like it,' she says, 'and I'm not going to have it on my conscience that we didn't do everything we ought.' So we come along, and we meet the maids from Abbottsleigh in the Lane, coming up from the late bus."

Frank said quickly,

"Are you on the telephone at the farm?"

"Well, yes, we are. I had it put in after the war."

"Then I think we'll give Mrs. Stokes a ring and find out if your niece has come in. There's an extension in here."

Maggie Bell heard the tinkling sound of the signal which brought Mrs. Stokes running out of the kitchen, where she had been sitting with the door open and the dog for company. On the party line everyone knew when anyone else was being rung up. Maggie's sofa by day was her bed by night. She slept badly, and burned her light till midnight or even later, though there would be no telephoning after eleven o'clock. She had only to stretch out her hand and lift the receiver to hear Mr. Stokes say,

"That you, Mother? Is Mary home?"

Mrs. Stokes' answer came all in a hurry.

"Oh, no, she isn't. What can be keeping her?"

Mr. Stokes said, "I don't know," and hung up.

The click came to Maggie along the line. She hung up too. Not much to be made of that, not even in the way of scandal. Quarter to eleven wasn't all that late. There was a first-class picture on at the Rex in Lenton—ever so many people had gone over to see it from the village. All the maids in the houses round had Saturday for their day out, because of the late bus. It didn't run other nights, only Saturdays, and what's the good of a half day if you've got to be in before nine? Maggie wondered why on earth the Stokeses were putting themselves in a fuss about Mary. If there was ever a girl for the last bus home, it was Mary Stokes. You wouldn't see her coming home in a hurry if she was out with a young man. Maggie didn't blame her for that. Fusses, that's what the Stokeses were, and old-fashioned enough to have come out of the ark. Came from not having any young people about. Pity about them losing those two sons in the war. And the one that was left didn't care for farming. Mad about aeroplanes, and doing well at the job. Nice-looking too. Might have livened things up a bit if he'd stayed on the farm. That stuck-up Mary wasn't any good to anyone. They'd no call to fuss about her—she'd be back all right. Let her alone and she'll come home, and bring her tail behind her, like it said in the nursery rhyme.

But when Mary Stokes came home it was feet first on a hurdle.

CHAPTER 13

They found her in the morning, under a pile of hay in a disused stable across the yard, with her neck broken.

Maggie Bell had a very interesting morning listening to the messages that went to and fro. A call to the Superintendent at Lenton—that was the first she heard of it. Inspector Smith, that was—very short and sharp, and no wonder either. Maggie went cold right down to the tips of her fingers as she listened to the curt sentences. Then there was Mr. Frank Abbott on a London call— Scotland Yard, to speak to Chief Detective Inspector Lamb.

Maggie never let go of the receiver, and before long the Chief Detective Inspector was on the line, and Mr. Frank's voice answering him from Tomlin's Farm. Sergeant Abbott he might be up in London, but down here he was Mr. Frank and wouldn't ever be anything else. She listened entranced to the conversation.

"Abbott speaking, sir. I thought you'd want to know at once— that girl's been murdered."

There was a grunt from the other end of the line.

"The girl who told the tale?"

"Yes, sir."

"Done to shut her mouth?"

"Might be—might be just coincidence."

"You do get them—sometimes. Pretty funny business. Think I'll come down. You can meet a morning train at Lenton. I'll give you a ring when we've looked it up."

Out at Tomlin's Farm the routine that waits on murder held its way. Doctor, photographer, fingerprint man came and went. The ambulance last of all. If the dead girl had found it dull at Tomlin's Farm, at least she was leaving it in a burst of notoriety.

In the kitchen Mrs. Stokes, her eyes red and swollen with weeping, made tea for everyone and cut large slices of homemade cake. Not battle, murder, nor sudden death could break the bonds of hospitality. Josiah came and went, grimly shepherding the official flock. Every time she was alone with him the tears ran down her cheeks and she said the same thing.

"I couldn't have believed it of Joe Turnberry."

Josiah's response never varied. He rumpled his hair with a vigorous thrust of blunt fingers and growled out,

"Who says it was Joe?"

"Seems like it must ha' been. Dog never barked. Wouldn't he have barked if there had been a stranger about?"

Josiah tugged at his hair.

"Mightn't have been a stranger, Mother. Needn't be Joe."

A big sob came up in Mrs. Stokes' throat.

"I went to school with his mother," she said, and turned away to fill the kettle again.

Well before noon everyone in Deeping had his or her own version of the murder. A good deal more than half of their neighbours were quite ready to believe that Mary Stokes had pushed Joe Turnberry too far, and that he had done her in. Mrs. Mayhew, the matronly cook at Abbottsleigh, held forth on the subject to Ruth and her sister Gwen.

"The way you girls carry on I wonder there isn't more of you get yourselves murdered. A young man'll stand just so much and no more. That's what I told my Emmy when she had Charlie coming after her. 'You make up your mind, my girl,' I said, 'if you're going to take him, take him, and if you're going to give him the go-by, you tell him straight. You're getting him all worked up,' I said, 'and that's when things happen. So don't say you haven't been warned.' "

Ruth looked scared, but Gwen giggled and flounced. She'd got a young man in Lenton, and she didn't mind if she did work him up—only not as far as murder, that went without saying.

The morning wore on. Frank Abbott met his Chief by the 10.45 at Lenton. Miss Silver finished the meanderings of the Reverend Augustus Grey. Cicely played the organ at the morning service.

Eight days since Mary Stokes had run screaming down the track from Dead Man's Copse. A great deal can happen in eight days.

CHAPTER 14

Chief Detective Inspector Lamb sat at the pedestal table in the parlour at Tomlin's Farm. The two photograph albums and the family Bible had been removed with their attendant mats, leaving the whole shining walnut top to a blotting-pad, an inkstand, a pen-tray, and an attaché case, which lay open, disclosing a pile of papers.

Frank Abbott, sitting across the corner of the table, pencil in hand and notebook before him, was struck with the complete harmony between his Chief and these surroundings. The large man in the large overcoat, with his florid colouring and the strong curling dark hair a little gone back from the temples and not quite so thick on the crown, might very well have passed for a farmer in his Sunday clothes. Mrs. Stokes' parents, looking down from their photographic enlargements on either side of the hearth, could have accepted him as a relative in an effortless, matter-of-course kind of way. The big feet planted squarely upon the old flowered carpet, the square capable hands, the heavy face, the shrewdness of the eyes, would have passed him in any English market town. Nothing surprising about it either, since he came of farming stock and had learnt his A.B.C. in a village school. When he spoke, the country lingered on his tongue.

"Well, then, here we are," he said. "This young fellow Joe Turnberry, he's the natural suspect. Trouble with you college boys is, the more a thing's shoved under your nose, the more you're too educated to see it's there. It's not clever enough, so you've got to go rummaging and raking around for something else. Like those French words I've warned you about. The plain English of a thing isn't good enough—you've got to have something fancy!" He gave a kind of snort. "Puts me in mind of the breakfast I had this morning, at that hotel—a lot of muck served up with Frenchified names!"

Frank laughed.

"I can assure you, sir, that it would have horrified the French."

Lamb grunted.

"When I see a lot of foreign words on the menoo of a country hotel I know what I'm in for. It's a cover-up, and pretty fools they must think anyone is to be taken in by it. Now let's get back to this Joe Turnberry. He's the natural suspect, and I'm taking him first. We'll have him in."

Joe Turnberry brought his reluctant feet, his shaking hands, and his tallowy face into the room and across the floor. Arrived over against this formidable London police chief, he made an attempt to straighten his sagging shoulders. Lamb let him stand for a bit before he looked up from the papers on his blotting-pad.

"You are Joseph Turnberry?"

"Yes, sir." The words knocked against one another.

"H'm—police service—h'm—good character—age . . . Local man, aren't you?"

"Yes, sir."

"Any service in the Army during the war?"

"Yes, sir."

"How long?"

"Two years."

"Joined up when you were eighteen—I see. Well then, you knew this girl Mary Stokes?"

"Yes, sir."

"Keeping company with her?"

"No, sir."

"You say no—other people say yes."

Joe Turnberry gave a gulp.

"It isn't true, sir. She wouldn't have me."

"Meaning you wanted to keep company and she didn't? But you met her yesterday afternoon. Go on—tell us what you did. Here, you'd better have a chair."

Joe sat down, the large bucolic frame balanced uneasily on the edge of an upright chair, the big red hands hanging helplessly between the knees. He gave another gulp and said,

"She told me she was going in to Lenton. She's got a girl friend there. I told her, 'What's the sense of coming home in the dark by yourself?' So she said all right, we'd have tea and do a picture and I could see her home, so we did."

"What terms were you on?"

"Terms?"

"You heard me. What sort of terms were you on? Did you quarrel?"

Colour rushed into the tallowy face, mounted to the edge of the dark hair, receded slowly.

Lamb said, "Well? Did you quarrel?"

Joe Turnberry said in a wretched voice,

"No, sir."

"Now look here, my lad, telling lies isn't going to get you anywhere, you'd better stick to the truth. You met Mary Stokes and her friend Lily Ammon and had tea with them." He picked up a paper. "This is what Lily Ammon says. 'Mary told me Joe Turnberry was meeting us for tea, and he did. She told me he was wanting to go with her, but she wouldn't. Not likely, she said. She told me he was ever so jealous. When we were having tea he got all worked up with Mary—something about her meeting somebody else. I don't rightly know what it was, because there was a girl the other side of the room, she'd promised me a jumper pattern, and I went over to remind her. When I came back they were at it hammer and tongs—something about fingerprints and her meeting this chap, I don't know who. He said she'd left these fingerprints all over the place, and who was she meeting? And she said it wasn't his business, was it? So then I said, "Well, I'm meeting Ernie"—that's my boy friend—and I left them to it.' Do you still say you didn't quarrel with Mary Stokes?"

There was a convulsive movement of the throat. What had been a gulp became a sob.

"I never touched her, sir—I swear I never!"

The Chief Inspector's eyes, which Frank Abbott had been known to compare irreverently to those hard bulging peppermint sweets known as bullseyes, neither softened nor wavered. Fixed, brown, and slightly protuberant, they maintained their enquiring stare.

"I'm asking you if you quarrelled with her."

Joe Turnberry lifted a terrified gaze.

94

"We had words—"

"Anything you'd like to add to that?"

"She told me off—said what she did wasn't no business of mine—said if she liked to go with a chap, I'd got a nerve to say anything—asked me who I thought I was—" He stuck.

Lamb helped him out.

"So then?"

"I said I was sorry, and she said, 'All right,' and we went along to the Rex."

"H'm. Any more quarrelling?"

"No, sir."

"Well then, you came home in the bus that gets in at ten minutes to eight. We've got statements from the other passengers. They say you and Mary Stokes never said a word to one another all the way in."

"There wasn't anything to say, sir."

"And then you walked home with her through the village and up the track between the Common and Dead Man's Copse?"

"Yes, sir."

"Still not speaking?"

"There wasn't a lot to say."

"Any sweethearting?"

"No, sir."

"Kiss her goodnight?"

The boy's face twitched.

"No, sir."

"Well, what happened when you got up to the farm?"

"Nothing, sir. She said, 'Goodnight, Joe,' and I said, 'Goodnight, Mary,' and she went in and shut the door and I come away."

"Did you see anyone, or hear anything to suggest that there was anyone else about—either coming or going?"

"No, sir."

Lamb had been sitting back in his chair, a large square hand on either knee. He leaned forward now, both arms on the table.

"You served in the Army. Taught you that trick of how to break a man's neck, didn't they? Taught you how to do it quick and quiet?"

"Sir—"

"They did—didn't they? You could have done it easy enough when she turned to go into the house."

Joe stared at him.

"Why would I want to? I thought the world of her." The words came slowly spaced. When they were out he lifted his head. "I swear to God I never touched her, sir!"

Lamb let him go.

When the door had shut he said,

"It's likely enough it happened that way, but there's no proof. It'd be a thinnish case—unless something more turns up. A peaceable kind of chap by all accounts, but you never can tell what a man'll do if he's pushed too far. Would you say she was that sort of girl?"

"Well, yes—" Frank Abbott sounded reluctant.

He got Lamb's formidable stare.

"Too easy for you—that's what, isn't it? Not enough of the high-class mystery touch."

"No, sir—but look here—"

"Well?"

Frank Abbott ran his hand back over his immaculate hair.

"Well, sir, if he killed her, why did he open and shut the door? There's no sense in it, is there? If you were killing a girl you wouldn't exactly draw attention to the fact by slamming her front door."

"Who says it was slammed?"

"It must have been shut pretty hard, or the Stokeses wouldn't have heard it in the kitchen."

Lamb grunted.

96

"Suppose the girl had opened the door and was just going in—he'd shut it, wouldn't he, for fear of anyone coming along before he got the body out of the way?"

Frank cocked an eyebrow.

"Well, he wouldn't bang it. But the girl might."

"Why?"

"She might have had enough of Joe in the sulks. Not one of our brighter conversationalists at any time. Or—have you thought of this? Suppose she was meeting someone else, it would be a signal to him and, perhaps she may have thought, a bit of a safeguard for her. I don't think we can entirely keep the Louise Rogers business out of it. If there was any truth in what Mary Stokes said she saw, then there was someone in the neighbourhood with an interest in shutting her mouth. There is also quite undoubtedly someone whom she had been meeting at the Forester's House. And that wasn't Joe Turnberry—we checked up on his fingerprints at once. It seems to me we've got to find the chap she was meeting before we can get any farther. As a preliminary, I suggest getting the fingerprints of Grant Hathaway, Mark Harlow, and Albert Caddle, and asking them what they were doing last night."

Lamb pursed up his mouth in a soundless whistle.

CHAPTER 15

It was a little later on in the morning that Maggie Bell was tantalized by a brief conversation between that Miss Silver and Mr. Frank. First there was the signal which meant a call for Tomlin's Farm, and a policeman's voice saying "Hullo!" Must have been someone from Lenton, because it wasn't Joe Turnberry. As likely as not Joe was arrested by now. Maggie quivered with anticipation as she heard a slight cough, and then a woman's voice asking for Sergeant Abbott.

"Miss Silver speaking. Will you be so kind as to ask him to come to the telephone? I have something of importance to say."

But when Mr. Frank had been fetched, Maggie got no more out of it than that Miss Silver would be glad to see him with as little delay as possible.

"What is it?"

"I think, my dear Frank, that I will say no more until I see you."

Maggie gritted her teeth. Wasn't that an old maid all over—making mysteries and wanting to have a finger in everyone else's pie! Mr. Frank wasn't best pleased either—you could hear it in his voice.

"Well, I don't know—"

That silly cough again.

"Mrs. Abbott asked me to say that she hoped you would bring the Chief Inspector here to lunch."

Mr. Frank sounded doubtful.

"Well, I don't know. Got an ace up your sleeve?"

"It might be."

Funny way of talking, Maggie thought. She waited while Frank Abbott went away, and she had to wait quite a long time.

Lamb's reactions to the news that Miss Silver was at Abbottsleigh were of a mixed nature. He wanted to know what she was doing there, the tone of his voice suggesting that if he had been in the habit of using strong language, it might have been, "What the devil!" On being assured that she was on a private visit to Mrs. Abbott he relaxed.

"My aunt has a very good cook, sir. It will be a great deal better than the hotel."

Lamb grunted.

"Well, I won't say anything about lunch. It depends how we get on. You say Miss Silver wants to see you?"

"Well—I thought she'd got something up her sleeve."

Maggie was feeling very impatient by the time he got back to the telephone, and then there was nothing worth waiting for— no more than an "All right, I'll be along."

Miss Silver looked up from her knitting as he came into the morning-room. After a brief greeting she said gravely,

"I hope you do not imagine that I would have intruded on your time without a very special reason. I felt that it would be indiscreet to say any more than I did upon the telephone. There is a young woman in the village who, I am informed, makes a regular habit of listening in. Since she is a cripple she has plenty of time at her disposal, and on an occasion like this she would be particularly interested. So I thought if the Chief Inspector could spare you—I hope he is well?"

Frank laughed.

"I've never known him anything else. They turned them out tough where he came from. Well, here I am. What are you going to spring on me?"

She deposited the infant's coatee in her lap and handed him a small leather-bound book open.

"What's this?"

Resuming her knitting, she informed him.

"It is the book which Miss Grey so kindly lent me—written by her father, the Reverend Augustus Grey, formerly Rector of this parish, and privately printed in 1868 during the early years of his incumbency when he was a good deal interested in local superstitions. If you will begin at the top of the left-hand page, I think you will find something which may give you food for thoughts. Perhaps you would care to read it aloud."

He pulled up a chair, sat down at a little distance, and began to read.

A slight cough checked him.

"I have not troubled you with the preliminaries, but what you are about to read is a transcript from the Day Book, or diary, of Sir Roger Peel, a local landowner and magistrate who was a contemporary of the Edward Brand who hanged himself in Dead Man's Copse. Mr. Grey was able to copy it by the courtesy of a descendant, Sir Humphrey Peel. Sir Roger had been approached by a widow of the parish whose name is given as Thamaris Ball, which the Rector supposes to be a mistake for Damaris. Now, if you would care to begin—"

Frank looked at the yellowing page and read:

" 'This Thamaris Ball said and deposed that her daughter
Joanna was picking of blackberries in the wood by the
Common, and being venturesome she came as far as the
edge of the clearing where the Forester's House is. And
this Joanna did say and swear that she did there see the
man Edward Brand a-making of clay mammets—' "

He looked up with a quizzical smile.
"What in the world is a mammet?"
She was knitting briskly now.
"It is rather an interesting derivation," she said—"from Mahomet, whom the Crusaders ignorantly supposed to be an idol worshipped by the Saracens. They brought the word back to England, where it became corrupted into mammet or mommet and was used to describe a small image or doll."
He murmured, "Revered preceptress—" under his breath and went back to the book:

" '—did see the man Edward Brand a-making of clay
mammets in the likeness of divers gentlemen of the
neighbourhood and their ladies and putting them to dry
in the sun. And said further that some of them that were
dry he took into the house and after a while came out and

went away through the wood. Then the said Joanna, being curious to see what was done with the said mammets, went privily to the back of the house and so entered. When she could not see the said mammets in any of the rooms she went down into the cellar and there found them with many others. And one in the likeness of a Bishop with a cope and mitre, and others like the Parson and the Clerk. And some with pins thrust through, and some with rusty nails. And one that was all scorched from burning at a fire. Then did this Joanna become very fearful and ran out through the house and through the wood, and so came sobbing and weeping to her mother, the said Thamaris Ball—' "

Miss Silver reached out a hand and resumed the book.

"Well, my dear Frank?"

His very fair eyebrows rose.

"Am I expected to know what you are getting at?"

"Indeed you are."

He shook his head.

"I'm at the bottom of the class, unless it's some coincidence between the 'said Joanna' and Mary Stokes—they both ran through the wood in hysterics. But you're not asking me to believe that Mary was frightened by a mammet, are you?"

"Think, Frank!"

He looked at her blankly.

"You'd better tell me."

The knitting-needles clicked.

"You have allowed yourself to be distracted by a number of picturesque details. The point is, what did Joanna do? She went into the Forester's House to look for something, and when she couldn't find it in any of the rooms she went down into the cellar."

Frank Abbott sprang to his feet.

"Gosh—what a fool! The cellar—she went down into the cellar!"

Miss Silver coughed.

"Old houses always do have cellars—I ought to have thought of it immediately. And if Edward Brand was occupying himself with forbidden arts, it is very probable that the entrance to this cellar would be masked. I would suggest an immediate search of the premises, and especially a thorough investigation of the panelled side of the staircase. It is where I should expect to find a continuation of the stair to the cellar."

Neither Sergeant Abbott nor Chief Inspector Lamb was to partake that day of the excellent lunch prepared for them at Abbottsleigh.

The Forester's House echoed to the tramp of policemen's boots, to knocking, tapping, hammering. In the end they broke down the panelling where it gave back a hollow sound, and disclosed a narrow stair which went steeply down to a bare cellar. Lamb stood on the bottom step and saw the light of a powerful electric lamp go to and fro over old stone flags. He stood there frowning, intent, and silent. After quite a long time he said,

"There's a lot of dust—"

Inspector Smith spoke from behind him.

"That's what you'd expect, sir, isn't it?"

Lamb grunted, then spoke over his shoulder.

"Get that lamp down here, Frank—I want it lower!"

As the light came down, he said the same thing over again and amplified it.

"There's a lot of dust, and as Smith says, it's what you'd expect. But what I wouldn't expect is for it to look like it does. Here, get the light more this way! See what I mean! Looks to me as if it had been swept. I don't reckon broom marks 'ud last getting on for a couple of hundred years, which would be about the time since there was any call to use a broom here. But if it's been swept lately, that'd mean somebody wanting to sweep his footprints out." He swung about and began to go up the stair

102

again. "We'll have those flagstones up, Smith. Get the men on to it at once!"

Louise Rogers was under the flags in the far corner. She wore the black coat described by Mrs. Hopper and by Mary Stokes. Her skull had been fractured by a heavy blow. Her fair hair hung down as Mary Stokes had seen it hang, a single diamond earring bright in the stained tangle—an earring like an eternity ring.

CHAPTER 16

On Monday morning Chief Inspector Lamb interviewed Miss Lily Ammon, typist and stenographer, a little creature with a turned-up nose and wiry dark hair in a frizz. She looked as if she had been crying, and Lamb, who had three daughters of his own, thought the better of her for it. He had her statement in his hand and took her through it—the lunch with Mary Stokes— the meeting with Joe Turnberry—the scene in the tea-shop.

"You knew her pretty well?"

"Oh, yes, sir. She used to work where I am till she got into Mr. Thompson's office."

"Friends—eh?"

"Oh, yes, sir."

Nice little thing—rather taking. Little earnest way with her— pretty voice. He wondered what she had in common with Mary Stokes.

Lily was going on.

"Of course we didn't see so much of each other after she went to Mr. Thompson's. And then lately she'd been ill, but she was better again. I was ever so pleased when she rang up and said couldn't we lunch together. I couldn't go to the pictures like she wanted me to because of my boy friend—I was meeting him at half past four—so we took our time over lunch and did a bit of shopping, and met Joe Turnberry like I said."

She wasn't a bit nervous now. The big man from London that she'd been so frightened about was as easy as easy to talk to. Put her in mind of Uncle Bert, that wasn't really an uncle at all but they called him Uncle when they were children—sweets in his pocket, and sixpences at odd times—a real kind man and fond of kiddies. Funny this big policeman should put her in mind of him, but he did. Something about the way he looked at you. Uncle Bert used to look that way when he was going to make a joke—ever so grave and solemn. Only this wasn't any joke— poor Mary—She blinked damp lashes.

"Now, Miss Ammon, you say you took your time over lunch. I expect you had quite a lot to talk about."

"Oh, yes."

"I want you to go over it all in your mind very carefully. A lot of it would be just girls' talk between friends, but I want you to think whether there was anything said that would help us to find out why she was murdered, and who murdered her. Will you try?"

"Oh, yes—" The word didn't get its full value. She took a quick breath before it was really out.

He said, "You've thought of something?"

"I don't—know—"

"Well, suppose you tell me." His voice was kind and encouraging.

"Oh, I don't know—she did say—"

"Just tell me everything you can think of. Don't mind whether it seems important or not."

Lily fixed brown serious eyes upon his face.

"It was just I said something about her being out of her job for three months and I supposed she'd be glad to be earning again, and she said maybe it didn't matter so much. So I said what did she mean, and she looked the way you do when you've got something you could tell if you liked but you're not sure if you will—" She paused, looking at him.

"Yes, Miss Ammon?"

"I thought—well, I didn't think, I wondered—whether she was going to be married. So I asked her right out—I'm not much of a one for secrets—and she tossed her head and said she wasn't in such a hurry to take an unpaid job, and she thought any girl was a fool who couldn't do better for herself than that. I thought she was hinting at me and Ernie—we're saving up to get married—and I said I didn't look at it that way."

Lamb grunted.

"What did she say to that?"

The colour came brightly into Lily's cheeks.

"She said I'd be a fool all my life, but it wasn't her style. So I asked her, 'What do you mean?' and she laughed and said she liked a bit of fun with a chap, but she'd no notion of paying for it working her fingers to the bone cooking and scrubbing. Then she said, 'And I don't want a man to keep me either—at least not that way.' I said, 'Whatever *do* you mean?' and she laughed and said, 'Well, I might be coming into a nice little bit of money, but you needn't say I said so.'"

"You're sure she said that?"

Lily nodded.

"Oh, *yes*. She looked funny too. And then she began to talk about something else. Afterwards I thought—well, I didn't know what to think. I wondered—" She hesitated.

"Yes—go on."

"Well, I wondered about that money—whether she was trying to get it out of someone and—and—"

"That is what we are trying to find out. Now, Miss Ammon—did she tell you anything about a fright she'd had?"

Lily's eyes were as round as a kitten's.

"Oh, no!"

"Nothing about seeing something that frightened her in a wood and running down to the village in hysterics?"

"Oh, no, sir."

"Just this hint that money might be coming her way?"

She nodded and said,

"When we were shopping there was a model coat in Simpson's, ever so expensive, and she said, 'Next thing you know I'll be buying myself one like that.' "

"Sure she said that?"

"Oh, yes, sir."

"H'm—anything else?"

"Yes, sir. I did think I ought to have put it in my statement, but it was all so dreadful—it didn't really come to me at the time that it might be important. I was so upset—"

"Well, you can tell me now. What is it?"

She blinked away a tear.

"I made sure she'd be staying till the last bus. I don't remember how it came up, but I said something like that, and she said oh no, she and Joe were going out by the seven-fifty. Well, I suppose I was surprised. She laughed and looked out of the corners of her eyes. 'I'm the good girl, getting in early! Something new for me, isn't it?'—that's what she said. So I teased her a bit—about Joe Turnberry, you know—and she said, 'Joe Turnberry indeed! I should hope I could do better than that?!' Then she looked funny again, and she said, 'I shall get home nice and early, and I don't suppose I'll kiss Joe good-night, and then—' I said, 'Oh, Mary—*what?*' and she said, 'Wouldn't you like to know, my dear?' And I said I would, but she shut right up, so I let it drop."

106

Lamb leaned forward.

"Miss Ammon, what do you think she meant—all that about going home early, and being a good girl, and saying goodnight to Joe Turnberry? What sort of impression did you get from it? Come on—honest! What did you think?"

Lily said without any hesitation at all,

"I thought she'd got a date with someone else."

CHAPTER 17

The Chief Inspector was telling Sergeant Abbott about his interview with Lily Ammon, when the telephone bell rang. They were in the Superintendent's office at Lenton police station, and for the time being only calls for the two Scotland Yard men would be put through to them. Frank Abbott therefore lifted the receiver, listened for a moment, then handed it to his Chief.

"For you, sir. Wilton speaking from the Yard."

Standing by the table, Frank was aware of Sergeant Wilton's voice, thin and small but perfectly distinct.

"That you, sir? Wilton speaking. They've traced the young fellow who was going about with Louise Rogers. Name of Michel Ferrand. French national. Got on to him rather a funny way. Car found abandoned in Hampshire. Traced to him through the registration number. He says he lent it to Mrs. Rogers last Friday week, the eighth. That's the day she disappeared."

Lamb was leaning forward, one elbow on the table, the receiver to his ear. He grunted.

"How do you mean, abandoned?"

"Well, it was left in front of a garage near Basingstoke some time after dark. They say someone rang them up and said the car would be called for in a day or two. They didn't attach any importance to the matter, and they'd no idea where the call came from."

"H'm—what make of car?"

"Old Austin Seven."

"What day was it left?"

"Friday night. The call came through about half past eight."

"What about fingerprints on the car?"

"Not a hope, sir. It's a fairly big garage and every mechanic in the place must have been handling it. You know how it is in those places—they just push the cars about. The doors and the driving-wheel are a mess."

"We'll have to have this fellow Ferrand down to see if he can identify the body—Mrs. Hopper's coming down on the two-thirty. Send someone with them."

He went on talking for a few minutes.

When he had rung off Lamb turned to Frank Abbott.

"I expect you could hear what he was saying. I've told them to send the fellow down. Now about that car. It explains how Louise Rogers got here, but—Basingstoke's a good twenty miles away. Whoever took it there and left it would have to get back again. The question is how. Train to Lenton—just take a look at the timetable and see what sort of a connection he could get. What time was it that girl Stokes ran screaming in on your tea-party?"

"Just after six. The church clock had just struck—but that was Saturday. Louise Rogers would have been murdered before then. We haven't managed to find anyone who saw her after she left Mrs. Hopper's on Friday morning. We don't know what was going on between then and the time when Mary Stokes saw her lying dead. Look at it this way. It doesn't seem likely that Mary saw the actual murder. It looks to me as if she'd come to the Forester's House to meet the man she was in the habit of meeting there. Instead she bumps into a murderer in the act of transporting a corpse to a place of concealment. I don't think there's any doubt now that she really did see what she described—it all fits too well. Her footprints show that she ran away from the Forester's House in a frantic hurry, so it is reasonable to suppose that she saw the corpse in or quite near to the house. But that's not to say that the murder had only just happened. I can't believe that Louise was still alive when her car was driven over to Basingstoke and left there. Much more likely that she was already dead and the body hidden somewhere till Saturday evening when arrangements had been made for burying it in the cellar. In the course of moving it the murderer discovered that one of those very noticeable earrings was missing. It must have put the wind up him. I'd give a good bit to know how it came off and where, and whether he found it again."

The Chief Inspector turned a stolid face and said,

"Teach you to talk at college, don't they? Or maybe it comes natural. Now how much of that did you think up for yourself, and how much did you cook up with Miss Silver?"

Frank looked down his long nose.

"I really couldn't say, sir."

Lamb chuckled.

"You come down off your high horse and look up those trains same as I told you! Remember he'd have twenty miles to cover in an Austin Seven, and the likelihoods are that it would be dark all the way. He'd got to get to the outskirts of Basingstoke, drop the car, and catch a train. Now what is there for him to catch?"

Frank was turning over the pages.

"Here we are. Let's see—she's not so likely to have been murdered by daylight. If you put the murder at five o'clock on the Friday, he'd got to hide the body and get the car off the map. It would be pretty good going if he got to Basingstoke station by a quarter past six. If he did that, he could get a train at six-twenty that would get him to Lenton, with one change, by half past seven. He could ring up the garage from there. Why do you suppose he risked calling them up?"

"Didn't want them turning the car over to the police. Wanted to gain time—get any fingerprints well messed up. Even if he wiped off his own, or wore gloves, he wouldn't want the girl's prints identified."

"Yes, I suppose so—but it seems a bit of a risk."

"No risk at all. A garage isn't going to bother about where a call comes from. He'd not want anyone making inquiries about that car for as long as he could put them off. He'd want time—time for people to forget they'd travelled with him or seen him taking a ticket. Well, Basingstoke'll have to get busy and see if anyone noticed a man taking a ticket in a hurry for that six-twenty. The people here can tackle Lenton."

Frank's eyebrows rose.

"What a hope!"

Lamb nodded.

"It narrows down at the Deeping end, my lad, and this second murder's going to help. We've got to find the man Mary Stokes was meeting. He may be the murderer, or he mayn't, but I expect he could tell us a thing or two, and we've got his fingerprints. Now are you going to tell me that that girl was carrying on like we know she was carrying on and no one knew anything about it?"

"They don't seem to."

"H'm! Villages must have changed a lot since I was a lad!"

"There's another way you can look at it. There must have been some very strong reason for secrecy. Someone was being particularly careful."

Lamb nodded.

"Who fills that bill?"

"Not Joe Turnberry."

110

"We know it wasn't Joe she was meeting, because of the fingerprints. And it wasn't Joe that was shifting Mrs. Rogers' body on Saturday just before six, because he was home at his lodgings—Mrs. Gossett says so. Between you and me, I think Joe's out of it. He couldn't have taken that car to Basingstoke on Friday evening, because he was on duty. You'd better check over the times with Smith, but I don't think he could have done it—let alone being able to drive."

"Oh, he can drive all right—did a year or two in a garage as a boy before he joined the Army."

"Well, if Joe's out, who's in? That Mary Stokes thought herself a cut above the village, didn't she? There's a Mr. Mark Harlow not so far from that Dead Man's Copse, isn't there? What about him? And the other chap, the one that's doing experimental farming—what's his name—Hathaway?"

Frank's face was expressionless.

"He's married to my cousin, Cicely Abbott."

"H'm—happy couple?—united?"

In a voice as expressionless as his face Frank said,

"No—they're separated."

"Well, we'll have his fingerprints—Harlow's too. Either of them could have been carrying on with the girl. Smith is seeing to it now and finding out what they were doing when Louise Rogers was being murdered and her car being driven to Basingstoke on the Friday, and when her body was being moved on the Saturday."

111

CHAPTER 18

Mrs. Hopper, in floods of tears, had identified her lodger, and fortified by strong hot tea, was now on her way back to Hampstead. At Lenton police station Michel Ferrand, tinged with green under a swarthy skin, was making a statement. There was a bright, hot fire in the Superintendent's office, but he shivered continually—a thin, frail young man with a prematurely lined face. He too had identified the body and wept over it as profusely as Mrs. Hopper. Now his eyes were dry. He sat close up to the fire and couldn't keep his hands still. In fluent English but with a strong accent and a foreign turn of phrase he poured out the statement which Sergeant Abbott was taking down.

"You knew Mrs. Rogers well?" This was Lamb leading off.

Ferrand threw out those shaking hands.

"If I knew her well! *Mon dieu*—who should know her if I do not! Our parents are friends—we are like brother and sister. I am a little younger. I adore her—I follow her about always like a little dog"—a shudder took him—"that is when we are children."

Lamb's eyes bulged. Foreigners were so excitable. He said in his driest voice,

"I'm not asking you about when you were children, Mr. Ferrand."

"But you wish that I tell you what I know. How can I do that unless I tell you how I know it? I substantiate myself. I am not what you call pick-up—I am friend of the family. I am to tell you that Louise is of a family very respectable, very rich. Her

112

father is Etienne Bonnard who has a jewellery establishment in Rue de la Paix."

"Where's that?"

Sergeant Abbott took it on himself to say, "Paris," and received a quenching look.

Ferrand nodded in an animated manner.

"When I say he has this establishment, it is of course before the war. Monsieur Bonnard is dead. He could not survive the fall of France—he had a seizure on the day that the government left Paris. His wife, who is English, renders to him the last offices of affection—she is plunged in grief. The Germans advance daily. In the end she revives enough to think of her daughter—of the future. She decides to save herself and as much of the stock as they can conceal—"

"Look here, Mr. Ferrand, how do you know all this? Were you there?"

"Me? No. I am with my mother in the south. It is Louise who tells me this when we meet in London. Perhaps, monsieur, you know what it is like, that flight from Paris, when everyone has the same idea, and the trains are not running, and there is no petrol. Louise drives the car till the petrol is all gone. The roads are jammed with cars that will not move. There is not enough food. Sometimes the Boche comes over and bombs them, making a sport of it. There are children born by the side of the road, and there are old people who die there. Madame Bonnard is one of those who is dying. Louise is in despair. She has a case filled with diamonds in her hand—necklaces, bracelets, brooches, rings—and they will not buy her a bottle of wine or a crust of bread to save her mother's life. She sits by the side of the road and waits. Just before it is dark there is more bombing—she sits there and waits for death. When it is dark she is still there. All the time people are passing—pushing through the crowd, cursing, screaming, weeping, shouting. Then, figure to yourself, she hears a man who swears in English—she gets up

113

and runs to him. She is, I think, a little mad. She has seen some dreadful things. She catches hold of his arm in the dark, and she says, 'You are English. My mother is English too. Will you help me?' He says, 'What can I do? I cannot even help myself.' Then, I think, she is quite mad. She says, 'This case is full of diamonds. I will give you half.' He says, 'Show me!' He takes a torch out of his pocket and turns it on. She opens the case. He puts his hand down into it and turns the diamonds over, very bright and sparkling under the light. Then suddenly it is all dark again and the case is gone. She feels it wrenched out of her hand and it is gone. All her fortune is gone, and the man is gone."

He threw out his hands in a wide gesture.

"Imagine to yourself her despair. She goes back to her mother. In the morning Madame Bonnard is dead. Shock—exposure—fatigue—I do not know—there was no one to say. Louise goes on walking. In the end she comes to a place she knows. There is a family who takes her in. She has lost everything in the world except a string of pearls and a necklace she is wearing. They are valuable and she is able to sell them—not at that time but later. When the war is over she marries an English officer, one called Rogers. It is not very happy. They separate. He goes to England—she stays in France. Then she hears that he is dead. She comes to England to settle his affairs. There is a little money, but not much—he has left it to her. That is how I meet her again."

Frank Abbott's hand travelled to and fro across the paper. Lamb said,

"You were in England at the time? What were you doing here?"

The young man had steadied as he told his tale. The fire had warmed him, his hands no longer shook. His answer was quite an animated one.

"Oh, yes, monsieur. My father, he is *hôtelier*—hotel-keeper. When Louise and I are children he is manager of a hotel in Paris.

Now he has his own hotel at Amiens. He has a friend who is manager of the Luxe in London. He sends me there to make my English perfect—to gain experience, you understand—it is done all the time in the hotel business. That is where I meet Louise whom I have not seen for ten years."

Lamb goggled at him.

"Are you telling me you recognized her?"

A smile changed the dark, thin face, flashing out for a second and then gone again.

"But no, monsieur—I cannot say that. I see her—it is in the evening—she wears a black dress, very chic. I see the blonde hair, the brown eyes, and I think that is not so common. Then I think that she reminds me of someone, and before I have time to think who it is I see the earrings and I know that it is Louise."

"The earrings—"

Michel waved pale, expressive hands.

"Yes, yes, monsieur—the earrings! It is Monsieur Bonnard, the father of Louise, who designs them and gives them to her when she is eighteen. There is a little what you call 'tiff' about it. Monsieur Bonnard, he does it for a surprise, but Madame Bonnard says Louise is too young—a young girl must not wear diamonds. But Louise is enchanted. She weeps, she begs, she cries, and in the end she has them. They are, you must under-stand, of a design quite unique, so when I see them I know that it is Louise. I approach her—I speak. I say, 'Is it that you have forgotten Michel Ferrand?' and at once she knows me. If we were not in a so public place we would embrace. She tells me she is dining alone. We cannot talk there. We make an appointment to meet—she tells me everything. After that we meet often. One day I find her very pale, very agitated. She has been away for a few days. Her business takes her to Ledlington, where the parents of Captain Rogers had a house, and where they died. The house is rented and the furniture put in store. Louise goes down to see what is to be sold. She is in a hotel

115

there which is called the Bull—three, four hundred years old. There is an archway going into a courtyard and the hotel is built round it. Louise is in a room looking on to this courtyard. She is undressed, in her nightgown ready to get into bed. It is not late, not much after nine o'clock, but she is fatigued. She puts out the light, approaches the window, and opens it. It is a fine night— the stars are beautiful—she regards them. Then all in a moment she is turned to stone. Under her window a man stumbles— something drops and he swears. Monsieur, she tells me—she protests to me—that the words, they are the same which she heard on the road from Paris. She says never will she forget them. The man under her window brings it all back. It is the same voice, he uses the same words. She swears to me that it is the man himself—she cannot be mistaken."

Lamb gazed at him with a stolid air.

"Come, Mr. Ferrand—that's a bit of a tale!"

The hands moved in a quick nervous gesture.

"It is not my tale, monsieur—I tell you what Louise tells to me. She says it is the same voice, the same words, but that is not all. She says the man takes out a torch and turns it on to look for the thing which he has dropped. It is a cigarette-lighter. It lies before him on the stones, he puts his hand down into the light to pick it up. And it is not only the voice and the words, but the hand of the man on the Paris road. Monsieur will remember that he turned on a torch to see the jewels, and put his hand into the light to turn them over. There was a mark on that hand, monsieur. I do not know what it was—Louise did not tell me. But she sees it on the night that the jewels are stolen, and she sees it again that night at the Bull. Then, on the instant, the man is gone. She cannot run down in her bare feet— in her nightdress. She puts on some clothes quickly, quickly— she runs down to the courtyard. It is all dark, all quiet. She asks the hotel porter to find out who has been there. She gives him a very large *douceur*—what you call 'tip.' He comes back and says a car has just gone out—two gentlemen who come in for a drink whilst their chauffeur changes a wheel. She asks what are their names, and he says they are strangers—they come in for a drink, they go out again—no one asks where they come from or where they go. She is in despair. She asks if anyone has noticed the number of the car. Because the tip is so good, the porter takes trouble to find out. It seems that no one has noticed it. Louise is at the end of her forces—she turns to go away. She goes up to her room, she weeps. Suddenly there is a knock at the door. It is the porter. He says one of the gentlemen has dropped an envelope in the garage—it has just been brought to him. It is only an empty envelope, but—Louise takes it, she gives him another tip. The envelope has upon it a name and an address—"

The Chief Inspector said in a hearty voice,

"Well, now we're getting somewhere! Let's have them if you please!"

Michel Ferrand threw out his hands.

"Alas, monsieur, I do not know them. Louise tells me everything else—but the name—the address—that she does not tell me."

Lamb stared in heavy displeasure.

"She didn't tell you?"

"No, monsieur." He leaned forward. "She is like that always from a child—she tells something, but she does not tell all—the thing that matters, she keeps it always in her own hand. She does not like that anyone says to her, 'See, this is the way that you must do.' She tells something because she is lonely, because she is a little fond of me, my poor Louise, but she does not wish to be advised, to have me say, 'No, that is imprudent—that you must not do.' "

Lamb said, "H'm!" Really very excitable people the French. But he thought the boy was speaking the truth. He said,

"What about the car? When did she borrow it—how long after this Ledlington business?"

Ferrand considered.

"The *jour de l'an*—New Year's Day. That was when she told me she was going to Ledlington. She was there three, four days. Then she comes back to Hampstead. I see her on the sixth—we dine together—she tells me what I have told you. She asks me to lend her my car—she says she is going away. I say, 'You are going to find this man. Do not do it, I beg of you. Put it in the hands of the police.' She laughs and says, 'Men are all the same—whatever a woman wishes to do, they always say don't.' I say to her very seriously, 'Louise, I beg of you, wait at least until next week. I will get permission to come with you.' She looks at me and she says, 'Concern yourself with your own affairs, my friend.' Then she laughs again and tells me it is not that at all, I jump at the conclusion. She borrows the car to pay a little visit to the aunt of her husband Captain Rogers who is his only surviving relative. She tells her name, Miss Rogers, and she says she inhabits a village six miles from a railway. 'If I am to go by train,' she tells me, 'it will take all the day—one changes continually.' I do not know whether I believe her or not, but I lend her the car. It is not the first time. If she wants something she must have it—Louise is like that." He plunged his head in his hands and groaned. "That is all, monsieur."

CHAPTER 19

Several things happened that afternoon. For one thing, the weather broke in a violent downpour which came on just after Mrs. Caddle had put on her hat and coat and shut the door of Rectory Cottage behind her. She had laid Miss Grey's tea and left her supper in the larder. The first few heavy drops came spattering down as she latched the garden gate, and then, before she had gone twenty yards, the clouds opened and the rain came down. For a few minutes she stumbled on. Then even the state of dazed misery which for the past ten days had sealed her off from human contact was penetrated by sheer physical discomfort. She had neither umbrella nor waterproof. The rain ran into her eyes and down her neck, heavy as a thunder-plump, and of an icy, searching cold. She turned round and ran back to the cottage, her feet splashing in the wet.

It was about this time that Chief Inspector Lamb, Inspector Smith, and Sergeant Abbott were looking at the fingerprints obtained from Grant Hathaway and Mark Harlow. Frank Abbott was experiencing some relief. Whoever it was who had been meeting Mary Stokes at the Forester's House, it was not Grant Hathaway—neither was it Mark Harlow.

Lamb grunted.

"That doesn't get us any forrarder. What about their movements?"

Smith's fresh-coloured face, never what would be called mobile, now assumed a rather more wooden expression than usual. He had not enjoyed his visit to Deepside, and he did not enjoy having to retail it now. He had wished very heartily that anyone else might have done his errand. If it had been a case of marching into the house and arresting Grant Hathaway—well, he hoped he knew his duty. But to ring the front door bell and ask a gentleman for his fingerprints, it was no use denying it was a bit awkward. The awkwardness was in his voice as he explained himself to the Chief Inspector.

"Well, sir, I started at Deepside, and Mr. Hathaway wasn't there. Seems he'd been away for the week-end."

Lamb sat up and took notice.

"The week-end—eh?"

"Yes, sir."

"When did he go?"

119

"Well, not till the Sunday morning. Breakfast at eight, and off in his car by eight-thirty. That would be just about the time Mary Stokes' body was found."

Lamb grunted.

"Mean anything by that?"

"No, sir. At least what I meant was that he couldn't have known anything about her being murdered—unless—"

"Unless he did it himself—is that what you're getting at?"

If Smith's countenance had lent itself to expression, he would at this point have looked shocked. He said stiffly,

"It was not my intention to make any insinuations. I was merely pointing out that Mary Stokes' body was not found until well after eight, and the body of Louise Rogers was not discovered in the Forester's House until the Sunday evening. Such being the case, and Mr. Hathaway being absent from eight-thirty on Sunday until half past eleven this morning, there was nothing unbelievable in his not knowing what had been happening here."

Frank Abbott saw his Chief's colour deepen. Smith was beating about the bush, and it was not a pastime which commended itself.

"Oh—he said he didn't know, did he?"

Smith's solemn gaze rebuked him.

"Well, it was this way. I got there about twenty-five past eleven, and the housekeeper opened the door to me herself. She said Mr. Hathaway went away Sunday morning and wasn't back yet. Then while she was saying it he drove up, so I asked if I might have a word with him, and he took me into the study. Rather short in his manner, and wanting me to see he was busy. 'Well, what do you want?'—that's the way he spoke— a bit off-hand, I thought. And somehow that's where it struck me that he wouldn't know what had been happening whilst he was away. I thought I wouldn't say anything unless he did, so I put it we were making an inquiry about unauthorized use of the Forester's House and it would be helpful to us to have the fingerprints of those who lived along the Lane, and also an account of their movements so as to get a check on who had been about on the Friday and Saturday evenings, January eighth and ninth. Mr. Hathaway gave a sort of laugh and said, 'There's some cock-and-bull story that girl Mary Stokes has cooked up, isn't there?' So I said, 'That's what we're inquiring into,' and he laughed again and said he supposed we had to find something to do.''

Lamb didn't laugh.

"Said that, did he?"

"Yes, sir. So then I asked him if he had any objection to having his fingerprints taken, and he said he hadn't. But when it came to his movements, well, it wasn't so good."

He produced a notebook and read aloud:

" 'Friday, January 8th—Mr. Grant Hathaway states he left his house about 5 p. m. and returned to it some time later in the evening. Says he was walking, and doesn't know what the time was.' " He looked up and met Lamb's stare apologetically. "I didn't know if you would want me to press him. I was by way of asking him whether he had met or seen anyone up and down the Lane."

"By way of being tactful?"

"Well, yes. If I may say so, Mr. Hathaway isn't the easiest person to question."

"Put the wind up you?"

Smith changed colour.

"I wouldn't say that. I didn't find him very co-operative."

Sergeant Abbott, who was sitting chin in hand looking down at the fingerprints, was suddenly impelled to slide the hand up so that it covered his lips. The Inspector's euphemism tickled him, and euphemisms of superior officers must not be allowed to tickle a sergeant in the middle of an official interview—at least not obviously.

121

Lamb had no inclination to laugh.

"What about the staff?"

"No good at all. There's an old lady that's been housekeeper there thirty years—Mrs. Barton. She doesn't have a regular day off, but on that Friday, the eighth, she'd gone down to the village to have supper and spend the evening with the postmistress. And the house-parlourmaid, Agnes Ripley, that generally goes out on a Saturday, she'd changed her day and gone into Lenton, coming back on the bus that gets in at ten to nine. Well then, she went round to the post office, put in a few minutes talking, and walked home with Mrs. Barton. Neither of them noticed the time, but it would be all of half past nine when they got in. Cold supper had been left for Mr. Hathaway, and he had had it, but they didn't see him. They went to bed about half past ten, and heard him come up half an hour later."

Lamb grunted.

"Louise Rogers was probably killed round about five o'clock—the medical evidence says between three and four hours after her last meal. We don't know where she had that meal. She may have brought food from London and eaten it in the car, or we may find someone who noticed her at a restaurant. There's not much doubt she came down here to find this man who had stolen her diamonds. She thought she had a clue to his whereabouts in the envelope which the porter gave her at the Bull. If she had taken Mr. Ferrand's very sensible advice and turned the whole matter over to the police, she'd be alive today. I've nothing against women in general, but there's no getting away from it, they get into a lot of trouble through thinking they can do things better than the people whose job it is. This is just another case that proves it. Well now, here's this woman, with a name and address on an envelope. Say for argument that it was Mr. Grant Hathaway's name and address. She's got to find the house. Houses in the country don't have names on the gates. She's got to ask her way—she isn't going to find it by instinct. We've got to find the person who told her how to get to Deepside—if it was Deepside. We'll get the B.B.C. to give us a hand there. Starting on the assumption that the man we're looking for is Mr. Hathaway, how do the times fit? He goes out of his house about five, and he doesn't say when he comes back to it. The first we really know of his being back is the housekeeper and the house-parlourmaid saying they heard him come up to bed at eleven o'clock. So far as any evidence to the contrary goes, he had six hours to play with. . . . What about Mr. Harlow?"

Inspector Smith went back to his notebook. The word which had tickled Frank Abbott occurred again almost immediately.

"Mr. Harlow was very co-operative—very pleasant and anxious to do what he could to help. On the Friday, he says, he was working at his composing—he writes songs, you know. He says he was working on one that wouldn't come right, and in the end he went out to get some air and clear his head a bit. He says he didn't notice the time. It wasn't dark yet, but getting on that way, which would put it at between five and half past. He says he came out of his back gate into the Lane and walked straight up the Lane across the main road, and on up the Lane past Deepside. He says as far as he knows he didn't meet anyone."

Lamb growled.

"What does he mean, 'as far as he knows'?"

"I asked him that, and he said his head was full of this song of his which he couldn't get right, and he might have met anyone or passed anyone and not noticed."

Frank Abbott murmured, "Our old friend the artistic temperament."

Smith nodded.

"That's about the size of it. Well, he says he went on walking till he saw the lights of Lenton. Then he thought he might as well go on. He turned into the Empire cinema, saw the picture, had a snack in the café, and walked back, getting in about ten."

"What about the staff? What has he got?"

"Mother and middle-aged daughter—very respectable—name of Green. They say he rang up from Lenton to say he was having something to eat there. They heard him come in about ten. Mrs. Green says it wasn't anything out of the way his going off like that when his music went wrong. She says they were used to it."

Lamb leaned forward.

"What time did he ring up?"

"Well, it was after half past eight, but not much. Mrs. Green says it was just on the half hour the last time she looked at the clock, and it wouldn't be much after that."

"H'm. Then as far as time goes, your co-operative Mr. Harlow could have done the job just as well as Mr. Hathaway. Both these men served in the Army, I take it. Either of them in France in 'forty?"

"I believe so."

Lamb turned to his sergeant.

"Know anything about that?"

"Hathaway was in the retreat at Dunkirk. He was attached to the Blankshires—taken prisoner—did a bolt and got away west. I don't know about Harlow in detail, but I believe he was in France during the retreat. There was something said about it the other day."

"Either of them ever serve with Commando troops?"

"Hathaway did—got a D.S.O."

"Either of them got a mark or a scar on the right hand?"

Frank Abbott began to say, "I don't know—" and then stopped, because all at once he saw, not Grant Hathaway's right hand, but his left, with a thin white scar running between the knuckles of the first and the second fingers. And Lamb had got it wrong. It wouldn't be the right hand—he'd have the torch in his right hand and be rummaging in the suit-case with his left. Or would he? With a shrug he concluded that it might be either way, and said so.

Lamb merely grunted. Smith said in a tentative voice,

"Mr. Hathaway has an old scar on his left hand. Mr. Harlow has a strip of sticking-plaster across the back of his right—says he caught it on some barbed wire."

Lamb shifted in his chair, turning his heavy body to face Smith again.

"Well, as I said, either of the two could have murdered Louise Rogers, driven her car to Basingstoke, and caught that train back to Lenton. There's nothing to show that either of them did it, and nothing to show that they didn't. They had the opportunity, and either of them might have had the motive. That's as far as we've got. And so much for Friday the eighth. Now we come to Saturday the ninth—the day Mary Stokes ran screaming into Rectory Cottage to say she'd seen a corpse. I think we may take it now that she did see what she described, and that the place where she saw it was either inside or just outside the Forester's House. She was meeting someone there, and she seems to have stumbled on the murderer moving the body to the cellar, where he meant to bury it. Well, I suppose it struck you both that it isn't so likely the murderer was the chap she was going to meet. You don't make an appointment with a girl and then bring a murdered body along. That's one thing. And here's another. Whoever the murderer was, he knew that cellar was there. You didn't find it for more than a week, and you wouldn't have found it then if it hadn't been for something about the cellar turning up in an old book and Miss Silver getting hold of it. But this chap didn't have to wait and scratch his head—he knew the cellar was there. We had to chop down the panelling to find the door, but he didn't have to so much as scratch it— he knew the trick. And that means one thing, and one thing only. It means a local man, or a man that's in a position to tap local knowledge. That would go for Mr. Grant Hathaway, and for Mr. Harlow too. Either family might have a copy of the old Rector's book—" He swung round on Frank. "Know if either of them did?"

125

"Old Mr. Hathaway had one, I believe. They were probably pretty well sprinkled about the neighbourhood."

Lamb nodded.

"What I said." He turned back to Smith. "Now what about Saturday the ninth? What were these two gentlemen doing between five-thirty and, let us say, six-thirty to seven o'clock?"

Smith hesitated.

"Well, I put the question rather in a roundabout way, and I didn't press it. Mr. Hathaway says he started out on a bicycle to go down into Deeping about ten minutes past four. I asked if he saw anyone in the Lane—casually, if you take my meaning—and he said he had a few words with Mrs. Hathaway, who was out with her dogs."

Lamb's eyebrows rose.

"His wife?"

"Yes, sir."

"Seems funny to me. Separated, aren't they? Well, he had a few words with his wife and went on down into Deeping."

"No, sir, he says he changed his mind and went home."

"H'm—bit of a queer start. Did he go out again?"

"He says not, sir. Says he had tea, and then wrote letters and did accounts in his study. But of course nobody would know whether he went out or not. The maids wouldn't disturb him."

"And Mr. Harlow?"

"He says he had tea at home, played the piano for a bit, and then went out for a short walk—says he didn't look at the clock, so he doesn't know what time it was. He says it's what he does most evenings when he's at home. He says he went out by his front gate, so he wasn't anywhere near the Lane. He didn't meet anybody."

Lamb lifted a large hand and let it fall again on his knee.

"Well, that leaves us just where we were before. Either of them could have slipped out to the Forester's House as soon as it was dark. Nothing to show they did—nothing to show they didn't."

There was a pause. Frank Abbott looked at Inspector Smith and said in his cool voice,

"What about those other fingerprints?"

Lamb turned his head.

"What fingerprints?"

"Some I asked Smith if he'd get out."

"Some *you* asked! What's it got to do with you?"

"Just being co-operative, sir. As a matter of fact—"

"Well, come along out with it! What have you been up to?"

Frank subdued an inclination to smile. That he was about to produce a red rag and might be called upon to face a charging bull, he was amusedly aware. He got on with it.

"There was an idea that these fingerprints might be of interest."

Inspector Smith had left the room, Lamb therefore felt no need to restrain himself. His colour deepened to plum as he said in an alarming voice.

"Look here, what's all this? Whose fingerprints are they, and whose idea was it—yours, or Miss Silver's?"

"Oh, not mine, sir."

Lamb's fist came down on the table.

"When I want amateurs to give me advice I'll ask for it!"

"Well, not advice, Chief—fingerprints."

The fist came down again.

"Whose fingerprints—and how did she get them?"

"Albert Caddle's—he's Harlow's chauffeur. I believe she dropped an envelope and he picked it up."

Still in that stormy voice, Lamb said,

"Harlow's chauffeur? Why? What makes her think he had anything to do with it?"

Judging the worst to be over, Frank set himself to appease the official mind with facts.

127

"Well, sir, he's married to a woman considerably older than he is, and I gather that he's a bit of a lad. Mrs. Caddle has been going about looking as if the roof had fallen in on her. I suppose I ought to have thought of it for myself, but that is where Maudie scores—she gets the tea-table gossip. As a matter of fact I suggested to my aunt that she might have one or two of her more talkative friends to tea. They seem to have talked about the Caddles—quite a lot."

Inspector Smith came quickly back into the room.

"Ashby's just got them done," he said. "Look here, sir!"

Frank got up and came round the table. The three men leaned together over as clear a set of prints as the law could wish for. Lamb brought them side by side with the prints from the Forester's House. They all looked, they all saw.

After a moment Lamb spoke.

"Well, there's one thing cleared up at any rate. We needn't look any farther for the man who was meeting Mary Stokes."

CHAPTER 20

The rain-storm which had turned Mrs. Caddle back to Rectory Cottage had, after the first ten minutes, subsided into a drizzle. Mrs. Caddle, who had hung her coat in the scullery in order that it might not drip on the kitchen floor, now put it on again and, accepting the loan of Miss Alvina's second-best umbrella, went out into the dusk and resumed her homeward way.

It was about a quarter of an hour later that Cicely Hathaway, answering the telephone, heard an agitated voice enquire if Mr. Frank was at home.

"I'm afraid he isn't. It's Miss Vinnie, isn't it?"

"Oh, yes. Oh dear—what shall I do!"

"Is there anything wrong?"

She heard Miss Alvina catch her breath.

"Oh, my dear, yes! I'm afraid so—I'm really dreadfully afraid so. But I don't know what to think—I feel I must have someone to advise me. It's too much responsibility, and I'm afraid it may be very serious indeed. I don't like to think what it may mean, only of course one can't help—and I did so hope that Mr. Frank would come down—"

"But, Miss Vinnie, what is it?"

"My dear, I couldn't possibly say—on the telephone—so public. I have always said that it was a very bad arrangement, and it's no good pretending that there are not people who take advantage of it, because we all know that there are. I wouldn't like to mention any names, but everybody knows—" The sentence ended in a sob.

"Miss Vinnie—"

There was a faint twitter from the other end of the line.

"Oh, my dear, I don't know what to do. I feel quite giddy."

"Miss Vinnie, listen! I could drive Miss Silver down in my car. If you're worried about anything, I expect she would be able to help you. Frank thinks a tremendous lot of her."

Miss Vinnie gulped.

"I must tell someone," she said.

Miss Alvina had not much more than ten minutes to wait, but they were the most dreadful ten minutes of her life. She would herself have piously excepted the time spent at her father's deathbed, but it was not in nature that the peaceful departure of a good old man should raise the feelings of horror and distress which now invaded her. Until she had spoken to Cicely on the telephone she had not found it possible to realize the full implications of her discovery, but in these endless minutes of waiting this realization became more and more dreadfully clear.

129

She was white-faced and shaking as she opened the door to Miss Silver. Cicely Hathaway, it appeared, had gone on to the church. "She won't need me," she told Miss Silver. "I want some of the music to take home, and I can always put in an odd half hour practising. I'll leave the little side door open and the light on, and you can just let me know when you are ready."

Miss Silver came into the cottage with a reassuring air of competency and calm. There was something so ordinary, so everyday, so perfectly normal about her that Miss Alvina's sense of security, which had been rudely shaken, began to return. Dreadful things happen to other people—they don't happen to us. It is on this simple foundation that most of us build. Murders are things you read about in the newspaper. Murderers are people whose pictures you see there. They are always caught, and when they are caught they are tried and executed. They are not people who walk about in your own village. A murderess couldn't possibly be a person who made your bed, and washed up your breakfast things, and cooked your dinner. She couldn't possibly be someone who had a unique recipe for strawberry jam, and whom you had taught in Sunday school when she was a little girl. The monstrous idea receded, only to be followed by the distressing thought that she had been making a fool of herself. A flush of embarrassment came to her face.

"Oh dear—I am afraid you will think me very foolish. I am all alone in the house, and it gave me such a shock."

Miss Silver said with authority,

"Then it was certainly very wise of you to ring up. Now suppose you tell me what gave you this shock."

"Oh, yes—I will. How kind you are! But I mustn't keep you standing here."

They were in the little square hall which had been contrived by sacrificing one room of the cottage. On the right a door led into the living-room, and on the left another gave upon the kitchen.

Both doors were old and solid, each with its iron latch. In the background a steep wooden stair went up to the two bedrooms above, its treads worn and polished by the feet of many generations, its handrail smooth as glass from all those sliding hands. Miss Alvina lifted the latch of the kitchen door and switched on an incongruous electric bulb. A modern cooking-stove stood small and lonely in the big inglenook. A black beam crossed the ceiling. Under the light stood a Victorian kitchen table, its top protected by a spread of green American cloth. There was a strip of carpet on the floor. The tick of a solemn old wall-clock came upon the warm air. There was an agreeable smell of cooking—bacon, perhaps, with just a hint of cheese. No room could have looked or smelled more homely.

Just short of the middle of the room Miss Alvina turned. Her flush had faded, she was pale again. Because after all she had been very much frightened, and now she had to talk about it. Her hands shook, and she caught at the top of a kitchen chair to steady them.

"Pray tell me what alarmed you," said Miss Silver.

Miss Alvina began to twitter.

"It was Ellen Caddle—Mrs. Caddle, you know, who does for me. She comes in every day from nine to four, but if I have friends to tea she will stay on. And I have always thought how fortunate I was, because she is really an excellent cook and so nice, and I have known her ever since she was a baby. It really isn't possible that she can have anything to do with it." The last sentence had a quite desperate sound.

Miss Silver laid a firm hand in a black woollen glove upon Miss Alvina's shoulder.

"Anything to do with what?"

Miss Vinnie fixed her eyes upon her and said in a shuddering voice,

"It was the—blood—"

Miss Silver said, "Dear me!" And then, "What blood, Miss Grey?"

The shoulder jerked under her hand.

"It was on the scullery floor—"

Miss Silver said "Dear me!" again. "There was blood on the scullery floor?"

Miss Alvina burst out crying. Words, sobs, and tears all came gushing out together.

"Oh, *yes!*" she said. "It was there on the scullery floor. She laid my tea and she went out, but it came on to rain and she hadn't an umbrella, so she came back for the storm to go by, and she hung up her coat in the scullery because it had got quite wet. Such heavy rain, but it didn't last very long, so then she borrowed my umbrella and went away. And I went into the scullery—oh dear, I can't remember what I went for, but I took a candle—there's no electric light in there—and I saw the pool on the floor where her coat had dripped. There is a row of pegs, and I could see where the coat had hung, because of the pool on the floor."

"Pray go on."

The shoulder jerked again. The voice caught.

"I put the candle down on the table and took a cloth to wipe the floor. It's a brick floor, not stone like it is in here—that's why I didn't see. Oh dear—I only thought it was careless of Ellen. But she wouldn't have troubled to light a candle—she would just have felt for a peg and hung her coat there, and so of course she wouldn't have noticed that there was a pool, or she would have wiped it up. She would feel for the coat. It's not like having a switch that you just turn on."

Miss Silver's hand exerted a little pressure.

"Pray, pray continue."

There was a quick sobbing breath.

"Oh, *yes!* Oh dear—it was so horrid! I mopped the floor and—oh, it was dreadful! The cloth was all—red. Not the sort of red that would come off the bricks, but blood. Oh dear, oh dear! You can't make any mistake about blood, can you?" Her voice had sunk to a horrified whisper.

Miss Silver coughed.

"What did you do?"

"I'm afraid I was very foolish. I dropped the cloth—I didn't feel as if I could touch it again. I washed my hands at the scullery sink. The most terrible thoughts kept coming into my mind—about poor Ellen Caddle—because the blood must have been there on her coat—quite a lot of it. It's an old black coat and very shabby—it wouldn't show—until it got wet and dripped out on to the scullery floor. She got so wet in the rain. Oh, Miss Silver, how did all that blood get on to her coat—that's what I keep thinking. And she's been looking so dreadful, poor Ellen, only I thought it was something to do with her husband—we all thought so. But all that blood—I thought—I thought suppose it had something to do with that poor girl who was murdered—not Mary Stokes, but the poor girl she said she saw murdered in the wood—the one they found in the Forester's House. It was very foolish of me, I expect, but I couldn't help it coming into my mind."

If she was looking for reassurance, she found none. The small, neat features were gravely set. The hand in the black woollen glove was withdrawn. Miss Silver said,

"Perhaps you will kindly allow me to use your telephone."

CHAPTER 21

The knocking on the door came through the fog which had settled over Ellen Caddle's mind. It would lift a little when she was down at the Cottage with plenty to do and Miss Vinnie fidgetting in and out the way she always did, but when she'd got home and done what there was to do, and Albert not back till after closing time, then it would come down on her thick and heavy until she was lost in it. Come getting on for a fortnight Albert hadn't been in for his tea—

The knocking came through the fog. She got up and went to the door, and all at once she was dreadfully afraid. They came in out of the darkness, and the darkness came in with them—came right in and stayed, like you heard it read in church: "Outer darkness, there shall be weeping and gnashing of teeth." But it was the outer darkness that had come in. It clouded her eyes, but through the cloud she saw Mr. Frank Abbott, and the big man who was a high-up London policeman, and the little lady who was staying at Abbottsleigh. There was no way to keep them out, so she stepped back, and the big man said,

"Can we have a word with you, Mrs. Caddle?"

She took them into the sitting-room which she had been so proud of when she married Albert and he let her furnish it out of her savings. He had grumbled about it afterwards, but you can put up with a bit of grumbling when you've got a good bit of Axminster on the floor, and real nice curtains, and a suite from the best shop in Lenton. It was icy cold, and the air felt dead in the room, because Mrs. Caddle only used it when she had company, but even now a faint half-animate pride stirred in her breast. Everything was good, everything was new, everything that could be polished was polished till you could see your face in it.

As she closed the door, the big man asked where Albert was. "Where's your husband?"—just like that. She thought of all the times she would have given her soul to be able to answer that, and opened her pale lips to give the only answer there had ever been.

"I don't know."

"He's out?"

"He's always out of an evening."

"Down at the local?"

"I don't know."

Lamb turned to his sergeant.

"Go out and tell the man with the car—what's his name, May?—to go down and see! If Caddle's there, he's to bring him back!"

Frank Abbott went out, and presently came back again. Lamb put down his hat on the arm of the couch and lowered himself into the corner seat. It was a tribute to the best shop in Lenton that the springs made no protest.

Mrs. Caddle remained standing. She had grown very thin. The black dress she was wearing threw up the hollows in her cheeks, her deathly pallor, her reddened eyelids. At Miss Silver's touch on her arm she gave a painful start.

"Pardon?"

"I think you had better sit down."

It didn't matter to Ellen Caddle whether she stood or sat. She took the chair which was indicated. It was what the Lenton shop had described as an occasional chair—small, stiff, upright, with a line of yellow inlay on the back and a seat of bright artificial silk surrounded by gold-headed nails.

Miss Silver took the other corner seat of the couch, and Frank

135

Abbott the smaller of the two easy chairs. Lamb, sitting up square and grave in a voluminous overcoat, allowed the silence to settle before he said,

"How did you get all that blood on your coat, Mrs. Caddle?"

The question ripped through the darkness and the fog like a stab of lightning. For a horrible moment it lit Ellen's mind so brightly that she could see all the things which she had been trying so hard to push down and away out of sight. There they were, blindingly clear, so that it was like seeing them for the first time. It was only for a moment, and then they were gone again, hidden in the fog. She didn't know whether she had cried out or not. She found her hand at her throat. She found her dry lips parting to say,

"What coat?"

Lamb looked at Miss Silver, who gave a little cough.

"Your black coat, Mrs. Caddle—the one you have just taken off. I think Chief Inspector Lamb would like to see it presently. You got wet in it this afternoon and you hung it on a peg in Miss Grey's scullery. It dripped on to the floor and made a pool there. There must have been quite a lot of blood on the coat to make the pool so red."

Ellen Caddle stared, her eyes open and glassy. Lamb said sharply,

"How did all that blood get on your coat?"

Something was happening to Mrs. Caddle. All the feeling was going out of her. It was like a hand or a foot going numb. The part which had agonized in pain and terror was going numb—it hurt less and less. In a little while it stopped hurting at all. It was a most extraordinary thing to happen, and a most blessed relief. She sat up stiffly on her occasional chair as if her body was holding her up just by itself without any help from her mind, and said,

"It must have been when I knelt down in the wood."

136

Miss Silver said, "Dear me—" under her breath. Lamb leaned forward.

"If this a confession, I have to tell you that anything you say may be taken down and used in evidence. You understand that?"

She nodded.

"Well then, are you going to tell us how it happened?"

She kept her eyes on his face and said,

"It was Albert—"

Frank Abbott's pencil dinted the page. Lamb said quickly,

"You say your husband killed the woman who was found in the Forester's House?"

She shook her head.

"I don't know who killed her. It was Albert I was looking for."

"When were you looking for him—what day are you talking about?"

She said, "Friday—it was the Friday evening."

"Friday, January eighth?"

"That's right."

"Well, you say you were in the wood. What wood?"

"Dead Man's Copse—across the other side of the Lane."

"What were you doing there?"

"I went after Albert."

"What made you think he would be there?"

Her hand went up to her throat. Nothing hurt any more, but just for a moment she remembered how bad the pain had been. She said,

"I'd known a long time he went into the Copse. There wasn't anything to take him there, only a girl. People don't fancy going there. I didn't know what girl would fancy it. Then I thought of Mary Stokes—she was one of the don't care sort—I thought it might be her. She used to come round with the butter and eggs, and I'd see the way Albert looked. She'd been round on the Wednesday. I took some eggs, and I left her whilst I got

137

the change. In the kitchen she was, and when I come back she was putting Albert's pouch up on the shelf—the one he keeps his tobacco in. I was outside the door. She didn't know I saw her—I didn't make any noise. When she was gone I looked in the pouch. There was a screw of paper in among the tobacco. It said, 'Friday—same time, same place.' "

She heard herself saying the words which had been like a twisting knife in her heart. There was no feeling there any longer. They were just words which she had seen on a scrap of paper, but they had taken her to Dead Man's Copse. Her voice ceased.

Lamb said,

"You thought that was a note making an appointment for your husband to meet Mary Stokes at the Forester's House on Friday? You needn't mind answering that, because we know he used to meet her there. They left their fingerprints all over the place."

Ellen Caddle shook her head. She didn't mind anything at all. She said so.

"I don't mind."

"Well, you're doing nicely. Just go on and tell us about Friday."

"I got back from Miss Grey's about half past four. Albert had been washing the car—the yard was all wet. I called up to him to know if he would be in to tea. When he's in we have it at half past five. I thought I'd cook him something, but he said no, he was going out. I asked him when he'd be back, and he said to mind my own business. When he came down he didn't look at me and he didn't speak. He got his bicycle and went out by the back gate."

"What time was this, Mrs. Caddle?"

"It would be after five. I'd made up the fire and tidied round a bit, and then it was a bit of time before he came down."

"Can you tell us what clothes he was wearing?"

She nodded.

"His blue serge. That's how I was sure he was going to meet her—he wouldn't put it on to go to the local."

"Did he take a coat?"

"Yes, he took his uniform coat. It was cold out." A tremor went over her, as if the remembered cold had power to shake her. But it was only her body that shivered. Her mind was quiet and numb.

"Go on, Mrs. Caddle. Your husband went out on his bicycle. What did you do then?"

"I went after him. I hadn't put my things away. I took my coat and hat and ran out of the gate. I thought I'd see his rear light, but there wasn't anything, it was all dark. I hadn't thought about its being so dark. I went back to get my torch." She stopped for a moment, looked at him in a distressed sort of way, and said, "I couldn't find it. It ought to have been on the shelf, but it wasn't there. I looked everywhere, upstairs and down, but I couldn't find it. It must have taken me the best part of half an hour."

"What did you do?"

She was still looking at him with the same expression.

"I went without it, but when I got down by the Copse I put my hand in my coat pocket without thinking, and there it was. I must have put it there myself, ready to go out. I don't know how I came to do a thing like that."

"Your mind was taken up—that's how you came to do it. No need to worry about it. Just go on telling us what you did."

"I put on the torch to find a way through the bushes, and I went into the wood—"

"Just a minute, Mrs. Caddle. Did you pass a car in the Lane or see one there at all?"

"No, sir."

"If there had been a car there, would you have seen it?"

She said in a wavering voice,

"I'd have seen the lights—"

139

"I suppose you would. But if there hadn't been any lights? How dark was it—would you have seen a standing car?"

She shook her head.

"It's all trees there. It was very dark."

Lamb leaned back again into his corner. The light shone down on his stiff black hair with the thinning patch on the top where the scalp was beginning to show.

"All right, go on. You went into the wood. What were you making for?"

She said in a failing voice,

"I thought they'd be at the house—"

"Well, go on."

"I kept the torch down. The wood isn't so thick once you get in. I'd gone a little way, when I heard something. I put out the torch. I saw a light among the bushes. Then it went out. I heard someone go off through the wood."

"Which way?"

"Towards the fields. I heard him go right away. If it was Albert, I thought maybe he'd left his bicycle on the field path—it runs out into the Lane. But I didn't know if it was Albert. I went on to where I'd seen the light. There's a clump of hollies—when I came up to them, that was the place I'd seen the light. I thought maybe they'd been meeting there. I went to see if there was any sign of it. I put my torch on. There were some leaves piled up among the hollies. I moved them with my foot, and I touched something. I put the torch on the ground and went down on my knees and pulled the leaves away. There was a girl there with her head smashed in. There was blood on the leaves—I suppose I knelt in it. I thought it was Mary Stokes, and I thought Albert had killed her. Then I saw it was a stranger. She had a diamond earring in her ear all set round with little stones. I didn't know why Albert should have killed her. It wasn't her he was going to meet, it was Mary Stokes. So then I thought it wasn't Albert, and if it wasn't Albert it wasn't none of my business, so I put

140

the leaves back and went home. But I couldn't get it out of my mind."

Lamb turned the frown of authority upon her.

"It was your duty to inform the police."

She hadn't anything to say to that—just sat there on the hard, uncomfortable chair with her hands in her lap. He said sternly,

"You did very wrong, Mrs. Caddle." And then, "Well, that will do for the present. You'll have your statement read over to you, and you'll be asked to sign it. I'll be glad if you'll stay in the kitchen." He turned to Frank Abbott. "I think that was the car. Just go and see if May has got Caddle there and bring him in!"

CHAPTER 22

Albert Caddle came into the room with a jaunty air. He was not very tall, but he was very well built and beyond all question a handsome young man. His curly dark hair was now rather longer than he had been allowed to wear it in the Army. His bold dark eyes looked over Lamb, looked over Miss Silver, and didn't think much of either of them. He said in a defiant tone,

"Here, what's all this?"

Lamb stared him down. A man who is sure of his authority and who has a thousand years of solid English law behind him has got something, and knows it.

Albert Caddle's eyes did not fall, but they shifted. Then, and not till then, Lamb spoke.

"You are Albert Caddle?"

Albert Caddle hitched a shoulder up and said,

"That's me."

"You are employed by Mr. Harlow as his chauffeur?"

"That's right."

"Well, I just want to ask you a few questions. You can sit down."

Albert's look said plainly, "This is my house, isn't it? You've got a nerve, telling me to sit down in my own house!" With a smile which showed some fine white teeth he crossed to the large easy chair and flung himself into it. If there had been any doubt before, it was now quite clear that he was the master of the house, taking his rightful place, and taking his ease in it.

Lamb had met his sort before. He said sharply,

"I should like particulars of your movements from half past four on Friday, January eighth."

"Really?" Tone and accent were in impudent caricature of Sergeant Abbott.

Lamb said, "That sort of thing isn't going to get you anywhere, Caddle."

"And suppose I don't want to be got anywhere?"

Lamb sat up straight.

"That will be enough of that! There have been two murders in this neighbourhood, and I'm inquiring into them. It's everyone's duty to co-operate with the police. I can't force you to answer questions or to make a statement, but if you're an innocent man you'll be glad to do so. I don't mind telling you that you've got something to explain. I'm giving you the opportunity of explaining your actions, and you can begin with the afternoon of Friday, January eighth. If you can't explain them, I shall have to detain you."

Albert Caddle sat up too. He sat up and said,

"What are you getting at?"

"I've told you. I want to know your movements after four-thirty on that Friday afternoon."

Albert put his hand on his hip and stuck his chin in the air.

"Why?"

"I'll tell you why. You had an appointment to meet a young woman that evening. You were in the habit of meeting her at the Forester's House in Dead Man's Copse. You went out about five o'clock to keep that appointment."

Albert showed those white teeth again.

"Well then, I didn't."

"You went out—"

Albert laughed scornfully.

"Here, here—what's wrong with going out? This is a free country, isn't it? That's the bother with you cops—you're too clever. A young lady may have made an appointment with me—I'm not saying whether she did or whether she didn't— but that's not to say I kept it. I suppose my wife's been tattling. Well, she's jealous—a jealous woman'll say anything."

"Look here, Caddle, you had an appointment with Mary Stokes—"

"What if I did? I'm not saying one way or the other, but what if I did?"

"Your wife followed you. She saw a light in Dead Man's Copse, and she heard someone going away. She found the dead body of a young woman named Louise Rogers hidden under some leaves. She got blood on her coat—that's how it has all come out. I think you must realize your position. You are not obliged to make any statement that will incriminate you."

Anger blazed in the black eyes. A surge of colour ran up to the roots of the dark hair. The voice rang.

"What do you mean, incriminate? I haven't done anything! You seem to know a lot about my affairs! All right then, I'll tell you some more! This Mary Stokes, she wasn't any good, and I was through with her. She had me on, and she had me off, and then she wanted me on again, and I wasn't for it—see? There's lots of other girls if you want them. Well, I've got another girl— over in Lenton. Mary Stokes, she left a note for me to meet her

143

Friday. I didn't meet her, I went into Lenton, and she could put that in her pipe and smoke it! Saturday morning she comes round with the butter and eggs and pushes a note in my pocket as she goes by—says she'll give me one more chance and I can meet her at the old house between half past five and a quarter to six. Did me a lot of good, that note did—when half past four come round I got on my bike and went to see my girl in Lenton!"

Lamb maintained a hard, impassive stare.

"You had quarrelled with Mary Stokes?"

"I'd done with her—that's that! And don't you go trying to make anything out of it either—when I've done with a girl I've done with her—I don't come sneaking back to break her neck!" He laughed. "I've never cared enough for any woman to swing for her, and I wouldn't begin with Mary Stokes! I'm sorry for the poor devil who did her in and I hope he gets away with it, but it wasn't me—I wouldn't take that much trouble. And if you think you can pin it on me, you can think again! Joe Turnberry saw her home, didn't he—round about eight o'clock? They come off the ten to eight bus. Well, I didn't break her neck, because I wasn't there to break it. And I wasn't there, because I couldn't have been there—see? I was in the Rose and Crown at Lenton, and I was playing darts—properly on my game I was. Me and my girl, we were there from eight o'clock till ten, and a matter of fifteen to twenty people will tell you so if you ask 'em. So what price arresting me now?"

Lamb said, "Let me see your hands, Caddle—both of them. Lay them out flat."

"Look here, what are you getting at?"

"Lay them out!"

Albert said, "Play-acting, aren't you?" But he laid his hands out, one on either knee.

The top joint of the left forefinger was missing.

CHAPTER 23

Mrs. Barton was a good deal troubled in her mind—angry too. She hadn't been housekeeper at Deepside for thirty years without learning to hold her tongue and control her temper. Old Mr. Hathaway wasn't one of the easiest. There had been troubles, like when his wife died, and when Mr. Roger the only son was killed out hunting. And there had been other things—things you didn't talk about, though she supposed everyone would know. There wasn't much people didn't know in a village. But if Mr. Hathaway sat emptying the decanter till it was all he could do to get himself upstairs, no one had ever had word or look about it from her, poor lonely old gentleman. Then they'd had a thieving maid once—with good references too and wonderful smooth manners. Everything just a bit too good to be true when you looked back on it, but it seemed all right at the time, and then off she went with the silver candlesticks out of the dining-room and a gold box that Mr. Hathaway set a lot of store by—given to his great-grandfather by some French gentleman that he saved from one of their nasty revolutions. But they had never had anything like this before—

The colour flushed up to the roots of her grey hair as she thought about it. If it hadn't been for Mr. Grant going off early on the Sunday morning and staying the night, she wouldn't have been into his room once the bed had been made—she would have helped Agnes and had no call to come back again. But today being Monday and the bed not slept in, there had been no need to make it, and nothing to take her into the room if it hadn't been that it came to her to drop a word to Agnes about a hot bottle to air the sheets. Perhaps she had got fidgetty, living so long with an old gentleman, but it was nasty cold weather and a bottle in the bed would take the chill off.

Her flush deepened as the scene rose quick before her eyes—Agnes in the room, the door not quite shut to, and herself going to it and pushing it a little so that she could see in. And what did she see? She couldn't have believed it if it hadn't been her own two eyes telling her it was true—that Agnes stooping over the bed kissing the pillow, and the tears running down off her face on to it! It made her right down ashamed—sobbing and crying and kissing Mr. Grant's pillow. She didn't know how she kept herself, but she did. Pulled the door to without making any noise and back to her kitchen. And when Agnes came down for her elevens she had given her her notice—no reason named, just that they were thinking of making a change. Queer how the girl stood there and never said a word—funny sort of smile on her face, funny sort of look in her eyes. And not a word out of her till she was going through the door. It made Mrs. Barton angry all over again to call back the way that Agnes looked at her. "Think yourself someone!" she said. "Don't you?"

It might have been expected that both Mrs. Barton and Agnes would have had other things to think about on this Monday morning. A double murder had been committed, the bodies of two young women discovered, yet here was Agnes weeping over Grant Hathaway's pillow, and Mrs. Barton unable to think of anything except this scandalous behaviour. The fact is that, for most of us, what happens to ourselves is so much more important than what happens to other people that the smallest mote in our own eye will prevent us from being unduly harrowed by somebody else's beam. When Mr. Stokes' cowman arrived late with the milk on Sunday morning and brought the news that Mary had been murdered and her body found in one of the barns, Agnes had cried hysterically, and Mrs. Barton had been quite suitably shocked. When, on the Sunday evening, a

146

second body was discovered in the cellar under the Forester's House, the impersonal thrill which the news provided was not very much more horrifying than if they had read about it in the paper. As far as Mary Stokes was concerned, Mrs. Barton had always been persuaded that she was a fast young woman and would come to a bad end, while Louise Rogers was just a nameless stranger who had somehow got herself murdered in Deeping. But a scandal in the house which had had the benefit of her presence and moral example for thirty years was quite another matter. Fast young women got themselves murdered every day, but a scandal in the same house as Mrs. Barton was so unthinkable that at the threat of it every fibre of her thought stiffened in protest.

It was in this frame of mind that she descended to the study after lunch and requested the favour of a few words with Mr. Grant.

He looked up from the letter he was writing.

"If it's important, Mrs. Barton. I'm rather busy."

She stood like a rock—massive in form; grey hair brushed smooth on either side of an immaculate parting; black dress neatly buttoned over swelling contours; a snowy collar pinned with a cameo brooch depicting a female with snaky hair. Incredible that Mrs. Barton should be wearing a head of Medusa but nevertheless true, the explanation being that classical mythology was a sealed book to her, and that the brooch had been a legacy from a most respectable great-aunt. Her own features being regular, her eyes very fine, and her manner one of dignity, she had a handsome and imposing presence.

Grant resigned himself, laid down his pen, and said,

"What is it?"

"I will not detain you, sir. I thought it right to let you know that I have given Agnes her notice."

Grant said, "Oh?"

147

He was aware of scrutiny. Mrs. Barton's grey eyes dwelt upon him in a steady and purposeful manner. He was unaware that his unguarded expression of mingled surprise and boredom was the most satisfactory thing those eyes could have beheld.

Never for a moment would Mrs. Barton be prepared to admit that she had suspected Mr. Grant of so far forgetting himself as to encourage that Agnes, but there he was, a gentleman separated from his wife, and why, nobody knew except their two selves. And a very great pity it was. A nicer young lady than Miss Cicely Abbott there couldn't be, nor a happier couple. Dreadfully quiet it left the house when she'd gone, after brightening it up the way she did—she and that Bramble dog that got around you whether you liked it or not, galloping up and down the stairs like a little colt and sparkling his eyes at you when he wanted a bone. A nasty kind of a hole they had left, he and Miss Cicely— and when gentlemen are lonely it's surprising what they'll do. Farther than that she wouldn't go.

These thoughts were in her mind between Grant Hathaway saying "Oh?" and going on with, "What's the matter with Agnes? A little on the gloomy side, but I thought she was doing all right."

"I have no fault to find with her work."

"Well?"

"I would rather not say any more, Mr. Grant."

"Oh, well, it's your affair."

"Yes, sir."

He went back to his letter.

When Agnes brought tea to the study at half past four he was still writing. She switched on the light as she came in, and then stood for a moment looking at him as he sat at the writing-table. She could not see much more than the rough tweed of his coat, the set of his shoulders, the back of his head, and the hand which moved across the paper as he wrote, but these things her eyes devoured. She was a thin, dark woman with a sallow skin and thick, straight black hair. Her eyes had a brooding expression.

As if conscious of the intensity of her regard, Grant checked suddenly and without turning said over his shoulder,

"All right—just leave it, will you? I want to finish this."

After a momentary hesitation she went silently out of the room and shut the door. He wrote three or four more lines, signed his name, swung his chair about, and poured out a cup of tea. Whilst it cooled, he put his letter into an envelope and addressed it to James Roney, Esq., Passfield, Ledstow, near Ledlington.

All the time he was having his tea he was thinking about the decision which he had just taken. James was ready to pay a handsome premium with young Stephen, and the money would come in uncommonly handy. He liked the boy too—brains, and keen on using them this way. You'd got to mix your farming with brains nowadays if you wanted to make it pay. You couldn't do without them, but you couldn't do without money either.

He sat on, making plans. In the end, with a queer twist of the mouth, he came to wondering what Cicely would say. In the curious and intricate game that they were playing, Stephen Roney represented a small but useful trump. He looked forward to seeing his wife's face when he played it.

He was still sitting there when Agnes came back to draw the curtains and take away the tea. She approached the table, but made no move to pick up the tray.

"If I might speak to you, sir—"

Until that moment he had hardly been aware that she was in the room. The routine of her entrance, the sound of the curtain rings sliding smoothly into place, had made the vaguest and most surface impression. It was only when she spoke that he became definitely aware of her, and of an impending scene.

He said, "What is it?" and heard his voice sharper than he had meant it to be.

Agnes stood there staring—there really was no other word for it. The overhead light made shadows on her face, the bony ridge of the brows darkening the eye-sockets, the cheekbone shading the hollow of the cheek, the tightened under lip doing something odd to the contours of the chin, the whole effect being one of plainness cruelly intensified. A throbbing atmosphere of emotion began to fill the room.

Feeling singularly defenceless, Grant got to his feet, and the scene broke. In a choked voice Agnes said,

"Mrs. Barton has given me my notice. I want to know why."

"I'm afraid you must ask Mrs. Barton."

Agnes clasped her hands.

"Are you going to let her send me away?"

What an impossible situation! He found himself getting out his cigarette-case, lighting a cigarette, putting the case away again—anything to occupy his hands as he said,

"I'm sorry, Agnes, but I leave all that sort of thing to Mrs. Barton."

She looked at him curiously, opened her lips to say something, and then seemed to change her mind. She spoke, but he had the strongest possible impression that what she said was not what she had been going to say.

"Mr. Grant—don't let her send me away! I haven't got any-one—" she choked—"I haven't got anywhere to go. I haven't done anything to be sent away like that—she hasn't even said what she's doing it for—if I done anything you don't like I'll do it different."

It was extremely embarrassing—all this emotion on the sur-face, and under it what? He had a feeling that there were uncomfortable depths, and made his voice brisk.

"Look here, Agnes, this won't do. There are lots of good places to be had. I can't possibly interfere with Mrs. Barton's arrangements. You're only upsetting yourself."

She fixed those shadowed eyes on him and said,

"I can upset more than me."

150

Grant was beginning to be angry. He disliked scenes in general, and this one in particular. It began to occur to him that Mrs. Barton was displaying her excellent good sense in getting rid of this obviously neurotic female. He moved away to the writing-table, ostensibly to find an ash-tray, and said in rather a final tone,

"There's really nothing to be done about it. Will you please take out the tea-tray."

She came after him, moving in an odd gliding way which gave him the creeps. When she had come right up to the writing-table she put her hands on it, gripping the edge and staring at him across the top.

He thought, "The woman's barmy," and was convinced of it when she repeated her previous remark with a slight but sinister variation.

"There's more than me would be upset if I was to tell what I know."

"Please stop talking nonsense and take away the tray."

She leaned right over the table and said in a weeping voice,

"Do you think I'd hurt you? I won't say a word, but you mustn't send me away. It makes me feel I don't care what I do or who I hurt."

He went over to the hearth and put up a hand to the bell.

When he looked round at her Agnes had turned. She still gripped the table edge, but she had her back to it now. Her eyes blazed from a colourless face.

"If you ring that bell you'll be sorry! You won't be able to take it back, not however much you want to. If there was a Bible here, I'd put my hand on it and swear. If you ring that bell, I'll go to the police!"

He kept his hand where it was, quite still, quite steady.

"I suppose you know what you're talking about. I don't."

Her voice went down to an almost soundless whisper. She said,

"They've found her—they've found them both—"

"I still don't know what you mean."

She said, "Hasn't anyone told you? Hasn't she told you? It isn't in the papers yet, but it will be tomorrow. The girl that Mary Stokes said she saw murdered Friday week, they found her in the cellar under the Forester's House last night."

Grant said nothing. Everything in him toughened and stood to take the shock. He said nothing at all, but his hand fell from the bell. He heard Agnes say,

"Everybody said poor Mary Stokes had made it up, but she never. Pity they didn't believe her before she got murdered herself."

He called out in an angry, incredulous tone,

"Mary Stokes murdered?"

"Saturday night, after Joe Turnberry saw her home—but they didn't find her till Sunday morning, and you'd gone off early. I thought perhaps you didn't know they'd found her—and the other one."

"No, I didn't know. How should I?"

She went on looking at him.

"They were bound to find Mary. But not the other one—that was bad luck. If they hadn't found *her*, they'd have thought Joe Turnberry had done Mary in. Everyone thought it was him till they found the other one in the Forester's House, and then they could see how Mary had been put out of the way on account of what she'd seen. Saw the murderer's hand, didn't she, in the beam of her torch? Might have seen something on the hand that she'd know if she saw it again—might have seen something that would make the chap think he wouldn't be safe till she was dead."

He said, "Be quiet!" in a sharp hectoring tone, and she fell into an angry silence, leaning back against the table, staring at him out of those hollow eye-sockets.

She saw his face set and frowning, heavy with thought. He wasn't looking at her—he didn't seem to be looking at anything. She felt a surge of furious pride because it was her doing. She'd stopped him with his hand on the bell—she'd given him something to think about. And there was more to come—a whole lot more. She had never felt so much alive in all her life, or had such a sense of power.

His voice came curtly across her mood.

"All right, that will do. You'd better take the tray."

Get rid of her, would he? Let that damned old woman send her away? Not much! She gripped the table till her palms were bruised, and flung the words at him.

"You can't get rid of me like that! I know too much!" Then, as she saw him turn again to the bell, "Don't! Don't ring it! Why do you make me say things to you like that? I don't want to hurt you! But I know you saw her—I know she came here— I heard what she said!"

He turned back rather slowly and stiffly.

"Explain yourself."

She said, her voice tripping and faltering,

"I only don't want you to send me away."

"Don't start that again. Explain what you said just now."

"I saw her."

He gave a short laugh.

"Is that what you call explaining?"

Her thin chest rose and fell.

"You don't listen—but you've got to. I don't want to hurt you."

"If you've anything to say, will you say it!"

"Yes, I will. You don't give me a chance. It was last Friday week. Mrs. Barton went out, and she made me change my day so as I'd be out too. Never gives anyone a chance, the old devil— always see me start, she would, before she'd go herself. But I banged the door, and she thought I'd gone and off she went.

Well then I come back—I didn't see why I should be driven out like that—and as I come out on the bedroom landing the telephone went."

The heavy thinking look had gone from Grant's face. It was angry now. He said in a cutting tone,

"So you thought you'd listen in."

Another of those sobbing breaths.

"It wasn't like that. I wanted to know if it was *her*—Mrs. Hathaway. I wanted to know if she rang you up, or—or if anyone else did. I—I liked hearing you talk."

"Oh, you've done it before? What did you get this time?"

She flung up her head.

"I heard a woman say, 'Mr. Hathaway—I want to speak to Mr. Hathaway.' "

CHAPTER 24

Mark Harlow turned round from the piano.

"How do you like it?"

Cicely was in front of the fire, standing there in a short brown skirt up to her knees and a high-necked russet jumper. Only the light over the piano was on. Except when the firelight blazed up she was in shadow. Her curls were rumpled. At her feet, as near the fire as he could get, Bramble lay stretched out, his head tilted sideways on one paw, his little crooked black legs straight out behind him like a seal's flippers. He had had rabbit for his dinner, and slept the deep untroubled sleep of the virtuous and young.

The house round them was quiet. Colonel and Mrs. Abbott were having tea at the Rectory, the one house in the neighbourhood to which he could be lured. The Rector and he would by now be playing the easy-going brand of chess to which both were addicted. Frank Abbott and Chief Inspector Lamb, after turning up at Miss Vinnie's cottage, had departed into the blue, taking Miss Silver with them. Cicely had driven herself home to find Mark on the doorstep. Since everyone was making mysteries and practising concealments from which she was excluded, she was a good deal more pleased to see him than she would ordinarily have allowed him to suspect. They had just had tea, and he had been telling her that he was to do the music for Leo Tanfield's new revue.

Cicely came out of some fastness of her own and said, "What?"

"Darling, how too abrupt!"

"I wasn't listening."

If he was angry he didn't show it, only smiled and said, "Will you listen if I do it again?"

"All right."

He did it again. Some brilliant execution, a catch-as-catch-can of sparkling notes, and then one of those half-said, half-sung trifles, cleverly rhymed and accented and not without wit. Melody negligible, performance well up to the mark. He struck a final chord and repeated his "Well?"

Cicely said, "Slick."

"And what do you mean by that, my sweet?"

"You are not to call me 'My sweet.' "

His eyebrows rose.

"Not even when we're alone?"

"Certainly not when we are alone."

He burst out laughing.

"It's all right in front of the assembled parish gossips, but highly improper when it's just you and me? Funny little thing—aren't you?"

"I'm not set on your doing it in front of anybody, but it wouldn't mean anything if you did."

"And it hasn't to mean anything?"

"No, Mark."

He got up from the piano and came over to stand beside her. The lazy teasing note went out of his voice.

"Look here, Cis, how long is this going to go on?"

"How long is what going to go on?"

"This marriage of yours. Why don't you get out of it?"

"That's so easy, isn't it!"

"Well, people are doing it every day."

Cicely said nothing.

"Well? What about it?"

She did speak then, tilting her head and looking up at him.

"I'm not talking about my marriage. It's my affair, not anyone else's."

"And a nice lot of ingrowing repressions you'll get that way! When you don't talk about a thing it gets you down. Civilized people talk these things out—they don't sit on them and hatch them into tragedies. I don't know why you and Grant split, but there it is—you're living in one house, and he's living in another. And you don't speak. You can't expect people not to notice. If you're going to make it up with him, make it up, and I'll be friends with you both as I was before. But if you're not going to make it up, there's no sense in going on like this. Get quit of what's only a farce and give yourself—and me—a chance."

Cicely raised her eyebrows. Her tone cut like ice.

"Is this a proposal?"

"Cis!"

"Is it?"

"My God, you're hard!"

"You asked for it."

"I asked you why you didn't get a divorce."

"Very well, I'll answer that. It's quite simple—Grant won't play. I can't divorce him unless he gives me cause, and he won't give me cause. He could divorce me in three years' time

156

for desertion, but he won't do that either. So that's where we are."

He stared at her, surprised and taken aback.

"Isn't there any way out?"

"No, there isn't." She went on without any break. "I think your last modulation was a bit abrupt. I've an idea it would sound better this way." She walked over to the piano and played a few chords. "Like this . . . Yes, that's better."

He followed her. They stood side by side looking down at the keyboard.

"I don't know—I rather want it to be abrupt. In fact I might even accentuate the discord. Cis, isn't it any good—you and me, I mean?"

"No, it isn't. And don't keep on making me say it, or I shall lose my temper. If you really want a discord, have it, but I think you're wrong. The stuff's too light to take it—you want to keep it light and slick."

CHAPTER 25

You can travel a long, hard way without any movement of the body. Grant Hathaway still stood by the hearth, the hand which had dropped the bell thrust deep into his trouser pocket. Agnes Ripley had not moved at all. She gripped the table edge against which she leaned as if she would never let it go. But she no longer knew that she was gripping it. Her mind was too disturbed, too tormented, to have room for sensations other than its own. In the short time which had passed the relationship between Grant and herself had changed immeasurably. they were no longer employer and employed, they were man and woman. And they were no longer the worshipping woman and the man who has no use for her. That was gone too—terribly lost and gone. There flared between them now that old fundamental antagonism which is implicit in the relationship of man and woman. Civilization has overlaid it with codes of conduct, religion has tamed and poetry sublimated it, but it is still there, a thing to be reckoned with, its native savagery ready to break out if once the barriers are let down.

They were down now. The words which Agnes had been pouring out could never be taken back. She had screamed them out with a naked lack of shame. There had been an awful pleasure in it. To stand there and say, "You killed them both, but I love you—I don't care how many people you've killed, I love you"—this was the relief for which everything in her had ached. It wasn't her love, it wasn't her rage which spoke. It was something that rushed through her, making her its mouthpiece, intoxicating her with its power. She heard her own words as if they were not her words at all.

"Louise Rogers—that was her name. How did I know that, if I didn't hear her say it? Perhaps even the police don't know it yet. But I could tell them—I could tell them a lot of things. I could tell them everything I heard. I could tell them what she said on the telephone. I could tell them how you watched for her to come and let her in. I could tell them some of the things she said to you, because I heard them."

Grant's eyes dwelt on her in an appraising manner. He said in a quiet matter-of-fact tone,

"You're crazy."

A new hot flow of words came rushing through her.

"Yes, that's true—I'm crazy—about you. Right away from the first—but you never noticed me. And what's *she* got that you wouldn't notice anyone else? A little bit of a brown thing that nobody could say was anything in the way of looks! And when she went away I thought, 'Well, maybe he'll notice me now,' but you *never!*"

"Agnes, you're crazy!"

Just for a moment the anger in her failed, as flame will leap and fail. Her voice broke.

"I'm not asking for much, but you could be kind to me. Why aren't you kind to me?"

A look of sharp distaste flickered across his face. The fire flared again. She pelted him with screaming words.

"I could hang you, couldn't I? If I went to the police and told them what I know, they'd hang you! Because you killed that Louise Rogers! And you killed Mary Stokes because she knew! You killed them both! You killed them—you killed them—you killed them!"

All at once he shouted at her, as angry as she.

"Be quiet, damn you!" He took a long stride towards her, and saw her flinch. He went on to the door and flung it open. "Get out and stay out! And you leave this house in the morning!"

She had straightened herself up. Her hands were numb when she let go of the table—she couldn't feel them at all. The hot words were all gone. She had let them loose, and they had done something, she didn't know what. They were gone. Now she was cold. Hot anger makes you feel wonderful. But the hot anger was all gone, with the hot words. Now she was cold. He had looked at her as if she was muck in the street, and she was cold. Words strung themselves in her mind—"Bitter cold—bitter—" The cold and the bitterness possessed her now, just as the hot fury had possessed her.

He told her what she had to do. She walked out of the room past Grant without looking at him and went to do it.

CHAPTER 26

Chief Detective Inspector Lamb sat in the Lenton police station with Inspector Smith to keep him company and Sergeant Abbott to take notes of what Albert Caddle's girl would say when Constable May had rounded her up and brought her in. Albert Caddle was not being charged—not just yet—but he was under detention. Whether he was charged or not would depend a good deal on what Miss Maisie Traill had to say.

Whilst they waited the Inspector held the floor. It became obvious that Scotland Yard had not a monopoly of bright ideas. Inspector Smith had some too. He had been having them all the afternoon. With a wooden face which concealed his opinion that Harold Smith was a very bright boy indeed and undoubtedly destined to rise to the top of the class, he now held forth, not dogmatically, but with a modest consciousness that he was worth listening to.

"There is an idea that has occurred to me, sir—I don't know if it has to you—about this Mr. Ferrand."

"What about him?" Lamb's voice could hardly have been less encouraging.

Frank Abbott leaned gracefully back on the hard wooden chair, crossed his legs in a negligent manner, and prepared to enjoy himself. The Chief wasn't liking this case. He was fogged, foxed, and flummoxed, to draw words from his own expressive vocabulary. When this happened someone was due to have his head bitten off. This time it wasn't going to be Sergeant Abbott's head. Smith, though he didn't know it, was a ram in a thicket. He proceeded in the voice that matched his face.

"This Mr. Ferrand—I don't know if it's struck you, but we've only got his word for all this story about Mrs. Rogers having her jewels stolen and coming down here to look for the man that stole them. To my mind it's a pretty thin sort of tale."

Lamb's eyes dwelt on him without pleasure, but he held his fire.

"Did you get through to the Bull at Ledlington?"

"Yes. She stayed there like he said. He wouldn't invent anything like that, because he'd know we would check up on it. She stayed there all right, from January second to January fifth. I spoke to the hall porter, and he says he doesn't remember giving her any address on an envelope. If she had dropped one, he would have given it to her. He wouldn't have given her anyone else's envelope—why should he? As for two gentlemen coming in for drinks, he would be more likely to remember an evening when they didn't come in—if it ever happened, which it didn't. So there's no corroboration of what Mr. Ferrand says, and it came into my mind to wonder whether he hadn't made the whole thing up."

"Why?"

"Well, what came into my mind was this. Suppose he'd killed the girl himself. In love with her, jealous of her—well it's the sort of thing that happens every day. Who says she borrowed his car and drove down here alone? Mr. Ferrand does. Well, suppose she wasn't alone, suppose he was with her—or suppose he met her somewhere. Then there's a quarrel and he kills her. All he's got to do is drive the car to Basingstoke and leave it there while he catches a London train."

Lamb's eyes bulged ominously.

"And who shifted the body to the Forester's House on the Saturday evening and buried it in the cellar? Do you think Ferrand came back? And if he did, how did he know about the Forester's House, and how did he know there was a cellar under it? It took us long enough to find when we knew it was

161

there, but a strange Frenchman with a corpse on his hands in the dark, he finds it as easy as kiss your hand. Tchah!"

Simultaneously with this explosive sound and the thump of the Chief Inspector's fist upon the table the door opened and revealed Constable May, large, fresh-faced, ingenuous.

"Miss Traill is here, sir."

Maisie Traill came into the room in a cheap tight-waisted coat, a skirt which cleared the knee, and high-heeled shoes which gave her a tilting walk. Her almost albino fairness had been carefully decorated. Lashes originally white were now quite unbelievably dark. Black eyebrows rose in a pencilled arch above pale grey eyes. A scarlet Cupid's bow was plastered unconvincingly over the thin line of the lips. She was bare-headed, the light shone down on a mane of brightened hair. She rolled her eyes, settled herself in a chair, and said,

"What's cooking?"

Frank Abbott sat up and took his pad.

Lamb said, "Just a few questions, Miss Traill."

"Pleased, I'm sure." Her voice was like all the rest of her, thin and brittle.

Lamb, who had a weakness for girls, being a good deal under the influence of three affectionate daughters, found himself for once inclined to severity. He had to make a conscious effort to speak with his usual bluff kindliness.

"Perhaps you wouldn't mind telling us what you were doing between nine and ten o'clock on the evening of Friday, January eighth."

Miss Traill giggled.

"I don't keep a calendar in my head. Friday—well, let's see— that's last Friday week. Five o'clock? I work at Brown and Felton's. They close at half past five in winter, so I come out and meet my boy friend—see?—and we have a bit of a snack and go to the pictures."

"I'm afraid I must ask your friend's name."

She gave him a hard stare.

"Whatever for? Hasn't done anything, has he?"

"His name, Miss Traill."

A shrewd, niggardly astuteness prompted her. If Albert had been getting himself into trouble, she was through. It didn't do to get on the wrong side of the police. She tossed her head and said,

"Albert Caddle. Know him?"

"You say he met you at half past five on the afternoon of Friday the eighth?"

"That's right."

"How long was he with you?"

Maisie giggled again.

"We went to the pictures like I said—had something to eat first—come out about half past ten."

"He was with you the whole of those five hours?"

"Well, except for five minutes here and there."

"Known him long?"

"Not so very."

"How long?"

"Couple of weeks."

"Know he's a married man?"

The light grey eyes stared hardily.

"What's that got to do with me?"

Lamb grunted. He hated to see a girl that way. Real bad bringing-up she must have had. Wanted smacking. He drummed with his fingers on his knee.

"Well, what about the next day, Saturday the ninth—did you meet him then?"

"Yes, I did."

"What time?"

"He came to my place about five. Saturday's our half day."

"Stay there?"

163

"For a bit."

"And then?"

"Went to the pictures—the other house. We were there till half past ten."

"And day before yesterday, Saturday the sixteenth—see him then?"

"Why shouldn't I? I told you it's my half day. We went to my place for a bit, and then we were at the Rose and Crown playing darts."

"What time did you go there?"

"Must have been getting on for eight o'clock. We come away about ten."

He went on questioning her, and got the same short, dry answers, sometimes accompanied by a roll of the eye, sometimes by a mechanical giggle. There were no inconsistencies, no contradictions. If Maisie Traill was to be believed, Albert Caddle could not have murdered Louise Rogers at dusk on Friday the eighth, afterwards driving her car to Basingstoke. He could not have shifted the body and buried it round about six o'clock on Saturday the ninth. And he could not have murdered Mary Stokes after Joe Turnberry left her at eight-fifteen on Saturday the sixteenth.

For what Maisie's word was worth, Albert had three clear alibis. Unfortunately for him her word didn't seem to be worth a great deal.

CHAPTER 27

As soon as Maisie Traill had gone out Constable May came back.

"There's someone here from Deeping, sir. Says she knows who did the murders. Name of Ripley."

Frank Abbott's lips drew up in a soundless whistle. He had typed the name within the last few hours, and had an unfortunate recollection of its significance. He looked across at the Chief Inspector as May retreated and murmured,

"Hathaway's house-parlourmaid—"

She came in in her uniform dress with a winter coat thrown over it. She had done the three and a half miles from Deepside on her bicycle. Like Maisie Traill she was bare-headed, but the contrast in looks could hardly have been more extreme. They were both women, that was all you could say. The night air had added its damp to the lank, plastered strands of Agnes Ripley's hair. It had added a rather ghastly dew to her sallow skin. There was no colour in her face at all, except that under the dark eyes there were brown and purplish marks like bruises. She sat down, and said in a hard, controlled voice,

"I know who murdered those two girls. Do you want me to tell you?"

Lamb's bulging eyes were taking her in. She'd come away in a hurry—indoor shoes, that uniform dress, and the coat caught up where she had missed a button. Run out of the house on the spur of the moment—that was what it looked like. He took a little time before he spoke, and saw her bare right hand contract upon itself and stay like that. Then he said deliberately,

165

"Do you want to make a statement?"

"I know who murdered them."

"Very well, you can make a statement. Let us have your name and address please."

She gave them impatiently.

"Agnes Ripley—Deepside—near Deeping."

"That's Mr. Hathaway's house, isn't it? I think I remember your name. You work there don't you—house-parlourmaid?"

"I was—"

Her mouth twitched. Things went away into the past and were lost there. You couldn't ever bring them back, you had to go on.

Sergeant Abbott was writing on his pad. The Chief Inspector said,

"Well, Miss Ripley?"

She went on.

"Last Friday week—" the same words that Maisie had used, with all the difference that there was between her and Maisie Traill—"last Friday week a foreign lady rang Mr. Hathaway up. Ten minutes past four it was—"

Lamb interrupted her.

"How do you know she was foreign?"

"She spoke that way."

"You answered the telephone?"

"No—I was supposed to be out. I listened on the extension."

"Why?"

"I wanted to know who was ringing him up. I thought it might be Mrs. Hathaway."

"And just why did that interest you?"

Her eyes told him why. They had a momentary glow, a momentary anguish. She said,

"I wanted to know whether she rang him up."

"But this was a foreigner—you're quite sure about that? Did she give any name?"

"She said, 'Mr. Hathaway—I want to speak to Mr. Hathaway.' And when he spoke she said, 'My name is Louise Rogers, but you will not know that. I have something you dropped, and I would like to bring it back to you.' "

"You're quite sure she gave that name?"

"How do you think I know it if she didn't? It hasn't been in the papers—yet."

"Go on."

"She said, 'You were at the Bull at Ledlington on the evening of January the fourth. You dropped something there—a cigarette-lighter.' Mr. Hathaway said she had made a mistake, he hadn't dropped any lighter, and she said, 'Perhaps it was something else—it might have been a letter.' Then she said she was ringing up from Lenton, and she'd got a car, and would he tell her how to get to his house. And he said he thought she was making a mistake, but he told her."

She came to a full stop there and sat staring at Lamb, but not as if she was seeing him. When he said, "Is that all?" she started, and began to speak again.

"I heard the car drive up, about half past four, and I heard him go to the door and let her in. Mrs. Barton was out too—the housekeeper—we were both supposed to be out. He let her in and took her into the study, and I went along down and eased the door open so I could hear what they said."

Lamb grunted.

"You went downstairs and listened at the door. Why?"

Her eyes had that flickering glow again.

"She didn't know him. She'd seen him at the Bull. Anyone could see she was making up an excuse to get off with him. I had to hear what he said."

Lamb drummed on his knee. Crazy with jealousy, that was about the size of it. Sometimes a jealous woman came out with the truth, but if the truth wasn't damaging enough she wouldn't stick at a lie.

He gave her a short "Go on!"

"I couldn't make out everything she said—she spoke quick and foreign—but it was something about some diamonds. I didn't trouble about that. I thought she was making up to him. It was him I was listening to, and he was putting her in her place—said he didn't know nothing about it. She was all worked-up and talking fast and foreign, and she calls out, 'Show me your hand—then I shall know!'—like that. And he says, 'You're making a mistake.' Then she calls out very loud, 'Your hand!' and Mr. Grant, he come over towards the door, and I thought he was going to open it, so I didn't stay."

There—it was said. Mr. Frank Abbott that was Colonel Abbott's nephew and was staying at Abbottsleigh, he'd got it written down, and no way of taking it back again. The thing that had driven her ceased to scourge her on. She was empty, and cold, and tired. Her clenched hand relaxed. The big London policeman was asking her if that was all, and she nodded. She felt quite weak—she didn't know how she was going to get all that way back on her bicycle. And then it came to her that she wouldn't be going back, and that she hadn't anywhere to go. It felt like being dead. But when you were dead someone took care of your body and buried it. There wasn't anyone that would do as much for her. She sat there staring.

Lamb said, "You said you knew who murdered Mary Stokes and the other woman whose body has been found. Are you suggesting it was Mr. Hathaway?"

She stared.

"That would be a very serious suggestion to make, Miss Ripley."

In a voice like an echo she said,

"He killed them."

"What makes you think so?"

She stared.

168

"It was her diamonds. She kept on about them—said she'd been robbed. I couldn't get it all, but I got enough to know she thought it was Mr. Grant—out in France in the war, when she was getting away from the Germans."

"Did you hear her say it was Mr. Hathaway who robbed her?"

"I didn't get it at all. What did she come there for if she didn't think it was him? It's common talk he sold some diamonds to pay off what was owed on the land."

"And that's enough to make you think he murdered this woman. Did you hear her go?"

"I heard the door shut and the car drive off a little before five o'clock."

"Did you hear voices? Did you hear her speak—say good-night—anything like that?"

"No, I didn't."

"Did you hear Mr. Hathaway after the car had driven off? Careful, Miss Ripley—this is important."

Why was it important? She groped for that, and got it. If the car drove away, and after that she heard Mr. Grant moving about in the house, then he couldn't have killed Louise Rogers. He couldn't have killed her if she had driven away in the car and left him moving about the house for Agnes Ripley to hear. She focussed her staring eyes on Lamb and said,

"No, I didn't hear him at all."

There were a lot more questions, but she didn't mind. She didn't mind anything any more. He asked where she was the next day between half past five and half past seven in the evening, and where Mr. Grant was. Everyone knew it was just after six o'clock of that Saturday Mary Stokes had run screaming into Rectory Cottage, and it was easy to answer that she was in the kitchen with Mrs. Barton. But she couldn't say anything about Mr. Grant—he might have been in or he might have been out. He might have been moving Louise Rogers' body after killing her the night before, or he might have been writing in the study. She hadn't seen him between five and half past seven, and she couldn't say. No more she hadn't seen him this last Saturday evening, the sixteenth, when Mary Stokes was killed—couldn't have, because she had caught the three o'clock bus into Lenton and come back on the ten to nine along with Mrs. Abbott's maids. Only she didn't walk up the Lane with them, because she had to call at the post office for Mrs. Barton that didn't like coming back in the dark alone. She supposed it would be half past nine when they got in. And she couldn't say whether Mr. Grant was in or out. She didn't see him and she didn't hear him—not till she heard him come up to bed round about eleven o'clock.

There was a pause. She thought the questions were over. Then all at once the big man asked her another.

"What were your relations with Mr. Hathaway?"—right out like that.

Her heart banged and the slow, heavy colour came up in her face. Her tongue stumbled over the word as she repeated it.

"Relations?"

"You know what I'm asking you. Did he make love to you— were you his mistress?"

She flinched as if he had struck her. Her face twitched. She broke into bitter weeping.

"No—no—he didn't—I wasn't! Do you think I'd have come here if I was? He never looked at me—he didn't know I was there! I'd have done anything—I'd have helped him if he'd wanted me to! And he was going to let me be sent away. Mrs. Barton was going to send me away, and he was going to let her. I begged and prayed of him, but he was going to let her do it. I couldn't stop him—there wasn't anything I could do. You can't just sit still and let things happen—not things like that. I told him I knew—

170

what he done—about those two girls, and he said to leave his house in the morning. But I didn't wait for the morning, nor to pack my things nor anything—I come right away—" She broke off short as if the furious rush of words had been suddenly dammed, and stared at Lamb with a horrified expression. She stared, and said in a weak, fluttering voice,

"It isn't any good—"

CHAPTER 28

It was seven o'clock when Mrs. Barton came into the study with a look of distress on her face.

"Mr. Grant, I don't know what has happened, but Agnes has gone."

He looked up from the catalogue he was marking—farm implements and machinery, some of them too expensive to be managed this year, some which could be managed out of the premium which James Roney would pay with his son.

"Gone?"

There was offence as well as distress in her voice as she answered him.

"I'm sure I don't know what to think. She came down the kitchen passage some time after tea all in a hurry with her coat on, and off on her bicycle. I thought she'd slipped down to the post, and I've been looking for her back ever since, but it's turned seven and the tea not cleared or anything. I don't know what came over her, and I don't like it, Mr. Grant, with these nasty murders and all. I don't know what would be keeping her like this."

All at once Grant Hathaway knew. He sat for a moment, half turned in his chair with the light shining down on him. Then, as Mrs. Barton went over to pick up the tray, he said drily,

"I don't think Agnes has been murdered, but I daresay she won't be coming back. She was in rather a hysterical state—about your giving her notice. Has she friends she would be likely to go to?"

It became clear to Mrs. Barton that Agnes had still farther forgotten herself. She looked very much shocked.

"I don't know about friends, Mr. Grant. There's a Mrs. Parsons she has tea with once in a while when she goes into Lenton. Would you care about your supper in here, sir? It would be warm and comfortable in front of the fire."

He said, "Yes," and she went out of the room with the tray.

As soon as she was gone he pulled the table telephone towards him and gave the Abbottsleigh number. Cicely answered, as she had done an hour before. At her "Hullo!" he said,

"It's me again. Is Frank back?"

"No, he isn't—I said I'd ring you." She sounded a little breathless.

"Sorry to be a nuisance."

"Grant, what's going on?"

"I should very much like to know."

As he spoke he began to hear a faint throbbing sound. By the time Cicely was saying, "What do you mean?" a car was undoubtedly coming up the drive. It turned, slowed down, and stopped. There were voices and footsteps.

He said, "Goodnight. I think I have visitors," and rang off.

As he went to the front door, it came into his head to wonder how, when, and where he would speak to Cicely again. With a kind of nightmare relevancy, there came clanking through his thoughts two lines which had thrilled him when he was a boy:

172

"And Eugene Aram walked between
With gyves upon his wrist—"

The fact that he hadn't at that time the slightest idea what a gyve might be had merely added to the delightful gloom. As he opened the door to Chief Inspector Lamb he was wondering whether he was about to be given a practical demonstration of the manacle as used today. Hints on handcuffs.

There came in through the open door some very cold air just touched with mist, the towering bulk of Chief Inspector Lamb, and the slim elegance of Cicely's policeman cousin, Frank Abbott. Well, well—perhaps the handcuffs wouldn't be applied just yet—there would be some preliminary conversation. Life was certainly full of new experiences. Who said the post-war years were dull? Even in the heyday of the late European mix-up the jaded taste might have got a kick out of a situation like this. He saw no reason to doubt that Agnes had spilled the beans, in which case it was going to be up to him to stage something particularly convincing in the way of an explanation.

With all this in his mind he led the way to the study, watched Lamb divest himself of coat and hat and, refusing a proffered armchair, seat himself austerely by the writing-table. Then, and not till then, did he say,

"I wonder if you were expecting us, Mr. Hathaway."

Grant was still standing. He said in his ordinary voice,

"Well, I was wanting to see you. I have rung up Abbottsleigh twice to ask whether Abbott had come in, as I wanted to get into touch with you."

Lamb grunted.

"Sit down, Mr. Hathaway. I have just come from Lenton police station. As you have probably guessed, we have had a visit from your house-parlourmaid, Agnes Ripley. She made a very serious statement, and I have called to know whether you would care to comment on it."

Grant had drawn up a chair. They were all sitting round the table now—the Chief Inspector with his heavy face and serious air, Frank cold and impassive—and Grant Hathaway defendant. It really was very like being in the dock, only all at very much closer quarters, and he had no counsel. If he couldn't be sufficiently convincing he would be for it, and whatever happened afterwards, the deal with James Roney would fall through. You don't pay a good-sized premium to place a son with a man who has been arrested for two particularly brutal murders. And he wanted that money. It was part of the game of "showing Cicely." He wanted it badly. He said,

"May I see the statement if I am to comment on it?"

He took the typed transcript which Frank Abbott handed him and read it, frowning a little as he read. When he looked up it was to say,

"I think she's got a screw loose. My housekeeper gave her notice this morning. She came in after tea and made a scene about it—wanted me to say she could stay on."

"Why did your housekeeper give her notice? Why was she being dismissed?"

"You'll have to ask Mrs. Barton—I leave these things to her."

"You don't know?"

"No. I could see that Mrs. Barton didn't wish to say."

"Well, Mr. Hathaway, you have Agnes Ripley's statement before you. Is there anything you would like to say about it?"

"Yes. To begin with, I don't know whether you know that I've been away."

"From Sunday morning at eight-thirty till Monday morning at eleven—yes."

"Very exact. I want to say that I did not know of these two murders until Agnes herself mentioned them at about five o'clock this afternoon."

174

"You came back here at eleven, and had an interview with Inspector Smith. He questioned you as to your whereabouts on the evening of Friday the eighth—that is, last Friday week—and he asked you for your fingerprints. Why did you suppose he did that?"

"I knew—that is, I heard—that there was some cock-and-bull story going round. At least I thought then that it was a cock-and-bull story—something about Mary Stokes having seen what she described as a corpse. As no corpse was found where she said she had seen one, I concluded that it was a made-up story."

"H'm. You had heard the story?"

"Yes—Mrs. Barton said something about it, and my wife mentioned it—lightly, you know—not in the sort of way she would have done if she thought there was anything in it."

"You thought Inspector Smith was questioning you with reference to this story? You did not know then that Mary Stokes had been murdered?"

"Certainly I did not."

"Or that the body of Louise Rogers had been found at the Forester's House?"

"I had no idea that a body had been found there."

"What were your movements after Inspector Smith left?"

"I was out round the place. I was with my cowman most of the time. After lunch I went out and worked on a barn we're patching up—there's quite a lot of work to be done on a farm. Then I came in and started to clear up my table—there's also quite a lot of writing to be done. Then Agnes came in and played her scene."

"And no one happened to mention that there had been two murders?"

"The cowman didn't, nor did either of the other two men I spoke to. And Mrs. Barton didn't. You can ask them if you like."

Lamb drummed on his knee.

"Let's get back to the statement. What about it? Are you admitting that what she says is correct?"

"Some of it."

"Would you care to say which parts are correct?"

Grant looked down at the typed sheets and turned them over.

"The conversation on the telephone—that's all right."

"This woman Louise Rogers did ring you up and say she wanted to come and see you?"

"Yes."

"She did come and see you?"

"Yes."

"Any comment to make on Agnes Ripley's statement as to what she overheard?"

"Yes—certainly. She's got it all mixed up. I think I had better tell you just what happened. The woman who came to see me was in a very excited condition—fluent English but a foreign accent, and very much worked up. I'm not surprised that Agnes got it mixed. She had a long story about escaping from Paris and being bombed on the road—I don't really know quite where. She said she had a lot of valuable jewellery with her, and it was stolen, she said, by an Englishman. When I could get a word in edgeways, I said I was very sorry and all that, but it was rather an old story and what had it got to do with me. Not quite as bald as that, you know, but words to that effect. Well, then she came out with what sounded like a completely lunatic story about having seen the thief's hand when he grabbed the jewels. She said she would know it again. Well, I still wanted to know what it had got to do with me. She said she wanted to see my hands, so I put them on the table and she had a good look at them. That seemed to pacify her, and she went away."

Frank Abbott wrote, his face expressionless, the likeness to Lady Evelyn's portrait at Abbottsleigh very marked. As a tale he was judging it thin—so thin that it might almost be true.

Lamb shifted in his chair. He had been sitting well back on it, square and upright, now he set a hand on the writing-table and leaned forward.

"You say this woman went away. What did you do after that?"

Grant smiled faintly.

"From five o'clock onwards? You've got it written down, haven't you? At least I seem to remember Inspector Smith writing it down this morning, and I suppose you've got it. I don't propose to make you a present of any inconsistencies. I went out about five o'clock, and I was out for some time."

"Did you leave the house with Louise Rogers?"

"No, I did not."

"How long afterwards did you go?"

Grant Hathaway's shoulder lifted slightly.

"A few minutes."

"How do you account for the fact that Agnes Ripley didn't hear you go?"

"I'm afraid I can't account for anything that Agnes said or did."

"Were you on foot, on a bicycle, or in a car?"

"I was on foot."

"Where did you go?"

Lamb's inexpressive gaze, which missed nothing, noted a tightening of the muscles of Mr. Hathaway's face. It was so slight that it might not have been there at all.

Grant, aware of the involuntary stiffening, quite deliberately relaxed. He had taken a very quick decision, and he relaxed. It is better to exhibit yourself as a fool than to be arrested as a murderer, and if you've got to make an exhibition of yourself, it is better to carry it off with a good grace. Without any perceptible pause he said,

"I walked down to the cross-roads and round by Tomlin's Farm into Deeping."

"Did you see Mary Stokes?"

"No—of course not. I didn't see anyone. I wanted a walk."

"See anyone in Deeping?"

"No."

"How long were you out, Mr. Hathaway?"

"I got in—" he paused, frowning—"getting on for half past seven."

"H'm. It wouldn't take you all that time to do—what's the distance—three or four miles?"

"About three. No."

"An hour at the outside. What about the other hour and a half, Mr. Hathaway?"

Grant's smile flashed out.

"I was in church."

"On a Friday evening?"

He nodded carelessly.

"Yes. As I came by the church I heard the organ, so I knew that my wife was there practising—she plays extremely well. The side door was open, so I went in and listened."

"For an hour and a half?"

"Just about. She left at seven, and it takes me about twenty-five minutes from the church."

"H'm. Mrs. Hathaway can corroborate this?"

"Oh, no—she didn't know I was there."

"Is there anyone who can corroborate this account of your movements?"

"I'm afraid not. Mrs. Barton and Agnes were out—that is, Agnes was supposed to be out. Did she go after she'd finished eavesdropping?"

"Yes, she went."

"Then I'm afraid you'll just have to take my word for it—or not."

Lamb tapped on the table. He thought Mr. Hathaway was a very cool hand. Odd story that about his going into the church to listen to his wife playing the organ. Might be the best cover-up he could think of—might go down with a jury, if it ever came to that—might even be true. He frowned and asked what Mr. Hathaway was doing on the evening of Saturday the ninth between half past five and, say, nine or ten o'clock.

Mr. Hathaway was quite pleasant about it, but not in the least helpful either to himself or to the police. He stuck to what he had already told Inspector Smith. He had started to go down into Deeping on a bicycle soon after four. He caught up with his wife, who was out with her dogs, had a few words with her, changed his mind about going into Deeping, and went home, where he remained.

"You were back by half past four?"

"I should think so."

"You didn't go out again?"

"No—I had a lot of writing to do."

"Could your housekeeper vouch for the fact that you were in?"

"I had a meal at half past seven. She and Agnes could both vouch for that. May I ask why this particular time needs to be vouched for? I suppose nobody else was being murdered then?"

Lamb's gaze remained impenetrable.

"Louise Rogers' body was moved to the Forester's House between half past five and six. Mary Stokes saw it there and ran screaming down to Rectory Cottage. If she had told the truth, the murderer might have been caught and she probably wouldn't have been murdered. But she didn't want to admit that she had been to the Forester's House, so she said she'd seen the body somewhere else. Meanwhile the murderer got it down into the cellar, and either then or later on buried it there."

Grant was a little paler—not much, but enough to be noticeable. He said,

"I didn't change for supper. Mrs. Barton will remember that, I suppose—and that I was reasonably clean and tidy. I certainly hadn't been digging a grave in a disused cellar, which sounds like a particularly messy kind of job. But of course, as you were about to observe, I could have got into suitable garments and gone out and done it afterwards. You were going to point that out, weren't you?"

As he said it he had a short stabbing doubt. Temper and instinct alike had prompted the attack. Temper at least had a nasty way of letting you down.

Lamb's voice came across the thought, slow and pleasant, with the country burr in it.

"I don't know that I should have said anything of the kind."

Grant laughed.

"You'd have thought it—wouldn't you? Well?"

Lamb said, "Can you give me any account of your movements on the evening of Saturday the sixteenth, from half past seven onwards?"

All this time Grant had sat easily, legs crossed, hands lying naturally. He moved now, as if quite suddenly his whole body had become aware of constraint. Or perhaps it was his mind which had become intolerant. His voice had an edge on it as he said,

"I'm afraid I can't do very much for you. Mrs. Barton and Agnes were both out. I suppose they would get in about half past nine, but I didn't see them, and they didn't see me. Agnes informed me that Mary Stokes is supposed to have been murdered some time after a quarter past eight. Alibis don't seem to be my strong suit, do they? I was here in this room, but I'm afraid I can't prove it. Where do we go from there?"

Lamb said, "Nowhere at the moment, Mr. Hathaway, but there are some more questions I would like to put. To get back to Louise Rogers. You say the telephone conversation as reported by Miss Ripley is correct."

180

"I think so."

"Then you were at the Bull in Ledlington on the night of January the fourth. Perhaps you would like to give your own account of what happened there."

"As far as I am concerned nothing happened. I had been over at Ledstow seeing a friend, James Roney. The address is Passfield if you want it. It's the same man I've just been staying with. He drove me into Ledlington to catch the eight-twenty. He put me down at the station, and I found I'd missed the train—his watch must have been wrong. The next train to Lenton didn't go for another hour and a half, so I thought I'd go over to the Bull. As I came out of the station I met a man I know. He had come down from town and was expecting his car to meet him. He offered me a lift. Then his chauffeur came up and said he thought he'd got a slow puncture, he'd got to change a wheel, so we all went over to the Bull. The car was there in the yard."

"Who was your friend, Mr. Hathaway?"

"Mark Harlow. He's my next neighbour here, at the Grange."

The mental atmosphere received a slight electric discharge. Frank Abbott's face showed nothing. His thoughts clamoured. So Caddle was there. . . . Albert Caddle was at the Bull when Louise Rogers looked out of her bedroom and recognized the hand she had seen amongst her jewels.

Lamb was probably saying the same thing, if more soberly.

"You went over to the Bull with Mr. Harlow. How long did you remain there?"

"About half an hour."

"Were you and Mr. Harlow together during that time?"

"During most of it. We had drinks, and then I saw a man who served with me in France. I went over to speak to him. Presently Harlow said he was going to see if the car was ready. I followed him a few minutes later."

"You went out into the yard?"

"Yes—the car was there."

181

"Do you possess a cigarette-lighter?"

"I do, but I didn't drop it in the yard at the Bull."

"Sure about that?"

"Quite sure. I walked to the car, and found it ready and Harlow waiting. We got in, and he drove me home."

"When you say 'he drove me,' do you mean that Mr. Harlow drove, or that the chauffeur did?"

"Oh, it was just a way of speaking. Caddle drove."

"The chauffeur was Albert Caddle?"

"Yes."

"Mr. Hathaway, you talked to Louise Rogers in this room for about half an hour. I suppose you had the same light on that you have now—you must have had quite a good view of her. Will you give me as detailed a description as you can?"

All this time Grant's face had hardly changed at all. Now he looked surprised.

"Black coat and hat—if you can call a little round cap a hat. Rather dashing. Good ankles, good stockings, good shoes—"

"All black?"

"Not the stockings."

"But otherwise she was all in black, with nothing to relieve it?"

"Oh, earrings—rather noticeable ones—like those eternity rings women are so crazy about, I don't know why."

"H'm—a pair of earrings. You're sure she was wearing a pair?"

Grant looked surprised again.

"Oh, yes—a pair of eternity earrings—quite noticeable, as I said."

That seemed to be all about that.

Lamb went on with his questions. Just what route had Mr. Hathaway taken during his escape from France? Just where had he joined the Paris road? And where had he left it? The answers all carefully written down, but not very helpful, since

182

Michel Ferrand had been quite unable to say where the jewel robbery had taken place. Beyond establishing the fact that his road and that of Louise might have coincided, Mr. Hathaway's answers did not contribute very much.

"Just what did Louise Rogers say when she asked to see your hands?"

"She said she saw the thief's hand turning over the diamonds in her case. She said she would know it again. She asked me to show her my hands, and I did."

"Hand, or hands?"

"Hands, I think. Anyhow I put them both out."

"Do you mind doing so now?"

"Not in the least."

He laid them on the writing-table. The light shone down on them—large, well-shaped hands roughened with work, a thin scar showing white across the knuckles of the first and second fingers of the left hand. If the skin had not been so brown, the scar would have been less noticeable.

Lamb said bluntly, "How did you get that scar, Mr. Hathaway?"

"Monkeying about with a knife when I was fourteen. Your Mrs. Rogers would have to have pretty good eyes to see it in the courtyard of the Bull, if that's what you think she did."

Lamb was imperturbable.

"If she talked to you about it, I expect she told you that the man who dropped his lighter put on a torch to look for it, and that she saw his hand in the concentrated light of the beam. A scar like that would show up all right under a good torch."

Grant was warming to the game. There were even moments when he could enjoy it. This was one of them. He smiled.

"But you see, she didn't say anything about a scar. She only said she would know the hand. When I showed her mine she lost interest and went away." He picked up his hands. "I should like to point out, Chief Inspector, that the Bull was quite crowded

183

that evening. There were at least twenty people in the bar when we went in. Any one of them might have dropped a lighter under Louise Rogers' window and showed a hand which she thought she recognized."

Lamb struck, and struck hard.

"But it was you she followed to Deeping, Mr. Hathaway. It is proved that she did that. It is proved that she had an interview with you in this room, and that she asked you to show her your hands. It is also proved that she was murdered that evening, probably not very long after this interview—that her body was concealed in Dead Man's Copse, transferred the following evening to the Forester's House, and subsequently buried in the cellar underneath it. Are you suggesting that the other twenty people in the bar at the Bull a fortnight ago can be dragged in to account for this chain of events? You have no alibi for any of the times that matter."

Grant slid his hands into his pockets and jingled a bunch of keys.

"Neglectful—wasn't it? But then I had no idea that anyone was going to be murdered. I don't suppose that even you would always have an alibi for everything. Anyhow, there it is. What about it?"

Lamb got to his feet.

"We're expecting some more evidence. Meanwhile, Mr. Hathaway, I would rather you didn't leave the district."

Grant was astonished at his own relief.

CHAPTER 29

Maggie Bell, listening hard, had heard nothing more exciting than Mrs. Abbott calling up Miss Cicely to say they wouldn't be back to dinner because Colonel Abbott and the Rector had got into a game of chess which would probably keep them up all night—"So you'll just have to feed Frank and Miss Silver."

Mr. Frank wasn't back. Maggie could have told Mrs. Abbott that, because Mr. Hathaway had rung Miss Cicely twice asking for him. There now—Miss Cicely was saying so.

"Frank's not back."

"Then feed Miss Silver—and yourself. Do eat something, darling." Mrs. Abbott rang off.

The next to ring up was Mr. Frank—said he'd be late and not to keep anything.

"Nonsense—you must have something to eat!"

"I've got to drive the Chief back to Lenton—I'll have something there." He rang off.

Maggie Bell thought it was very dull stuff.

The next call was Mr. Mark Harlow for Miss Cicely. Maggie always listened to them with all her ears. Making up to her, that's what he was—you could hear it in his voice. And she was pretty short with him—most times—but if there was one of those divorces—well, he might have a chance all the same. Not one to do anything underhand, Miss Cicely. Too proud. Not the stuck-up sort of being proud, but the kind everybody ought to have a bit of.

Well, there was Mr. Harlow saying "Cis—" and her sounding a bit cross, like you do when the telephone keeps on.

185

"What is it?"

"Can I come round?"

"No, I don't think so."

"Why?"

"The parents are out."

"What has that got to do with it? I want to talk to you."

"You would have to talk to me and Miss Silver. Do you want to do that?"

"We could go somewhere else."

"No."

Quite definitely Mark Harlow wasn't pleased. His voice was loud enough to jar the line.

"How you say that! You're like a bit of stone!"

She laughed as if she was really amused.

"What have I got to be soft-hearted about?"

"Cis, I'm distracted—these damned murders! And the police all over the place. Would you believe it, they've actually been here! Apparently they want to know everything I've said or thought or done for the last fortnight. As if anyone could remember—as if anyone but a policeman would expect you to remember! And the result is my work has absolutely gone down the drain. I was just beginning to make a good job of the quartet—you know—" He hummed an air which Maggie didn't think very much of. Miss Cicely didn't either by all accounts. She said so right out.

"I don't think much of that."

Mr. Mark sounded quite angry.

"You never do, but it would have been all right if it hadn't been for all the damnable fuss that's going on! I can't work when the atmosphere is so disturbed. If one can't get peace and quiet, what's the point about the country? It's damp, it's dark, it's cold, it's dreary, and it's dull. The one thing you might expect is that you would be let alone there. I mean, if people are going to get themselves murdered, why can't they do it where they belong instead of coming down here and making our lives a perfect hell with Scotland Yard detectives?"

Miss Cicely didn't say anything for a minute. Then she said quite off-hand,

"A bit self-centred, aren't you, Mark?"

Mr. Harlow regularly blew up.

"That's damned nonsense and you know it! Everything you do has to start with yourself, hasn't it? You are the centre— naturally everything begins and ends there. If you're not your own centre, you're nothing—it makes nonsense. You have no point, no purpose—you're just the unbalanced sport of circumstance. Every artist has to work from his own centre, or he loses himself."

"That sounds like nonsense to me."

He laughed.

Maggie wasn't expecting that. It was a bit funny after being so angry. He laughed, and he said,

"You're the most self-centred person I know."

"I'm not."

"Oh, yes, you are."

Miss Cicely slammed down the receiver.

Maggie didn't know when she had enjoyed a call so much.

Cicely came back into the morning-room where Miss Silver sat knitting. The blue woolly coatee which had occupied her for the first day or two of her visit now reposed in the left-hand top drawer of the bow-fronted mahogany chest in her bedroom; a second jacket of a delicate shell-pink was rapidly taking shape. Cicely, who had been coldly exasperated by Frank's enthusiasm for his everlasting Miss Silver, had now travelled quite a long way in the opposite direction. Easy enough to dismiss the unwanted visitor as dowdy and governessy. Easy, that is, in the first five minutes or so. After that you could only go on doing it if you were very stupid or quite unable to rid yourself of a preconceived idea. Cicely wasn't stupid. Against her will,

Miss Silver impressed her. She was aware of an intelligence which she respected, and she observed that Frank not only respected this little elderly person, but, quite astonishingly, he had a real and rather humble affection for her. She found this odd, entertaining, and impressive.

Now, as she came back into the morning-room and Miss Silver looked up at her and smiled, something happened. She heard herself say in a puzzled voice,

"Would you say I was self-centred?"

Miss Silver kept her friendly smile.

"Has someone been telling you so?"

Cicely nodded.

"Yes—Mark Harlow. He said I was the most self-centred person he knew. Do you think I am?"

Miss Silver continued to knit. She also continued to smile.

"What do you think about it yourself?"

Cicely was now sitting on the floor in front of the fire, her hands in her lap, her head tilted, her eyes widely opened and a little anxious, like a child who isn't quite sure whether it has got its lesson right.

"I don't know—I never thought about it."

"And what do you think now?"

She said slowly, "I think—perhaps—I am." And then, "It's difficult not to be when everything goes wrong. You can't help thinking about it all the time, and that means you are thinking about yourself."

Miss Silver was accustomed to being the recipient of confidences. In the course of her professional career the most unlikely people had told her the most unlikely things. It did not surprise her that Cicely, who talked to no one, should now be talking to her. It was to surprise Cicely herself very much when she came to look back on it. At the time it seemed entirely natural, and it eased the pain in her heart.

188

Miss Silver did not speak, only looked at her gravely and kindly. If she had spoken, it might have checked Cicely's impulse. But there was nothing to check it. She went on.

"If things go wrong with you, that does mean that you keep thinking about yourself. I've been doing that. I expect it's been beastly for the parents."

Miss Silver said, "It is hard to see someone you love unhappy and not be allowed to help."

The dark eyebrows drew together over troubled eyes.

"Mummy adores Grant. It didn't seem fair."

Miss Silver coughed.

"To him, or to her?"

"Both, I think—and to me too. To be a proper mother-in-law she ought to have hated him and taken sides with me, but she didn't—she never does do things like other people. So that made me worse. And I couldn't drag Daddy into it—he does hate rows. Men do, don't you think, much more than women? I don't mean that they don't have rows themselves, but they think women make a fuss and have them about nothing—and of course it's true, only not always. And they think the woman is always bound to be wrong. Daddy is very fond of Grant too. He would only have thought I was making a fuss about nothing."

The needles clicked with a gentle soothing sound.

"And were you?"

Cicely blinked. She felt as if she had been hit quite suddenly and rather hard. The colour ran up into her cheeks, and she said in a crying voice,

"No—no—I wasn't! There isn't anything more horrible than to think someone loves you and find out that it's only your money." She blinked again quickly to keep back the angry tears. "It wasn't as if I hadn't been warned. Gran warned me. My grandfather married her because of her money, and look what it did to her! I think she was a little bit fond of me, I don't know why, but except for that she hadn't got a

189

shred of feeling for anyone. She quarrelled with both her sons, and she disliked their wives. Fancy not liking Mummy—but she didn't. She thought everyone was after her money except me— and she only didn't think it about me because I was too young. She put it in her will, you know—'My granddaughter Cicely, who is at present too young to be mercenary.' Of course anyone who could think that Daddy had a mercenary motive anywhere about him must have had a screw loose. But that's what she was like. She told me she was going to leave her money to me, and she warned me that everyone would try and get hold of it." Suddenly and shockingly, her colour drained away. "She said I was just a plain brown little thing, and men wouldn't fall in love with me, but they would make up to me and want to marry me because of the money."

Miss Silver coughed.

"An inexcusable thing to say."

"It's the kind of thing that eats into you. You remember it when you don't want to—you've forgotten all about it, and it crawls out of some horrid hole and gets you." She paused and took a long breath. "There was poor Ellen Caddle. Gran left her five hundred pounds, and she married that bounding Albert whom anyone could see didn't care tuppence about her. Why, she was at least fifteen years older than he was."

Miss Silver gave her gentle cough.

"That was sadly imprudent. A woman should have more self-respect. As Shakespeare says: 'Let still the woman take an elder than herself, so wears she to him.' "

"Well, she didn't. And of course that brought Gran's snake out of its hole, but not so that I couldn't boot it back again. Because, you see, when she died I wanted Daddy to have the money, and to give some of it to Frank. I wanted them to promise they would take it when I came of age—I couldn't do anything about it till then. But they wouldn't. So then I thought I had got rid of the snake. I thought if Gran had been wrong about that, I needn't bother any more. We came here to live, and I began to see Grant. He had just come in for Deepside. I thought he was falling in love with me. I was frightfully happy—I didn't think about Gran any more. We were married. I went on being frightfully happy for three months. Then I found out that it was the money after all. Gran knew what she was talking about all right—it wasn't me, it was the money. So I came back here." She sprang up with burning cheeks. "I've never told anyone about it—I don't know why I've told you. I suppose one has to tell someone—some time." She went over to the piano and flung up the lid. "Do you mind if I bang a bit?"

CHAPTER 30

It was after ten when Frank Abbott walked in upon Miss Silver knitting and Cicely making stormy music at the piano. She stopped on a crashing chord, let the sound die away, and got to her feet.

"Has anything happened?"

"No."

Bramble got up from the fire and came to sniff at Frank's ankles.

"Have you had anything to eat?"

"Yes, thank you."

"Have some coffee?"

"Oh, don't bother."

"I'll go and make it."

She went out, and Bramble after her.

Frank sat down by the fire. He was cold, he was tired, he had had a very bad dinner. He had never hated a case so much. He began to tell Miss Silver about it to the soothing accompaniment of warmth, the click of her knitting-needles, and a prospect of hot coffee.

Cicely, coming back with the tray, heard the murmur of their voices from the other side of the morning-room door. She set the tray down on one of those uncomfortable carved chairs so wisely relegated to halls. Then she did what Agnes had done on a previous occasion—she turned back the handle very slowly, evenly, and gently until the latch was free and the door swung in a little. If they noticed it, she was coming in with the tray. If they didn't, she meant to know what was going on. When you've been properly brought up you don't listen at doors. It was a revolting thing to do. She was going to do it. Something much stronger than anything she had been taught cried in her and was afraid. Something was happening, and she had to know what it was.

Almost at once she knew, because Frank was saying, "I'm clearing out of here tomorrow morning. They couldn't give me a room at the hotel tonight. The Chief offered to send me back to town and have someone else down, but I said I'd rather go through with it."

Miss Silver coughed delicately.

"I think that was judicious. To retire from the case would be tantamount to a public admission of Mr. Hathaway's guilt."

Cicely's left hand held the door knob. With her right she leaned hard against the jamb. Frank Abbott said,

"I can't stay here. He is Cicely's husband. If he did it, it's frightful for her, and for Monica."

"Do you think he did it?"

"He could have. I haven't got as far as thinking whether he did. Albert Caddle could have done it too. That little fancy bit of his gives him three lovely alibis, but I shouldn't think a jury would look at any of them—at least not after they'd looked at Maisie. Then there's Mark Harlow. The three of them were together at

192

the Bull on the night of the fourth when Louise Rogers saw and recognised the hand of the man who robbed her. The bother is, we don't know just what it was that she recognised. The lad Ferrand who gave us the lowdown doesn't know either. He could only say she was quite sure she would know the hand again, and that she did know it. Whoever it was, dropped a lighter in the yard at the Bull and switched on a torch to find it. Louise saw his hand in the beam and was prepared to swear to it. She was undressed. By the time she had put on some clothes and got down, two men and a chauffeur had driven away. One of them dropped an envelope addressed to Grant Hathaway. That's why she came down here. We now know that she had an interview with Hathaway between half past four and five on the eighth—that is, just before she was murdered. Agnes overheard part of it, and when Mrs. Barton gave her notice today she had a scene with Hathaway and rushed off to denounce him. It is pretty obvious that she was crazy about him and—"

Miss Silver coughed, and observed primly that hell had no fury like a woman scorned.

"As you say. Well, Grant has no alibis for the three important times. He could have killed Louise then and there in the study, though it would have been very risky. Agnes only heard part of the interview, but from the distance to which she then retired she heard the front door open and shut and the car drive away. Grant could have driven away in it—Louise may have been dead, or she may have been alive. Or his story may be true. He says that Louise drove away by herself, and that a few minutes later he went out, walked round by Tomlin's Farm to the church, sat there listening to Cicely playing the organ for about an hour and a half, and then came home."

Cicely pushed open the door with the flat of her hand, turned round for the tray, and walked into the room, her face colourless, her eyes amber-bright. She put the coffee down at Frank's elbow and went back to shut the door. Then she came round in front of him and said,

"I've been listening. If it's got to do with Grant, it's got to do with me. I want to know the bits I've missed."

Frank's fair eyebrows lifted.

"My dear child—"

She said very distinctly,

"I am not your dear child—I am Grant's wife. If you can tell Miss Silver you can tell me. I can hold my tongue, but I've got to know."

He looked involuntarily at Miss Silver, and received a slight nod.

Cicely stamped her foot.

"If you don't tell me I shall drive over to Lenton and see the Chief Inspector!"

He reached forward, touched her hand, and found it icy.

"All right, Cis—sit down. I don't know how much you heard, but this is how it stands."

She listened, sitting up straight and never taking her eyes from his face. Miss Silver knitted with an even click of the needles. She had heard some of Frank's narrative before, but it was interesting to hear it again. Her thoughts went to and fro as methodically as her needles, noting a loophole here, a small discrepancy there, a definite possibility somewhere else. Frank had an orderly mind and a lucid way of putting things.

Cicely listened, not just with her ears but with the whole of her. Everything except that listening was blotted out. The familiar room, her companions, Bramble illicitly curled up in Monica Abbott's chair, the firelight, the warmth, Frank pouring out the coffee she had brought and drinking it, the click of Miss Silver's needles—with all these things her contacts were broken. No sound reached her, no image, no sensation. Only Frank's voice, only the things it said—these were crystal clear.

194

He came down to the point at which she had entered the room.

"So there you have Caddle with three alibis which may or may not be fakes, and Grant with no alibis at all. Mark Harlow hasn't any either."

Cicely spoke for the first time.

"*Mark?*"

"He was one of the three at the Bull. We went on to him after seeing Grant. Well, on the Friday he says he went out for a walk and didn't meet anyone. Of course he might have met Louise and murdered her. He says he walked right into Lenton and went to a cinema. On the Saturday, when Louise's body was being shifted, he threw another walk and didn't meet anyone. On Saturday the sixteenth he lunched with people in Lenton and did a flick with them afterwards. Home by car, driving himself. Staff out—cold supper. He says he was in by half past seven, which of course would give him plenty of time to nip round to Tomlin's Farm on a bicycle and kill Mary Stokes— don't suppose he'd have risked taking the car. To sum up, Grant and Harlow had every possible opportunity of killing Louise on Friday, shifting the body on Saturday, and disposing of Mary Stokes on the Saturday following. There's only Maisie Traill's word to say that Caddle's opportunities were not just as good. Of the three, Grant leads a little as a suspect, because we know that he had an interview with Louise, and there's nothing to say that either of the others did. But if it comes to a show of hands, then I think Caddle has it. Louise Rogers told Ferrand that she would know the hand of the man who robbed her and recognise it anywhere. Well, Caddle has lost the top joint of his left forefinger—that's a thing you couldn't possibly forget. Grant has a scar which shows up white, and Harlow hasn't any noticeable mark. He had some sticking-plaster on the back of his right hand, but he peeled it off, and there's nothing but a deep scratch under it. He says he got it on some barbed wire—there's absolutely nothing to suggest that it was done to cover up an old scar. But he has got rather odd-shaped hands. The forefinger is longer than the others, and the thumbs—well—"

Cicely said with stiff lips,

"That's what gives him his stretch on the piano—they're double-jointed."

"The question is, would a thing like that show enough to impress itself on Louise Rogers all in a moment by the light of a torch? No—I think Albert definitely has the lead there. A whole joint gone would fairly hit you in the eye."

Cicely got up. She said, "Thank you, Frank," and went out of the room.

After a short silence Frank said,

"It's a nasty mix-up. You see, the murderer is bound to be a local man, because no one else would have known about the Forester's House, let alone the cellar under it, and no one else would have had any motive for killing Mary Stokes. He is almost bound to have been one of the three men who were at the Bull on the evening of the fourth. That is to say, he is almost bound to be Albert Caddle, or Grant Hathaway, or Mark Harlow."

Miss Silver coughed.

"What did you think of Mr. Harlow?"

Frank gave her a cool, shrewd look.

"Oh, Rome can burn as long as no one interferes with his fiddling—his music matters, and nothing else does. He writes revue tunes, and these nasty rough murders have put one of them out of his head. Too disastrous. If he had been Beethoven, Bach, and Brahms all rolled into one, I should have thought he was making rather too much of the catastrophe. We interrupted him when he was producing horrid sounds from a piano. He had an attack of artistic temperament, but rallied sufficiently to promise us his kind assistance. As he seems to be the sort of chap who never knows what o'clock it is or what he was doing yesterday, the result didn't amount to very much. Honestly, you ought to have seen the Chief. He reached an all time high in the colouring line, and I was afraid his eyes were going to pop out when Harlow said artlessly that he wasn't sure which cinema he went to on the all important Friday the eighth, or what picture he saw. Said he very often didn't look at the picture at all, just sat and thought about tunes. The old boy asked me seriously afterwards if I thought Harlow was quite all there. I told him there were lots more where he came from, and that it was mostly pose—very much so in this case, because when judiciously prodded he came off it sufficiently to identify the Empire, and to remember quite a lot about the film, including the fact that there was a new girl with marvellous legs. You won't have heard of her, but—is he right!"

Miss Silver smiled.

"Perdita Payne?"

He burst out laughing.

"You do know everything! Well, he condescended to remember Perdita's legs—and they're worth remembering."

A very slight frown replaced Miss Silver's smile. She considered that the emphasis on legs had been sufficient. She said,

"I heard the police message which was broadcast after the six o'clock news. It was given out just as I came in."

Frank sat up.

"Oh, yes, I was going to tell you—a café at Ledlington rang up at once. Louise lunched there rather late—didn't leave till half past two—asked the way to Lenton. She was alone, so bang goes Smith's engaging theory that she brought someone down to murder her at Deeping—the unfortunate Ferrand for choice."

"What is Mr. Ferrand like, Frank?"

"Are you going to join Smith? I thought he was a harmless youth—fond of her, and very much upset. I don't think there's anything there."

"No—perhaps not."

She coughed, and was about to speak, when the door opened and Cicely came a little way into the room. Her head was bare, but she was wearing a fur coat. Beyond her, where she had just set it down, a suit-case stood. Bramble jumped out of Monica Abbott's chair and ran to meet her, bobbing up and cocking his head on one side. She dropped a hand for him to nibble and said,

"Will you tell the parents when they come in—I'm going home."

Miss Silver said, "Dear me!"

Frank pulled round in his chair.

"Cis!"

She stood there, her colour brilliantly heightened, her eyes glowing.

"You heard what I said—I'm going home."

After his one surprised ejaculation Frank returned to the detached manner.

"Does one ask why? Monica will. Return of tigress—where is my cub?"

Cicely's foot tapped the carpet.

"You can tell her I've gone home."

"A little repetitive, aren't you? Hadn't you better wait and tell her yourself?"

She came slowly over to the hearth, bent down, put a log on the fire, and said,

"No, I don't think so. I don't want a fuss." She straightened up and looked from him to Miss Silver. "You can tell her. It's quite simple. Grant and I have got our own quarrel—it's got nothing to do with anyone else, it's between ourselves. If he's going to be suspected of these murders, then I'm going back. We can go on with our quarrel afterwards. I won't have people thinking I believe he's got anything to do with murdering people."

Miss Silver continued to knit, the pink wool revolved.

198

Frank Abbott got up. You couldn't drive Cicely—you never could even when she was a baby—but Monica would expect him to have a stab at it. He cursed the Rector, and the Rector's chess, and Uncle Reg. Let Monica do her own dirty work and get bitten by her own daughter. He said,

"Cis, it's one of those three men. Hadn't you better wait?"

She looked at him steadily.

"It's not Grant." She turned to Miss Silver. "Will you help us?"

"My dear—"

"Frank says you always know. You take cases professionally, don't you? I want you to take this one for me—and Grant."

The needles were momentarily still. Miss Silver looked up, and Cicely looked down.

"My dear, I can't take any case for this person or for that. I can only have one object, which is to find out the truth."

Cicely said, "That is what I want too."

"You are very confident."

"Yes."

"Suppose your confidence were misplaced. Suppose I took the case and the truth was a very unwelcome one—"

All Cicely's bright colour was gone. Under the brown skin there was a cold pallor. She said,

"Lies aren't any good. I want the truth. Will you take the case?"

Miss Silver said, "Yes."

CHAPTER 31

Frank Abbott watched the tail-light of the car dwindle to a spark and go out. He went back to the morning-room and said,

"Well, I've got a précis to make for the Chief, only I shall have to find an English word for it, or he'll go through the roof. He's had to put up with Ferrand being French, but he won't be taking any of it from me. By the way, what is the English for précis?"

Miss Silver obliged with the word "summary," and was thanked.

"All right then, I'm off to the study. You can tell Monica about Cis."

Miss Silver smiled and said, "I think she will be pleased."

He stopped on his way to the door.

"She would have been—I don't know about it now. It's—a bit tricky, isn't it? Well, it's no good worrying. I couldn't have stopped her."

He went out.

Miss Silver sat there knitting with the room settling into stillness round her. Bramble and Cicely seemed to have left the house very quiet. The old spaniel must have taken himself off to the kitchen, where scraps were strictly forbidden but the rule was perhaps not always as strictly kept.

It must have been well after half past ten when there were sounds from the hall—the clap of the front door, a man's voice saying, "Don't bother—I'll just go in," and upon that the dramatic entrance of Mark Harlow with wind-swept hair and an appearance of distraction. Somewhere behind him the house-parlourmaid Ruth murmured and withdrew to inform her sister and Mrs. Mayhew that he had just walked past her, and she didn't think it was right.

Mark Harlow shut the door behind him, stared, and said, "Where's Cis?"

In the ordinary way Miss Silver would have reproved the informality by one of those changes of manner which, though slight, leave no doubt that an offence has been committed. On this occasion, any displeasure she may have felt was not permitted to appear. Instead she smiled slightly and said,

"Come and sit down, Mr. Harlow."

He came a step or two nearer and repeated his question.

"Where's Cis? I want to speak to her."

Miss Silver lifted her eyes to his face. The artistic temperament alluded to by Frank Abbott was apparently still very much in the ascendant. She said in a calm and cheerful voice,

"Mrs. Hathaway has gone home."

"*What!*"

"She has returned to Deepside."

The news seemed to deprive him of the last vestige of manners. He said "*What!*" again, only much more loudly and rudely than before. And then,

"You don't know what you're talking about!"

"Mr. Harlow—"

Something in her look and manner halted him. It even produced a kind of impatient apology.

"Oh, I'm sorry! But there must be some mistake—she wouldn't go to Deepside if it was the last place on earth—especially now!"

Miss Silver coughed.

"Why do you say that, Mr. Harlow?"

He flung himself into the chair in which Frank had been sitting.

"What's the good of that fellow Abbott? Why didn't he stop her going? Don't you know that Grant Hathaway is in this business up to the neck? Frank Abbott knows it well enough. She had no business to go back! He ought to have stopped her!"

Miss Silver continued to knit. From her tightly netted fringe to her beaded slippers, she presented a perfect picture of the elderly English spinster whose means, like her ideas, are strictly limited, and her position in the social scale such that she may quite safely be ignored or taken for granted. To Mark Harlow she was merely someone to whom he could let off his nervous irritation. She said, "Dear me!" in a tone of mild protest, and he burst out with,

"She ought never to have been allowed to go! Suppose he is arrested while she is there!"

Miss Silver's expression became tinged with surprise.

"Is there any reason to suppose that he will be arrested?"

He went on angrily,

"I should think there was every reason!"

She gazed at him in what he took to be incredulity. He let himself go.

"I should think he was liable to be arrested at any moment! What are her parents thinking about?"

Miss Silver continued to gaze.

"They are dining out. They have not yet returned."

He made an inarticulate sound of anger.

"And that useless fellow Abbott—he must know what they've got against Hathaway if no one else does!"

Miss Silver said, "Oh—" It was the merest breath. And then, "What have they got against him, Mr. Harlow?"

The coffee-tray still stood beside the chair. Almost as if he did not know what he was doing, Mark Harlow filled the cup. Now he gulped down what must have been a nauseous lukewarm brew, milkless and sugarless, and set the cup back rattling on its saucer.

"Plenty, I should say. Not that I want to say anything—but Cis going back to him like this, it makes me mad. Did she tell you I rang up? I wanted to come round and see her then, but she said no, and like a fool I let it go at that. I oughtn't to have taken any notice of what she said. I ought to have come round— I had the strongest feeling—But I didn't want to offend her." He stared blankly at Miss Silver. "I'm in love with her, you know. That doesn't matter—I'm not thinking about that. It's Cis that matters—and that damned fellow Grant."

Miss Silver knitted. After a moment she said,

"What makes you think that Mr. Hathaway may be responsible for these two murders?"

He went on staring gloomily.

"It's not what I think—it's the police. All I care about is Cis getting involved."

"And what do the police think?"

He jerked a shoulder.

"They don't tell me, but it's pretty obvious, isn't it? It's the most damnable luck my having run into him at the Bull. I couldn't do less than offer him a lift, and look what it's dragged me into! I've had to tell the police that I left him in the bar, and that we had to wait for him. He turned up late, and he was putting something in his pocket. I haven't the slightest doubt that it was the lighter which this Rogers woman said she saw him looking for in the yard. On the top of that she comes down here after him. Well, I ask you!"

"She came down here after him?"

"It looks like that, doesn't it? I suppose Caddle and I ought to be thankful it was his name and address that she got hold of and not mine, or the police might be trying to stick it on to one of us. We were both in France along with about a million other people, and we were both at the Bull that night. But it was Grant Hathaway she came down here to see—and that lets us out."

"How exceedingly shocking!"

203

Miss Silver did indeed look as if she had received a shock. For the moment she had even ceased to knit. Her hands were motionless upon the cloud of pale pink wool.

"So you can understand why I'm worried about Cis."

Even in the midst of the distressing thoughts which were crowding in upon her, Miss Silver was able to feel distaste for this continued use of the diminutive. That young people nowadays rushed straight into Christian names was a mere commonplace of fashion, but that intimate "Cis" could still offend her. Even Monica Abbott did not use it as freely as that. She said,

"Oh dear ! Do you really think that Mr. Hathaway—"

"It isn't my business to think about Grant. I'm worried to death about Cis."

"Do you think Mr. Hathaway saw her when she came down—this Mrs. Rogers?"

He looked at her without troubling to conceal his contempt.

"Well, he must have done. He couldn't very well have murdered her if he hadn't."

"But you don't know that he saw her?"

He gave an angry laugh.

"There's such a thing as guessing! I can make a very intelligent guess!"

CHAPTER 32

Cicely drove up the dark Lane. She drove slowly, because now that she was clear of Abbottsleigh she was not quite ready to arrive at Deepside. She had wanted to get away before the parents came home, she didn't want to meet them. But she didn't know how she was going to meet Grant—and, as a stupid anticlimax, Mrs. Barton. However much you would like to conduct your private affairs in a vacuum, the domestic hearth is full of eyes, the spot you live in is full of ears, especially if it is a village. Relations and friends expect to have things explained to them, and if you have a housekeeper you have at least to tell her where you are going to sleep.

Cicely crawled up the Lane, fortifying herself. Her own thoughts left no room for what otherwise might have been the macabre suggestion that here or hereabouts Louise Rogers had been violently done to death, and not so far away to the left her body had lain under a pile of leaves between a Friday and a Saturday evening.

Any attention which she had to spare was taken up by Bramble, who stood on his hind legs and leaned out of the window giving short yelps and moans of excitement. At intervals she said, "No, Bramble!" and he turned round to lick the air rapidly in the direction of her shoulder before resuming what amounted to a running commentary upon their return. There was certainly no need to tell him that they were going home. His sleeping-box, complete with its paper mattress and its blankets, reposed upon the back seat. He hadn't the slightest doubt as to where they were going, and his quivering anticipation knew no bounds.

The back gate stood open as it always did. She drove slowly up to the side of the house and stopped there. She would have to get the key of the garage. She put the window up and slipped out on her own side, shutting the door quickly on Bramble, who did his best to slip out too and very nearly brought it off. She said "No!" several times very firmly, and left him there moaning with his nose pressed tightly up against the glass. Just for the moment she didn't want him at her heels, or bounding joyously on ahead to bark and hurl himself at the nearest door. It had just occurred to her that she didn't know how late it was, and that Mrs. Barton would probably have gone to bed. Suppose she was asleep, and Grant was asleep. It would be the most humiliating flop if she had to turn round and go back to Abbottsleigh. Of course she needn't because she still had her latch-key safe in the flap of her crocodile purse, only if Grant had shot the bolt, the latch-key wouldn't help her to get in.

She crossed the front of the house, passed the main door with its pillared porch and the three steps going up to it, and came round the corner to the opposite side from where she had left the car. If Grant was up he would be in the study, and if he was in the study she would be able to see the light through the curtains. She might even be able to see into the room, because those curtains were devils. Someone had economized over the stuff when they were made, and they weren't really full enough. If you got them to meet in the middle, it was ten to one they left a gap at the side, and if that snake Agnes had gone blinding off to Lenton, it was pretty certain no one would have had time to bother very much about them tonight.

She drew a quick breath of relief. The study was lighted. Both windows showed a glow, and the left-hand one, which was a door, a long gold streak. Her heart began to beat rather hard as she came up to it and looked in. There was all the strangeness of a dream about standing outside her own house and looking in. Just for a moment it made her feel like a ghost. Then something warm rushed over her and she was Cicely Hathaway and very much alive.

Grant was there. He could only just have come in, because he was wearing his old raincoat. What she had just seen was a bit of the sleeve moving as he crossed the room. The gap in the curtain showed her no more than a handsbreadth of the opposite wall and what lay between that wall and the window. She could see the width of the old dark wallpaper, the edge of a heavy gold picture -frame, the jut of the black marble mantelshelf, and, right in the middle of the space, the blue Chinese bowl which she had filled with *pot-pourri*. She remembered gathering the roses and drying them—all the same kind, Hugh Dickson, because he kept his scent better than any of the others. She had filled two bowls and put them one on either side of the mantelpiece because it wanted cheering up, with that dark paper, and the quite forbidding portrait of old Mr. Hathaway's grandfather glooming down on the room. She couldn't see the portrait, only the edge of the frame and the bowl of *pot-pourri*. And then she couldn't see the bowl, because a shoulder and arm and a lot of raincoat came between. The shoulder moved, the arm moved, the raincoat moved. There was a patch on the outside of the sleeve just above the elbow—quite a new patch, showing dark against the weather-bleached stuff. She wondered about the patch, and about what Grant was doing over there by the mantelpiece. His arm had lifted, as if he were doing something to the bowl of *pot-pourri*. But she couldn't see what he was doing, she couldn't see his hand.

And then all at once she had a horrid cold feeling. She didn't want to stand there looking in any more. She didn't want Grant to know that she had stood there looking in. She stepped back softly and ran for the corner. There was a flower-bed next to the house. She kept on the grass verge and made no sound, but she was shaking when she turned the corner and felt in her purse for the key. Mrs. Barton was almost sure to have gone to bed, but the door wouldn't be bolted, because Grant always did that the last thing. She stood just inside the porch and groped for the key. Her fingers shook. She groped for the key, and it wasn't there.

She felt a blank astonishment, because it had always been there, in the outer flap which wasn't used for anything else. She couldn't remember when she had actually seen it last, but it had always been there. It ought to be there now, but it wasn't. She had the feeling you get when you miss a step in the dark. It isn't a nice feeling. And on the top of that the feeling of being a ghost came back—a ghost locked out.

Well, there were two things she could do. If Mrs. Barton wasn't in bed, there would be a light somewhere at the back of the house. It might be in her bedroom, or in the sitting-room, or in the kitchen. If there was a light downstairs, she would hear the front door bell. If the light was upstairs, or if there wasn't a light at all, Cicely would just have to go back and knock on the study window, and she didn't want to. Quite inexplicably and unreasonably she didn't want to. She didn't even want to go back past the study window, but she made herself do it, because if she went round the other way she would have to pass the car, and Bramble would probably start screaming. She went as she had come, keeping to the grass.

Just as she was level with the study window, the light went out. She ran the rest of the way. Idiotic to be startled by a light going out in your own house, but she ran until she had to stop and grope her way under an arch heavy with ivy which gave upon the herb garden at the back of the house. There was a straggling ivy hedge, and a rickety gate under the arch. She had to stop and grope for the latch. Then when she was through, there were some evergreen shrubs to clear before she could get a good view of the windows. The kitchen was dark, but beyond it there was a chink of light at the edge of the sitting-room window. The sight was comfortable beyond all belief. In a revulsion of feeling she told herself just what an idiot she was and went briskly on round the house to collect her suit-case and Bramble.

After he had pounced and tried to lick her face he rushed joyously ahead, giving short excited screams and occasionally coming back to bite her ankles. The whole business of being shut out and feeling like a ghost now seemed too silly for words. Bramble certainly hadn't the slightest doubt about the joyfulness of the occasion. At the sound of footsteps approaching on the other side of the door he hurled himself against it, barking at the top of his voice.

208

Mrs. Barton hesitated for no more than a moment. Alone in the house she might be, and with two murders in the neighbourhood you did stop to think before you opened your door as late as this. But if it wasn't that Bramble dog pouncing and barking fit to burst his way in, then she'd lost the use of her lawful senses, which was a thing they'd never had in their family, thank God. She opened the door, and was overwhelmed, partly by a flurry of black dachshund nipping her ankles, pulling at her skirts, and making as much noise as half a dozen, and partly by the astonishing sight of the suit-case and Mrs. Grant Hathaway. She saw them in that order, and was bereft of speech.

It was Cicely who said very clearly and with a kind of young dignity,

"How are you, Mrs. Barton? I'm afraid it's rather late to arrive, but I have only just heard about Agnes and I thought I had better come home."

Mrs. Barton again thanked God, and was never certain whether she had done it aloud or not. She did not know when she had ever felt so much fervent relief. There was nothing that would put such a stop to people talking as for Mrs. Grant to come back to where she belonged—and a very proper answer to that Agnes and her mad goings on. There wasn't anyone could believe what there wasn't any call for them to believe—not with Mrs. Grant showing them like this.

Before she could assemble seemly words of welcome Cicely was saying,

"Mr. Grant will bring in Bramble's box and put the car away. I'll just go and tell him we're here."

Mrs. Barton looked distressed.

"But he isn't in. There's one of those Jersey calves not too good. He said he'd be late. That's why I'm up myself. I didn't fancy going to bed and the house not locked up properly."

Cicely stared.

"But, Mrs. Barton, there was a light in the study just now. I came round that way."

She walked past her into the hall and set the suit-case down. Then quite suddenly she ran round the corner and down the passage leading to the study. She ran, because if she stopped to think, it wasn't going to be easy to tell Grant that she had come back. She didn't stop to think. She ran down the passage and opened the door on a dark and empty room.

CHAPTER 33

Cicely's homecoming had fallen very flat indeed. She had braced herself for a scene, and there wasn't going to be any scene, because Grant wasn't there. It was the one possibility which had never crossed her mind. There ought to have been a scene, and there were all sorts of different ways in which it might have been played. Grant might have been angry, in which case the sparks would have flown, and oh, what a relief that would have been after bottling everything up for months. Or he might have been frightfully touched and grateful about her rushing back when he was in trouble. An odious small devil-imp cocked a snook at her out of a dark corner in her own mind and said, "So damn likely!" Well then, he would have been angry, or—Cicely didn't like the "or" very much, because he might have just been polite on top and sarcastic underneath, in which case she would have had to be polite and sarcastic too, and she wasn't as good at it as Grant was. Now there wasn't going to be a scene at all. Grant would just peter back into the house and sleep like a log, and scenes before breakfast are really only possible to the cold, vindictive, persevering type of nagger. All that would happen now would be Grant raising his eyebrows and saying, "You've come back?" and Cicely saying something on the lines of "As you see," and going off to help Mrs. Barton make the beds. All the time she was putting away the car and getting Bramble's sleeping-box in she was kicking herself for having come back when Grant was out, and turning her back on the oddest sensation of relief.

It was no good, the relief persisted, she couldn't down it. From the moment she had looked in through the gap in the study curtains she had had cold feet about the whole thing. If she could have put the clock back half an hour she wouldn't have come at all. Or would she? She didn't know. She knew perfectly well. She didn't want to see Grant. But you can't put the clock back ever. She couldn't put hers back now—not when it meant explaining to Mrs. Barton, and then going back and explaining to Miss Silver, and Frank, and the parents.

She came into the hall with Bramble's box and went upstairs. Mrs. Barton followed her.

"Mr. Grant must have stepped in for something and then stepped out again—that's how you must have come to see a light in the study. He could have come in with his key and gone out again, and I shouldn't have heard him down the other end of the house. Now I've a nice kettle on, and I've filled two of the stone bottles whilst you've been gone, and your bed shouldn't be damp, for I've aired it regularly. One of the last things I got that Agnes to do was to light a fire in your room yesterday and have the mattress out in front of it, so it shouldn't be damp. And I've got your sheets down by the kitchen fire."

Cicely would rather have slept in any other room, but the mattress was against her. You can't fling an aired mattress back in a housekeeper's face, especially when she's been thirty years longer in the house than you have.

She went into the big low-ceilinged room with its bow-window and its big stripped bed and found it bleak beyond words. The bright chintz curtains were drawn. Everything was quite dreadfully clean, and tidy, and bare. Nothing on the dressing-table, because months ago she had swept it clear with angry, shaking hands. Nothing in the wardrobe, or in the wall-cupboard where she used to keep her shoes. Nothing in the two chests of drawers. Nothing to show that Cicely Hathaway had ever come here as a bride and been quite terribly happy. There wasn't any happiness in the room now. There wasn't any unhappiness either—just a blank, empty feeling.

Mrs. Barton went down to fetch the sheets.

The minute his box was in its accustomed corner Bramble hurled himself into it and had to be pulled out again. This happened every night. He lay on his back, waved his paws, and gazed at her with melting eyes. She had to grope for the back of his neck and lift him out like a dead rabbit, after which he stood and watched his bed being made—well crumpled newspaper and a small blanket over it. At this point he was allowed to take a flying leap and curl himself up. Then a loose inner blanket, and a large outer one which went over and under the box, so that he could turn round without uncovering himself.

When he had given an ecstatic sigh and at once plunged into sleep, Cicely got to her feet and went over to the door of Grant's dressing-room. She remembered the cold feel of the key against her palm when she locked it. It was the last thing she had done before she left the house. She turned the handle now. The door was still locked. She pulled her hand away quickly and went to meet Mrs. Barton and the sheets.

It was midnight before Grant came home. She heard him cross the hall and come up the stairs. He walked as if he was tired. She wondered what he would say if she were to open her door and look out. It was what she would have done before the crash. She would have run to the door and said, "Oh, darling, how late! What will you have—coffee, or cocoa?" If it was as cold as this, he would say, "Cocoa."

And she would say, "The water's hot if you would like a bath." All those homely things which were part of being married.

She heard him go into his room and take off his boots. Extraordinary how much noise men contrived to make with their boots. Bramble gave a faint woof, a long way off in a dream. Grant was making too much noise to hear it, and anyhow the door was locked.

Presently there was silence on the other side of the locked door. Cicely lay in the big bed with two hot water-bottles and was perfectly comfortable and warm. Bramble slept. On the other side of the door Grant Hathaway slept. The night was cold and still. Cicely hadn't the slightest excuse for not going to sleep, but sleep refused to come. She heard the clock in the hall strike one, and two, and three.

Then, with no apparent transition, she was walking on a long, straight road which went away over an empty moor. It was dark, but that doesn't matter in a dream. She could see it ahead of her, going on, and on, and on. There wasn't a light, there wasn't a house, there wasn't even a star. There wasn't anyone else on the road. There was only Cicely Hathaway— Cicely Evelyn Hathaway—and she was all alone. Something blew against her face, and she knew it was her wedding-veil, only in the dream there was such a lot of it. It blew against her in muffling folds. She had to say, "I, Cicely Evelyn, take thee, Edward Grant—to have and to hold— from this day forward—for better, for worse," but the veil choked her. She couldn't speak, and she couldn't get her breath.

She woke sweating, with the sheet over her face and a horrid cold dawn coming up behind lead-coloured clouds. She turned away from it and went to sleep again.

CHAPTER 34

It was broad daylight when she woke again, and Grant was gone.

"Just swallowed his breakfast and out of the house with no time for anything."

Cicely sat up in bed and looked with dismay at Mrs. Barton in a dark blue overall spotted with white.

"Does he know I'm here?"

Mrs. Barton shook her head.

"Not without you told him." She crossed over to the blanketed box in the corner. "I should have thought that Bramble would have been up seeing what was what."

Cicely felt small, and cold, and lost. She murmured,

"Not an early riser—he doesn't care about it. But he ought to go out now. Will you call him?"

She dressed, breakfasted, and plunged into housework. The morning stretched before her like the endless path of her dream.

Monica Abbott rang up, obviously torn between a desire for confidences and the ever present possibility of Maggie Bell.

"Darling, how sudden! But I do hope you didn't sleep in a damp bed. They must all be wringing wet."

How exactly like Mummy to harp on beds. Cicely said,

"You'd better not let Mrs. Barton hear you say so. Mine had just spent a whole day in front of a fire."

"Cis—"

Cicely's voice had been casual. It now became that of a dreadfully polite stranger.

214

"Is there anything you really want? Because if not, I've got rather a lot to do here."

She heard Monica steady herself to say,

"No—no—nothing—it was just—" The sentence died there and the receiver clicked.

Cicely gave an exasperated sigh. Why on earth couldn't the people who loved you let you alone? She plunged back into housework, embarking on turning out the drawing-room, which hadn't been used since she went away. It languished in dust sheets and half-drawn blinds after the fashion of Mrs. Barton's youth, and reminded Cicely quite dreadfully of a morgue. Not, of course, that she had ever seen a morgue, but it gave her the same kind of feeling. There was quite a lot to do.

Grant came home at one. He met Bramble on the doorstep, and Cicely in the hall. She had just finished the stairs, which she had left to the last because they wouldn't really matter for once if she was put to it, and stood up very pale with the dustpan in one hand and a brush in the other. There was a moment when they couldn't have heard themselves speak, and another when Bramble's ecstatic screams of welcome were dying down.

Grant stood there frowning and looked at her. Then he said,

"What's all this?"

"I'm house-parlourmaid."

"And just what do you mean by that?"

"Agnes has gone, hasn't she? I heard last night. I thought I had better come back and help Mrs. Barton."

"When did you come?"

"Oh, last night—"

He gave her a long, hard look. Something inside her was shaking. What she would have liked to do was to sit down on the bottom step and burst into tears. Naturally she would rather have died. The sound of the telephone bell came as a blessed relief. Grant stopped looking at her and went off to the study with Bramble at his heels. Cicely put down the dustpan and brush and began to dust.

In about two minutes Grant came back, bleak and angry. This time he didn't look at her at all. His voice was like a northeast wind.

"You'd better go back to Abbottsleigh. You shouldn't have come."

"Why?"

"Because I say so."

She said, "Why?" again.

"If you had a grain of sense you would know why. You've been away for months, and you choose this time to come back!"

"Why shouldn't I?"

She was warming a little. If he could be angry, she could be angry too. But when he spoke again her anger dropped down dead between them.

"Because it's quite on the cards that I'm going to be arrested."

"Grant!"

"That was Lenton police station. They want me there. I said I'd be out by two—I can't make it before. I'm the leading suspect, you know. Joe Turnberry has been hanging about all the morning—to see I don't give them the slip, I imagine. I should think it is well on the cards that I shall be detained, if not arrested, this afternoon. You'd better get out and stay out."

She stood up straight and said,

"That's why I came back."

He gave a sudden hard laugh.

"I'm a fortune-hunter, but not a murderer—is that it? Quite a gesture, Cis, but I can't do with it. Better go home—there's nothing for you here. Do you mind asking Mrs. Barton to let me have something to eat—anything that's ready. I want to see Johnson again before I go off. He may have to manage on his own for a bit."

216

And that was all. The rest was a horrid meal, a few words about the calf which had hurt a leg but was doing all right now—nothing that came near to touching either of them, until at the end he looked back from the door as he was going out and said,

"Get along back to Abbottsleigh, Cis. Mrs. Barton can have someone up from the village for company if I'm kept."

"I'd rather stay here."

She was standing between her pushed-back chair and the table. She saw him frown.

"I'd rather you didn't. Get along back before it's dark!"

And with that he went out and shut the door. The front door banged.

When they had washed up together Mrs. Barton put on her coat and hat and walked down to the corner to catch the bus into Deeping, a saving of three-quarters of a mile over the straight walk down the Lane. Cicely's offer to run her down in the car was refused.

"I should prefer to be independent, Mrs. Grant. And the rain is nothing—I've my waterproof and a good umbrella, so I'll just be off. Annie Stedman will be very suitable to replace Agnes, and I know she would like to come. She's my second cousin Lydia Wood's daughter and a sensible age. She's with Mrs. Martin at the post office whilst she looks about her. It's not every situation she'd take, but no later than Saturday she was saying what a pity we hadn't a vacancy here. But I wouldn't like you to think that had anything to do with my giving Agnes her notice. Just is just, and I had no fault to find with her work. But she overstepped, and that is a thing I couldn't put up with— I've seen too much of where it leads to. So I gave her her notice."

Cicely said, "You were perfectly right," and Mrs. Barton departed, panoplied in virtue and able with an equable mind to combine family feeling and her duty to her employer.

Cicely watched her go and turned back to the empty house. She hadn't the slightest intention of returning to Abbottsleigh. When Grant came back they would have it out. If he didn't come back—she faltered over that, but forced herself to say it—if there was any frightful mistake and they wouldn't let him come back, then it was her place to be here looking after things whilst he was away.

With Mrs. Barton gone, she had a feeling of relief. The house was all hers. She could go where she liked and do what she pleased, with no one but Bramble to watch her.

She went all over the house. If Agnes was a snake she was a good worker. The house was one of those rambling, untidy structures which have been built on to piece by piece. There was a whole top floor which hadn't been used in two generations— five rooms opening one into the other, and the farthest room stacked with old furniture which they had always meant to go through, only they had never done it because there were so many other things to do and all the time in the world ahead of them. She stood looking in. They still had all that time. Something said, "No." Her foot wouldn't cross the threshold. She shut the door and ran down the steep attic stair.

Even up here there wasn't any dust. Agnes had done her job. Cicely wondered about Agnes—where she was, and how she had overstepped, and why she had gone into Lenton to tell the police about Grant. It came to her suddenly and sharply that Agnes mattered. If she went on saying that Louise Rogers had come here to see Grant and to accuse him—if she went on saying that she hadn't seen Grant or heard him about the house after Louise Rogers left, then the police were going to think, and everyone else was going to think, that Grant had killed Louise. Up till this moment the shock of indignation had numbed her perception of his real danger. She had been taken up with the situation as it affected their intimate personal relation. Now, sharply and clearly, there emerged the fact that if Agnes stuck to her evidence there would be a serious case against Grant.

All at once it became intolerable just to stay here and wait. Mrs. Barton would get back before it was dark, but that wasn't what mattered. When would Grant come back? Why hadn't she made him take her with him? She could have sat in the car and waited, and she would at least have known what was going on. If they arrested Grant, they would have to come and tell her. You can't just leave someone sitting outside in a car and not come and say that you have arrested her husband. What was the good of saying why hadn't she made Grant take her? You couldn't make Grant do things—it was like pushing a stone wall. And leaving her sitting outside a police station whilst he was being arrested was the sort of thing which would be likely to reinforce the stone with chilled steel. She knew very well that she couldn't have made him take her into Lenton.

The afternoon dragged unbelievably. She could have taken Bramble for a walk, but she couldn't bring herself to be out of earshot of the telephone. Grant might ring up. Or Frank. If it was Frank, that would be bad news. She let Bramble out, and presently let him in again. It was rather a relief when he went and scratched at the kitchen door. She opened it for him and watched him make himself comfortable in the armchair. Presently when Mrs. Barton came home she would scold him, and he would put his head on one side, lift a paw, and sparkle his eyes at her. Very undermining. Mrs. Barton was being systematically undermined. She had been heard in a weak moment to address the creature as "Darling."

Cicely left him to it and made her way to the study. If the telephone bell rang, she would only have to cross the room. She thought it must ring soon. It seemed a long time since she had heard the clock in the hall strike three.

She made up the fire. Grant would be coming in cold. As she straightened up from putting on a log she met the portrait's gloomy frown—old Mr. Hathaway's grandfather. Funny how she always thought of him like that, because he was Grant's great-grandfather, and sometimes when Grant was angry they had the frown in common. The portrait was practically all frown. Everything else had got swallowed up in a general murk.

The frown dominated the room. She looked away from it to her bowls of *pot-pourri*. She remembered them in August, full of the fresh red roseleaves, gay against the blue and white of the Chinese bowls and so sweet that you could smell them as soon as you opened the door. She put her nose down to the left-hand bowl now. That's what Grant must have been doing when she looked through the curtain last night. The dried roseleaves weren't gay any more, but they were still sweet. She put her hand down into the bowl to stir them up, and felt something hard. Just for a moment everything stopped—feeling, pulse, breath, thought. Then automatically her thumb and forefinger closed on the hard thing they had touched. Her hand moved and came up out of the bowl with a round bright ring, a little dusty from the roseleaves. It was the eternity earring.

CHAPTER 35

In the Superintendent's office at Lenton police station Chief Inspector Lamb read over the statements in the case. If it is asked where the Superintendent was, he was in bed with a chill, and very sorry for himself as far as that went, but perhaps not so sorry to be out of an affair which threatened to involve two highly respected local families.

Lamb went through his sergeant's neatly typed sheets from one end to the other, his face without expression, his big fingers turning the pages methodically and without haste. When he had finished he looked up and said in measured tones,

"I thought I'd come to him with everything fresh in my mind, but it makes no difference—looks worse if anything. The Commissioner was surprised we hadn't made the arrest. Gave me the feeling I'd made a fool of myself, going up there with the papers and getting that. 'What are you waiting for?' he said. 'An eyewitness? They come a bit short in murder cases.' "

He sat there with his bowler hat a little on the back of his head and his big overcoat taken off and thrown over the arm of a chair. He had been up to town and down again since breakfast. Outside a grey, cold day was settling into rain. But the police know how to make themselves good fires. The Superintendent's office was hot enough to remind Lamb of his mother's kitchen on baking day. He took off his hat and tossed it over on to the coat.

"Well," he said, "we'd better have him in. I don't quite know why you got him over here, but it'll save us going to get him."

Frank Abbott said, "Just a moment, sir—"

"Well, what is it?"

"Just something Miss Silver asked me to pass on."

He got a suspicious look, and a quick "Well, well—out with it! Pack of nonsense, I expect."

"That is for you to judge, sir. Mark Harlow came up to Abbottsleigh last night—he does quite often drop in in the evenings. He likes to play over his stuff to my cousin Cicely Hathaway—she's musical, you know. Well, last night he didn't see her, because she'd packed up and gone home."

Lamb pricked up his ears.

"How do you mean, gone home?"

"A gesture. It had come to her notice that things were rather piling up against Grant Hathaway, so she packed a bag and went home." This was thin ice. He skated on rapidly. "So Mark didn't get as far as playing the piano, but he did have a heart-to-heart talk with our Miss Silver. If you want to know why, I've got my own ideas."

Lamb gave a formidable grunt.

"Where's all this getting to?"

"I'm telling you, sir. Harlow seemed very much upset at the idea of Cicely going back to her husband—said that Grant was in this business up to the neck, that I knew it, and that I had no business to let my cousin go back to him. He said I ought to have stopped her. I may say that nobody could possibly have stopped her. Miss Silver asked him what made him think Hathaway was going to be arrested, and he gave her his version of the affair at the Bull, with a fancy touch about Grant putting something in his pocket when he turned up late at the car. Mark said he hadn't the slightest doubt it was the lighter which 'this Rogers woman'—his expression—said she saw him looking for in the yard. Harlow then said, 'On the top of that she comes down here after him. Well, I ask you!' Miss Silver echoed his words discreetly, and he enlarged upon them. He said, 'I suppose Caddle and I ought to be thankful it was his address she got hold of and not mine, or the police might be trying to stick it on to one of us. We were both in France along with about a million other people, and we were both at the Bull that night. But it was Grant Hathaway she came down here to see—and that lets us out.' " He made an impressive pause.

The Chief Inspector's eyes bulged.

"And what are you and Miss Silver cooking up out of this? Sounds like a lot of tittle-tattle to me."

"Yes, sir. But who told Harlow that Louise came down here to see Grant Hathaway? How many people knew about it? You and I and Smith, Hathaway himself, and Agnes Ripley—that's the lot. Which of them told Mark Harlow? Not you, or I, or Smith. Miss Silver asked me that at once—had we told Harlow that Louise Rogers had got hold of Grant's name and address on a dropped envelope—that she had come down here to see him, and that he admitted having an interview with her not very long before she was murdered. I said most definitely we had not. Did Agnes Ripley tell him? She had her scene with Grant about five o'clock yesterday evening and came blinding out here. Not likely she told anyone before that. She had a crush on him—she only talked because he turned her down, and she came straight out here to us. Can you believe for a moment that she had any communication with Mark Harlow? She was more or less in a state of collapse when I took her round to her friend Mrs. Parsons. That leaves Grant Hathaway. Why should he tumble over himself to tell Harlow that he had had a highly compromising interview with Louise? And if he didn't tell him, there's only one person who could have told him, and that is Louise herself."

Lamb maintained a perfectly stolid gaze. That this was often a screen behind which the mind worked forcibly and intelligently, Frank was well aware. He was not therefore discouraged. He stopped talking himself and awaited results.

After a considerable pause a remark arrived on a growling note.

"Might be something in it—might be nothing at all. We don't know enough about Agnes Ripley to say right off that she wouldn't have told Harlow. If they were strangers, it isn't likely. If there was any link, she might. She was in that state when she might have done anything. I don't think the ordinary rules would apply. She wanted to hit back at Hathaway. The same thing that made her come to us might have made her want to damage him with his friends. It's all of a piece with the thing that makes people write anonymous letters. I won't say it's likely she rang Harlow up, but I won't rule it out." He shifted in his chair and went on speaking slowly and impressively. "I won't rule out Hathaway either. He might very easily have rung Harlow up himself. Say it was this way. Louise Rogers asks him about the men he was with at the Bull—if she didn't recognise Hathaway himself she'd have asked him about the others, wouldn't she? She'd made up her mind it was one of those three—well, she'd ask about the other two."

A faint gleam came into Frank Abbott's eye.

"You are supposing that Grant is innocent?"

Not a muscle of Lamb's face moved.

"Just for the purposes of argument. Take it she asks who the others are, and he tells her. She goes off in her car. He might ring up a neighbour and warn him that trouble is on the way. She could have bumped into Caddle going in by the back way past the garage, or she could have bumped into Harlow, if he knew she was coming."

"And Albert's alibi?"

The Chief Inspector waved it away.

Frank Abbott said, "That theory doesn't seem to come out so very different from Miss Silver's, sir. If Grant was the murderer he'd hardly have rung Harlow up. So we're back at Harlow's knowledge that Grant had had an interview with Louise being guilty knowledge."

"That's going a bit far."

Frank leaned forward.

"Look, sir—Harlow knows what no one outside the police, Hathaway, and one witness knows. It's guilty knowledge, because he must have linked it up with the murder. Why didn't he give it to the police? He didn't know that we knew."

Lamb grunted.

"Friendly with Mrs. Hathaway. People do keep things to themselves. If he's guilty, why did he let it out to Miss Silver like that?"

"He was a good deal worked up, and—you know how it is when you don't know her—I expect he thought she was negligible. If he'd been talking to you, or even to me, he'd have watched his step, but just Miss Silver, sitting there and knitting, he let himself go and slipped up. What he was trying to put across was the idea that Hathaway was the murderer, and—he slipped up."

The Chief Inspector said,

"H'm—" Then after an interval of some length, "Putting Agnes Ripley on one side for the moment, it is difficult to reconcile Harlow's knowledge with Hathaway's guilt. If Hathaway were guilty he would not have informed Harlow that he had seen Louise Rogers. He might have rung him up if he was innocent. We'll have him in and ask him if he did. We will also ask Harlow how he knew that Hathaway had seen Louise. We can't count on either of them telling the truth, but now and again there's quite a lot of information to be got out of a lie. Just step along and ask Mr. Hathaway to come in."

CHAPTER 36

As her hand came up, Cicely turned quite automatically and instinctively to the light. It was rather dark in the study, because outside the clouds were low and it was raining—not hard, but with the fine drizzle which thickens the air. Even before she turned she could see what she was holding. She saw the earring, a quite round platinum ring set continuously with small bright diamonds. She saw it, but it didn't mean anything yet. There had been some kind of a shock, and the part of her that was going to think about the earring wasn't doing its job—it wasn't thinking. It left her to her eyes, which went on looking at the round, bright ring. Somewhere deep down inside her she was afraid.

She looked at the ring. It was about three-quarters of an inch across. There was the mark of an almost invisible hinge at one side and a tiny catch at the other. They wouldn't show at all when the earring was on.

With a piercing suddenness thought began again. This was the missing ring. Louise Rogers had worn a pair of eternity earrings, and Mary Stokes had seen the murderer tossing over the dead girl's hair to look for the one that wasn't there. He hadn't found it. Slowly and draggingly her mind repeated the word "then." He hadn't found it—then. Had he found it afterwards? The body had been hidden in the wood. It had lain there between Friday and Saturday evening. She thought he would have gone back to the place where it had been and looked for the earring, turning the leaves to and fro as he had turned the dead girl's hair. He would go on looking for it until he had found it.

Her thought halted there—seeing the dark trees, the dark wood, and a hand going to and fro, turning the leaves.

Whose hand?

He would have had a torch—dark wet leaves dazzling under the light—the ring dazzling—

He must have found it, because it was here—she had it in her hand. The deep-down thing that was afraid began to rise up towards the surface of her mind, like a bubble coming up through dark water. All at once she was shaking. She had seen Grant in this room last night—Grant with his back to her over by the mantelpiece, lifting his arm, doing something to the bowl of *pot-pourri*. She had wondered then if he was stirring it. It was that recollection which had put it into her mind to stir it now. The picture rose quick—the raincoat with the new patch upon the sleeve, the movement of the shoulder and the arm.

Something in her said, "No!" It was a thing she couldn't believe. There are things you can believe, and things you can't. She stopped shaking. There was nothing to shake about. The thing which had said "No!" spoke again quite loudly and firmly. It said, "Grant isn't such a fool." Of course it ought to have been, "Grant isn't a murderer." Perhaps that was just taken as said.

What the voice kept repeating in tones of scorn was, "Grant isn't such a fool." Would he, would anyone, bring a thing like that into his own house and keep it there? It had only been brought last night. The body already found, the other earring in the hands of the police—what sort of a fool would you have to be to bring the missing ring home with you and hide it in your own room, when you could drop it in the Lane or in the wood and be safely quit of it?

She was still looking at the earring. The light changed on it, darkened. With a little click the right-hand window which was a door swung in. She looked up and saw Mark Harlow come into the room. His raincoat glistened and there were beads of moisture in his dark hair. He said,

"I did ring, but I couldn't make anyone hear."

She said, "No—Grant's in Lenton and Mrs. Barton has gone down into the village."

He had an agitated air.

"Cis—I had to see you—"

At the first sound she had closed her hand. The ring was hard against her palm. Her "Oh!" was just the escape of startled breath.

He said, "I'm too wet—I'll get rid of my coat," and went towards the door.

It was then she saw the new dark patch on his sleeve. She saw it as he turned—shoulder and sleeve of a raincoat, and a new dark patch on the sleeve. Everything in her mind became quite clear and plain. She had been groping in the dark, but now there was a very cold, bright light. She said,

"No, Mark—wait! It doesn't matter about the wet. I want to speak to you."

He turned. She thought he was surprised. Perhaps it was something in her voice. She looked at him, and remembered that they had been friends, and remembered that he had said he loved her. The words she had been going to speak wouldn't come. She

227

tried for them, but they wouldn't come. She heard herself say,

"You could have let yourself in—you've got my key, haven't you? Will you let me have it back?"

He looked so exactly the same. How could you do—that sort of thing—and go on looking the same? He looked just the same. He said,

"Your key?"

"You took it out of my bag. I'd like to have it back."

"I?"

"Yes, Mark. You let yourself in last night, didn't you? You see, I came back while you were here—I saw you."

"Cis!"

"I was going to let myself in, but my key was gone, so I did what you did just now, I came round to the study window. There was a light inside. The curtain always hangs crooked over that door, so I looked in. I saw you, and I saw what you were doing."

His face changed. It went on changing. The colour went out of it, and the careless, confident look. He said in a voice she had never heard from him,

"There wasn't anything to see."

"I think there was. You see, I saw you. You were over here by the fireplace, and you were putting something into the bowl on the mantelpiece—into the left-hand bowl. I could see your arm going up—I could see the patch on your raincoat. I knew you were doing something to the bowl. I've just found out what it was."

"I don't know what you're talking about."

She felt rather sick—not frightened but just sick, because they had been friends. The thought struggled into words.

"The police will have to know. I'll have to tell them, but I'm telling you first. I thought we were friends—I'm telling you first." She opened her hand and held it out with the earring on the palm.

He looked at it, and looked at her, and went on looking. At last he said,

"So that's the way of it? And you're going to tell the police?"

"I must."

He nodded.

"Of course. And Grant—you'll have to tell Grant. Oh, Cis, what a fool you are!"

She said, "I must—" Her voice wavered.

He gave an impatient jerk.

"Haven't I said 'Of course'? You know, that's where it has you—you don't set out to do things, they do themselves. Something pushes you and you start off, and then you can't stop. It wasn't as if there was any harm in it. It was all just sheer bad luck. A woman with a bag full of diamonds on a road that was being bombed to blazes—she wasn't going to be able to get away with them anyhow. Why, her chances of survival were just about nil. If you'd seen the road choc-a-block and the bombs coming down! And she'd nothing but her flat feet to get away on. I had a motorbike—what was the sense of leaving the diamonds for the Boche?"

"So you took them?"

"Of course I did! Anyone would have! Why, the chances of her surviving—"

"Yes, you said that before. But she did survive."

"It was rotten bad luck. And then, after all these years, for her to turn up again, and to recognise me! Why, she only heard me speak once. She said I swore, and when I dropped that damned lighter at the Bull I swore again, and she said I used the same words and she recognised my voice. And my hands—now, for God's sake, what is there about my hands that a woman who's seen them once should say she could swear to them again?" He stretched them out towards her tense and quivering.

229

Cicely, who had seen them a hundred times, saw them now for the first time as Louise Rogers had seen them—the long, thin forefinger quite overtopping the other two—the thumbs splayed out, splayed back—the abnormal stretch. It seemed to her no longer strange but inevitable that they had been recognized.

He must have read her face. With an angry gesture he drove them deep into the pockets of his raincoat.

"If I hadn't lost my head I'd have told her to go on and do her damnedest. She couldn't have proved a thing. If Grant had rung me up and told me she was coming, if I'd had time to think, if I hadn't been taken by surprise—I owe him something for that—perhaps he'll think of it when he's being paid. It's all been the rottenest luck. I tell you I came out just to get a breath of air, and there was the car coming down the Lane. The headlights caught me, and she stopped. If it hadn't been for that, she'd have gone up to the house, and I'd have been out. You can't fight luck like that. I'd forgotten the whole damned thing—how could I imagine it would crop up again? I tell you it was all forced on me. She stopped the car and put on the light inside. All I saw was a good-looking woman in black. I hadn't the least guess I'd ever seen her before. I went up to the car, and she put the window down and said, 'That gate that you have come out of— what house is there?' I noticed that she had a French accent, but I didn't think anything about it. I said, 'It's called the Grange.' She said, 'That is the name he told me—Mr. Grant Hathaway— the Grange. It is where Mr. Harlow lives—Mr. Mark Harlow?' I said, 'Yes.' She said, 'Are you Mr. Mark Harlow?' and I said I was. She was sitting in the car with the lights on, and I was standing a little way back—not far, you know, but she couldn't really see me. She said, 'You were with Mr. Hathaway and your chauffeur at the Bull at Ledlington at nine o'clock in the evening on January the fourth?' 'Well,' I said, 'suppose I was?' She gave a sort of smile and said, 'Perhaps I saw you there. Perhaps you dropped your cigarette-lighter under my window, and perhaps

I have seen you pick it up.' I thought she was just making a pass at me, so I laughed and said, 'You couldn't have seen me—it was much too dark.' And she laughed and said,'You had a torch—I think perhaps it was you. It was not the Mr. Grant Hathaway who has dropped an envelope with his name and address—that is how I find him.' " He mimicked a French accent, a quick, light way of speech. " 'I have talked with him at his house, and it is not he. So I think perhaps it is you. Come a little near and I will be sure.' I came right up to the car. She had the window down. I put my hand on the ledge. She stared at it and she said, 'O mon dieu—it is you!' I didn't like the way she said it at all. I began to think if I had ever seen her before, and those damned earrings caught my eye. I thought, 'It isn't possible! Nobody's luck could be as rotten as this.' And then she was screaming at me in French, saying I'd taken her jewels, and calling me every dirty name she could lay her tongue to—'Infâme—scélérat—assassin!' Well, I had to stop her, hadn't I? Anyone might have heard her. I knocked her out—what else could I do? And then I finished the job with a stone. I couldn't let her come round and start screaming all over again. It was just the worst luck in the world."

Cicely said nothing at all. Her hand had closed on the earring and dropped to her side. She stood quite still and listened to what sounded like Mark's voice talking about things which couldn't possibly have happened except in a nightmare. The dreadful thing was that he didn't talk about them like that. He talked about them as if they were quite ordinary and natural.

He went on talking.

"I put her in the wood out of the way. And then of course I had to get rid of the car. I took it to Basingstoke and left it outside a garage there, and then I caught the six-twenty back to Lenton and went into the Empire. I walked out to a call-box at half past eight and put through a call to the garage telling them to look after the car for two or three days and I'd pick it up. I don't remember what name I gave—not my own of course. I

231

just didn't want them reporting a stranded car to the police. You see, I thought of everything. I went back and saw the rest of the picture, and walked home. Then of course I had to think out a way of getting rid of the body. I remembered the Forester's House. My uncle had a book with stories about it, written by Miss Grey's father when he was Rector here. I remembered reading them when I was a boy. The last time I stayed here when my uncle was alive we got on to the subject. He took me into the wood and showed me the house. He showed me how to open the catch of the cellar door. He knew about it because his grandmother was a Tomalyn and all the papers about the house came into the family with her. You know, he disputed the title with the Abbotts, but in the end they settled it between them. I expect you knew that."

Cicely said, "Yes."

It might have been quite an ordinary conversation. They might have been talking about any of the things which gave him that familiar intolerant look. They were talking about how he had murdered Louise Rogers and buried her body in the cellar under the Forester's House.

His hands were out of his pockets now. He used one of them to push back his wet hair.

"Then I had my second bit of bad luck. I waited till it was dark and I opened up the cellar and took along the tools I should want. I'd got it all most carefully planned, but you just can't fight your luck. It wasn't any too easy getting the body from where I'd put it, but I managed. I had to put my torch on at the Forester's House to find the doorway, and when the beam fell on her I saw that one of those earrings was gone. That put the wind up me and I started looking for it, and right away I heard someone give a sort of gasp. Well, I knew she was dead, but just for the moment it knocked me out. And then I heard someone running—I tell you she went like a racehorse. By the time I'd pulled myself together and got started I knew

232

I couldn't catch her. I got the body down into the cellar and shut up the door and went home. Whoever it was, couldn't have seen me—I knew that. I sat tight. In an hour or two the whole village was buzzing. Mrs. Green and Lizzie came home full of what Mary Stokes had seen and what everyone was saying about it. Fortunately she'd lied about where she'd seen the body, so they hadn't found anything. I went back in the middle of the night and made a good job of burying it under the cellar floor. I thought I was perfectly safe."

With a sudden change of tone he spoke to Cicely directly. She wasn't just an audience any more. He looked at her and he spoke to her.

"You see how it was." And then, "Why don't you say something?"

Frightful echo of the old Mark. He had given a performance, now he wanted her applause. How and in what words did you applaud murder? She said,

"You thought you were perfectly safe."

She saw him flush angrily.

"And so I would have been if it hadn't been for that damned girl! Everybody thought she had made the whole thing up, or else they thought she'd seen a ghost. She hadn't seen me, and I thought I was perfectly safe. It was the most frightful shock when she came up with the butter and eggs this last Saturday morning and tried to blackmail me."

Saturday the sixteenth—last Saturday . . . So that was what had happened. Mary Stokes had tried to blackmail him—and in the evening she was dead—

He made an impatient movement.

"Of course she was a perfect fool to try it on. I was coming in the back way when she came down from the house. She stopped and said good-morning. I stopped too. I saw her looking at my hands. I didn't try to hide them or anything like that. She went on looking. Then she said just what the other girl said—'So it was you. I thought so.' I said, 'My dear girl, what do you mean?' and she said, 'Come off it! I could swear it was you. Do you want me to?' I said, 'I haven't the faintest idea what you're talking about,' and she said, 'All right, then I'll go and talk about it to the police.' She began to walk on, and when she'd gone a little way she turned her head round over her shoulder and said, 'They'll be interested when I tell them about the cellar, won't they?' Well, of course, I couldn't let her go after that. I said, 'We can't talk here,' and she said, 'Where would you like to talk?' So then we fixed it up. She was going into Lenton, and Joe Turnberry was seeing her home. She said she would go in and shut the door, and when he had cleared off she could slip out again, only she wasn't coming any further than the porch." He gave an angry laugh. "She thought she was being frightfully clever about that—thought she'd be within call of old Stokes in case I got rough. What did she think they taught us in the Army?" He laughed again. "She never had a chance to call out. She never even knew I was there until she felt my hands round her throat."

Cicely shuddered from head to foot—just the one long shudder. Then the cold again, and the stiffness. It was Mark who was saying these things—Mark. He went on saying them.

"I couldn't possibly let her go round tattling, could I? You must see that. From beginning to end the whole thing was forced on me—absolutely. I don't see how anyone can blame me. It was just sheer bad luck—you must see that." He paused, and then said in exactly the same voice, "And now there's you."

Cicely said, "Yes—"

He threw out his hands.

"What on earth did you want to come back here for? I couldn't possibly have foreseen that you would do a thing like that! Grant was absolutely certain to be arrested as soon as the police found out that he had seen this Rogers woman, and then they were bound to search the house. And when they did that they would find the missing earring. It was dropped when I shifted the body. I went back and looked for it as soon as it was safe, and there it was. I thought it would come in useful—and it's going to."

Cicely repeated the last words.

"It's going to?"

"Of course. They'll find it clutched in your hand. That will make everything quite clear—you came on it by chance, and he killed you."

Cicely said, "He?"

"Grant of course. He killed the other two, and he killed you because you found out. Then he'll hang. That was part of the plan. I had to get him out of the way. I wanted to marry you— I really did want to marry you."

A quick, tingling life was driving away the stiffness and the cold. Kill her, and hang Grant—brush them out of his way as if they were a couple of flies . . . Everything in her rose up to make a fight for it. She was less than two yards from the writing-table. It was large and massive. If she could get to it and dodge round it she might be able to get out through the glass door, and then—

She would have no chance in the open. Make time—make as much time as you can—someone might come—

She said, "I don't call that very clever."

It was the voice which always nettled him when they had their arguments. It nettled him now. He flushed.

"How do you mean, 'It's not very clever'?"

"Well, is it? Grant is supposed to kill me because I find the earring. Well, he wouldn't be likely to leave it for the police to see. He isn't a fool, you know."

He seemed to wrestle with that. It was the way he had planned it. Mark always hated to give up anything he had planned.

"He might not have seen it—clutched up in your hand."

"Then why does he kill me?"

235

It was a crazy parody of one of their old arguments. He wasn't quick really—she always got the better of him, and he resented it. The resentment was in his voice.

"You think you're so clever! But there's a very good answer to that. He kills you for the same reason that Mary Stokes was killed—because you know too much. You haven't shown him the earring—you've got it clutched in your hand. But you've told him you know, and he kills you—to shut your mouth. Like this."

At the horrible change in his face and his sudden stride forward Cicely sprang. She reached the table and ran round it to the other side. She didn't know that she had screamed until she heard the light, high sound. She screamed again, much louder.

Mark Harlow leaned across the table with grabbing hands, and missed her by an inch. She put a desperate edge on to the next scream. Then she had no more breath. She was dodging, twisting, doubling, and he wasn't Mark any more but a mad wild beast, clutching, cursing, doubling when she doubled—horribly, ruthlessly set on her destruction. He touched her sleeve, he caught it. She wrenched free. On the outer edge of sound, beyond his trampling feet, their panting breath, beyond the cruel beating of her heart, there was something, she didn't know what. It might have been a throb in the air. It might have been a car.

She took all the breath she could and screamed again. She saw him swing a chair above his head and poise it. Her hand found the heavy glass inkstand. She threw it straight in his face. Then she turned and ran out through the glass door and into Grant Hathaway's arms.

236

CHAPTER 37

About the time that Cicely was finding the afternoon intolerably long Grant Hathaway was entering the Superintendent's office at Lenton and wondering whether he would still be a free man when he came out again.

Frank Abbott followed him into the room and shut the door. He sat down, and Frank sat down. Old Lamb sat there looking stuffed and florid, and no wonder. There was a raging fire. Grant put the temperature round about seventy. All very appropriate, since he was certainly going to be grilled.

"Good afternoon, Mr. Hathaway. There are just one or two points, if you don't mind."

"Oh, certainly."

"In the course of your conversation with Louise Rogers, did she mention how she obtained your name and address?"

"Yes. She said I had dropped an envelope. Someone picked it up and gave it to her when she made enquiries."

"That was how she came to you?"

"That is what she said."

"Did she ask who was with you in the car?"

"Yes."

"Did you tell her?"

"Yes."

"And then she went away."

"And then she went away."

"Did she give you the impression that she meant to follow the matter up?"

"She didn't say."

"You gave her Mr. Mark Harlow's name, and the name of his house. Did you tell her how to get there?"

"She asked me where he lived, and I told her."

"She didn't say she was going to see him?"

"No."

"Did you think she meant to?"

"I didn't think about it—I wasn't interested."

"Did you ring Mr. Harlow up and let him know she was coming?"

There was a faint effect of surprise. Grant said,

"Certainly not."

"You might have done?"

"I didn't."

"You were on friendly terms with Mr. Harlow?"

"I've never had any quarrel with him."

"That doesn't sound very enthusiastic."

"I've never quarrelled with him. He's not much in my line."

"But you accepted a lift from him on January the fourth."

Grant smiled.

"Ever try those cross-country trains from Ledlington? I wanted to get home."

Lamb grunted.

"So you didn't ring Mr. Harlow up and warn him there might be trouble coming his way?"

"No."

"To whom did you mention this visit of Louise Rogers?"

"I didn't mention it to anyone."

"Sure about that?"

"Quite sure."

"Sure you didn't mention it to your wife?"

"Why should I?"

"I'm asking you if you did."

"I didn't."

"You didn't mention it to anyone?"

"No."

"Why didn't you?"

Grant smiled again.

"Three reasons—all good ones. I wasn't interested. I'm a busy man. I was a good deal taken up with my own affairs."

There was a silence. Lamb's gaze dwelt on him. The temperature of the room was now certainly well over seventy. In all the best thrillers the villain developed beads of perspiration upon the brow. Grant became aware that he now displayed this attribute of guilt.

The silence went on, the gaze became overshadowed by a frown.

Lamb said, "Harlow knows you saw her."

"Not from me."

Lamb pushed back his chair.

"Well, I think we'd like to know where he got it from. He knows, and you say you didn't tell him—you say you didn't tell anyone. I think we'll go and ask him how he knows, and I think you can come along."

They drove down the Lane in the police car, Constable May at the wheel. Just before they came to Deepside Grant said abruptly,

"If you're going to detain me, can I go and get some things?"

Nobody could have known what hung in the balance whilst Lamb considered this. It was in his mind to say, "Who said we were detaining you?" It was in his mind to say, "You can get what you want on the way back." He didn't say either of these things, and he never knew why. What he did say was,

"All right—it won't do any harm."

Miss Maud Silver was afterwards to describe this as providential.

They drove in, and heard the distant insistent barking of Bramble, shut in the kitchen. They drove round to the front of the house, and just as Constable May stopped the car and shut off the engine, Grant heard Cicely scream. Three doors were wrenched open, and in a moment four men were running— Grant and Frank because they had heard the scream, Lamb because he thought Grant was getting away, and the constable because he was of an age to run when he saw other people running.

The scream had come from the study. The glass door was ajar. As they came up, it was pushed wide and Cicely ran out. She ran straight into Grant Hathaway's arms and he lifted her off the ground and held her. Frank Abbott, coming to the door, saw two things. First the eternity earring lying on the floor where it had dropped from Cicely's hand. And then, on the other side of the table, Mark Harlow getting to his knees. He had come down with the chair on top of him, the chair which he had swung up over his head to strike Cicely down. He was struggling to his knees, struggling to free himself. His face was a mass of ink and blood. His hands groped.

Frank went forward. Lamb, a good second, halted on the threshold. He heard Cicely say between panting breaths, "He killed them both—he was trying to kill me too!" His eyes focussed on the eternity earring and passed to Mark Harlow, on his feet now, leaning on the table, dashing the blood and ink from his eyes. His mind ruminated on these things. He said,

"What's been happening here?" and went straight on into the official warning.

Mark Harlow heard it, as you hear something shouted at you in the teeth of a high wind. The blood was pounding in his ears and he was dizzy with pain. The words came to him in snatches—"Anything you say . . . taken down and used . . ."

He cleared his eyes and stared at Lamb out of a ghastly face.

240

"What's the good of that? I've said it, haven't I?" He cursed Cicely and his luck. If Louise Rogers had been there she would have recognised voice and words.

Lamb said equably, "Well, I've warned you. Mrs. Hathaway says you tried to kill her. Is there anything you would like to say about that? Or about Louise Rogers? Or Mary Stokes?"

Mark Harlow said, "Oh, I killed them. I'm through. You can't fight your luck."

CHAPTER 38

They had gone. Cicely had made her statement, and they had gone. It was half an hour since the last sound of the car had died away, taking them back to Lenton with Mark Harlow handcuffed beside Frank Abbott on the back seat, and the Chief Inspector sitting in front with Constable May.

After the violent interruption, all the normal things had begun again at Deepside—Bramble being let out of the kitchen, where he was screaming his head off; Grant going to and fro, getting out of his raincoat, hanging it up; Cicely bringing in tea. The sooner you get down to doing things like that, the sooner the nightmare things slip away back to their own horrible place. They were in the study now, with the fire bright on the hearth and the curtains drawn. By being very careful indeed Cicely had got them to meet. Tonight if she had stood on the other side of the glass door and tried to look in, there wouldn't have been any chink.

The police had taken away the eternity earring, and Grant had picked up a few splinters of glass. There was a dark stain on the carpet where the ink had gone, but it wasn't going to show very much when it was dry. The inkstand was back in its place with fresh ink in it. No one would have noticed that it was chipped.

Cicely was glad of the hot tea. She didn't want to talk or do anything. Presently she would have to go and wash up the tea things, but not just now. The wood fire made small comfortable sounds. Bramble lay stretched in front of it with his nose on his paws and his hind legs out behind him.

Grant lay back in his chair with his head against one of the old brown tapestry cushions. Into the calm of release from danger there came seeping an ineradicable dislike for brown tapestry. For tapestry in the mass, and for brown tapestry in particular. People used to get it because it wore for ever, and as it would always look dirty when it was clean, they could go on pretending it was clean when it was dirty.

In a dreaming, drifting sort of way Cicely began to do the study over. The wallpaper must be at least thirty years old—blue and brown chrysanthemums on a dingy ground. She substituted cream distemper, and was trying to decide between green and claret for the curtains, when Grant opened his eyes and said,

"Like to talk?"

Cicely said, "No."

He stretched a little and sat up.

"I expect we'll have to."

She shook her head.

He got up, moved the tea-table out of the way, and came back again to sit on the arm of his chair and look down on her.

"We'll have to talk, Cis. Better get it over. All this nonsense of your going away and wanting a divorce—we've never had it out. Don't you think it would be better if we did?"

She shook her head again. A most deadly, weary loathing of the last few months rose up in her like a physical sickness. When she thought Grant was going to be arrested—when she thought Mark would kill her and Grant would hang for it—what had she cared for the things which she had built up into a barrier between them? They were like something that had happened in another world, in another life—they no longer had any substance. She shook her head.

Grant's voice came back with a determined ring in it.

"I'm afraid we must. I want to know what started the rot. Everything was lovely one minute, and the next you were walking out and giving me to understand that I had married you for your money, and that you had found me out. Now, apart from any natural feelings I might be supposed to have, I really should like to know what put it into your head."

Cicely sat up too. There was still fire in the embers. They began to glow.

"You can't sit there and say you don't know!"

"I do sit here and say I don't know. Now what about it?"

"Grant! When you gave me the letter with your own hands!"

"What letter?"

"From that cousin of yours—the one that was brought up with you, Phyllis Shaw. You said, 'Here's a letter from Phil—with any luck they'll be home by Christmas. She's a good sort—I hope you're going to like her,' and you opened the top right-hand drawer and rummaged about and got out a letter and threw it over to me. You were just going off for the day."

He nodded.

"Yes, I was going over to see James Roney. And when I got back you were gone, and there was a note to say you didn't intend to come back. After which you refused to see me, or to answer my letters, or to behave in any sort of a reasonable way."

Cicely's eyes sparkled.

"I didn't feel reasonable."

"No—I noticed that. And now do you mind telling me what it was all about?"

"You don't remember what was in the letter?" Indignation put an edge on to her voice.

"I don't remember anything to set you off like that."

"You've got a very short memory!"

He sat there very much at his ease, one foot on the ground, the other swinging. His tone hardened a little.

"I don't remember anything that could possibly have upset you. If there was anything I missed, don't you think you'd better tell me what it was?"

"You really don't remember?"

"If there was anything in that letter, it was something I hadn't read. Be reasonable—should I have shown it to you if I had? And now perhaps you'll tell me what it was."

Cicely sat up straight. She had been pale, but now her colour flamed. She said,

"I don't see how you can forget a thing like that! I don't know why you showed it to me. I've thought and thought, but I couldn't ever make out why. It was at the top of the second page. You had just gone. I came back from the window and began to read the letter. The beginning was all nothing—about how hot it was. Then I turned over the page. Your cousin writes a very clear hand. She said, 'A pity about Cis Abbott. I mean, I know you like them fair. Your "She's just a little brown thing" doesn't sound very enthusiastic, but I hear she's quite nice. One of Gerald's sisters, the fat one, Mary, was at school with her. That's how I heard about Lady Evelyn Abbott leaving her all that money. There aren't too many heiresses going, and you'll get used to her looks. Mary says she isn't what you'd call really plain.' "

Grant Hathaway's face, which could express as much or as little as he pleased, was now only too revealing. That he recollected the passage quoted was evident. That it evoked a lively horror and a desire to laugh was perfectly plain. He said,

"Oh, Cis!"

Cicely pressed her lips together until they were just a scarlet line.

"My poor child, I'm so sorry. It was the wrong letter."

"Yes? That doesn't make it any better."

"Darling, did you happen to notice the date?"

"No, I didn't."

"Have you got this frightfully incriminating document?"

Her eyes blazed at him.

"Of course I haven't! Do you think I'd keep it for a single second!? I tore it into shreds and burnt them!"

He said in a laughing voice,

"Moral tract about losing your temper, Cis! If you'd looked at the date you'd have seen it was written last January."

She came stabbing back at him.

"January! She said how hot it was!"

"So it is in South Africa. Didn't they teach you anything at that school of yours?"

She said, "Oh!"

"Yes, my child. Now listen to me! When I came here I wrote and told Phil I didn't see how I was going to pay the death-duties, let alone make a go of running the place. She wrote back that of course I would have to marry money—there were lots of nice girls. She instanced you—practically next door—old schoolfellow of Gerald's sister Mary—what could be nicer? When I answered the letter I had met you once at a perfectly frightful tea-party with Mrs. Bowse in full cry. You had obviously been dragged there. You were in a foul temper. You never uttered."

Cicely stuck her chin in the air.

"I was in a rage with Mummy. She wouldn't let me wear a hat I'd just bought. It was pretty fierce, but I'd bought it all by myself, and you know how it is—if you let yourself be downed, well, there you are, a slave for life."

"Poor Monica!"

245

"It wasn't—it was poor me!"

"All right—poor you. Let's say you weren't looking your best—people don't when they're having a hate. I wrote to Phil that evening and said you were a little brown thing who never uttered, and some more kind words like that, on receipt of which she wrote the fatal letter."

"And then?" She couldn't manage quite enough breath. The words were there, that was all.

"Then, my child, I fell in love with you."

He got up and stood over her, reaching down to take her hands.

"Cis—look at me! This matters a lot. If you don't believe me, we're through. Now think! Think of us together! Think of everything!"

He pulled on her hands and she stood up.

"I fell in love with you. I'm going to be dead honest—if you hadn't had a penny, I should have tried not to fall in love with you, because I wasn't in a position to marry a girl who hadn't got a penny. I should have kept away. Anyhow I should have tried to—it mightn't have come off. I weathered the death-duties by selling a lot of old jewellery that had been put away in the bank for about forty years. That was one of the things I hoped wasn't going to come out when the police got busy."

Cicely said, "Oh—"

He gave a sudden laugh.

"There was quite enough piled up against me without that, wasn't there? And now, Cis, that gets us right down to bed rock. We're here safe and sound, but it's only by the skin of our teeth. If old Lamb had been a little bit later, or if we hadn't come in here at all, where would you and I be at this minute? Just take a look at it. It isn't pretty, but it's—" He paused for a word, and made it "sobering." "You'd be dead, and I'd be in jail, and they'd be calling the evening papers to the tune of 'Triple Murderer Arrested.'"

246

Her hands went cold in his, her face went white.

"Don't!"

"Take a look at it. And now look at me! Do you believe that I love you? Truth and honest, Cis!"

She looked at him gravely, steadily. Then she said,

"Yes."

"And do you love me?"

She said, "Yes," again.

He dropped her hands and picked her up as he had done when she ran to him.

"Oh, Cis—what a lot of time we've wasted!"

CHAPTER 39

Miss Silver made her farewells. Chief Inspector Lamb paid a state call upon her before returning to London, remarking that they didn't live so far from each other in town, but they generally seemed to meet in the country.

Miss Silver coughed, smiled, and enquired after his family in detail.

"I hope Mrs. Lamb is very well? . . . . I am so glad. Last time we met she had had a troublesome cough. I hope it has quite gone?"

"Yes, thank you."

"And the daughters? Lily is very happily married, I know. Her baby was a boy, was it not? He must be seven months old."

Lamb's official manner was thawing fast. His daughters had always done what they liked with him. He said,

"Nearly eight months, but you'd think he was quite a year. Lil says he's like me."

"How very delightful. And Violet?"

"Going to be married at Easter. He's a very good chap—in a house-agent's office. The trouble is to find somewhere to live. It isn't a good plan to start at home with Mum and Dad, though my wife would like it."

Miss Silver hastened to agree.

"Oh, no—you are very wise—young people should be independent. And Myrtle? Is she engaged?"

Lamb grunted. Myrtle was his youngest and the core of his heart. He didn't want to part with her, but he wasn't easy in his mind. He found himself telling Miss Silver all about it.

"She gets engaged, but when it comes to the point she doesn't want to get married. Likes her own way—likes being independent. My wife can't understand it—says she ought to marry a nice boy and settle down to raising a family—says I've spoilt her."

Miss Silver smiled.

"And have you, Chief Inspector?"

He said, "Well, well—" and then, "I daresay I have. But she's a good girl and we're not all made alike." He got up to go. "I'm glad those young Hathaways have made it up. Too many marriages on the rocks these days, and mostly for the want of a little sense. Funny how hard people will work at their business or their pleasure, but they won't do a hand's turn towards making a good job of being married. Well, I must be off. I've to thank you for your being right on the spot with Harlow when he dropped in to see you and made the slip which put us on to him. And the Hathaways have to thank you too. That was a narrow escape she had."

"Providential," said Miss Silver.

She parted from Monica Abbott with sincere regret, and received a warm invitation to come again.

From Cicely she refused a fee.

"No, indeed, my dear. The case was solved before I had any opportunity of working on it."

Cicely looked at her with a warm light in her eyes.

"I think you saved my life."

Miss Silver smiled.

"I hope it will be a very happy one."

To Frank Abbott she did not say goodbye. When, a day or two later, he dropped in he found her unpacking a parcel. It contained a silver rose-bowl large enough to accommodate the pot of blue-and-white hyacinths which had arrived separately from a florist. The effect of the flowers in the bowl was all that could be desired. Contemplating it in a place of honour on the top of the walnut bookcase and immediately under a reproduction of "The Soul's Awakening," Frank wondered whether it was Grant or Cicely who had been inspired to select a gift so perfectly and solidly Victorian. That Miss Silver was very much gratified was apparent. The card with its charming inscription, "Our love and our very great gratitude," the handsome proportions of the bowl, its weight, the graceful flutings which adorned its surface, the charming addition made to it by the flowering hyacinths, all contributed to give her the greatest possible pleasure.

With an appreciative cough she turned to Frank Abbott.

"So very good of them. I am really quite touched. Such a fine bowl, and the flowers—so really beautiful. And the two together—so harmonious. Will you think me fanciful if I am reminded of Lord Tennyson's comparison, woman set to man 'like perfect music unto noble words'? Those hyacinths—so fragile. And the bowl supporting them—so strong."

Frank had thought he knew his Miss Silver inside out—her intelligence, her high principles, her competence, her senti-ment—but on this occasion he was rendered speechless. For the rest of his life his cousin Cicely would present herself to him as a hyacinth supported by a bowl of durable metal and handsome design. Nor would he scruple to tell her so. He enjoyed the pleasures of anticipation, and throwing over all the resources of his mother tongue, fell back upon the French language so often reprobated by Chief Detective Inspector Lamb.

"*Le mot juste!*" he said.

THE END